The Other Frankenstein

The Other Frankenstein

Melissa F. Olson

NEWCON
PRESS

NewCon Press
England

First published in the UK, July 2025 by
NewCon Press
41 Wheatsheaf Road,
Alconbury Weston,
Cambs, PE28 4LF

NCP347 (limited edition hardback)
NCP348 (paperback)

10 9 8 7 6 5 4 3 2 1

ISBN:
978-1-917735-01-8 (hardback)
978-1-917735-02-5 (paperback)

Cover Art by Caroline Harroe
Cover layout by Ian Whates

Editing by Gillian Redfearn
Typesetting and book layout by Ian Whates

A Note from the Author

Like the narrator of this novel, I have Ehlers-Danlos Syndrome, a joint disorder that causes a wide variation of symptoms and challenges. This book discusses some of those issues, including health difficulties around childbirth.

Heck's medical battles are inspired by my own – but only mine. Please do not assume this account is a universal depiction. I would never claim to represent the EDS experience, only my own EDS experience.

Remember: think zebras.

Melissa

One

Dear Madison,

It's Saturday evening, and at long last the cruise ship has left the port.

I almost can't believe it. I was nervous right up until the last second, worried that your grandmother would figure out my plans and stage some dramatic intervention. Or worse, knock on the door of my cabin with a shiny smile and a suitcase.

I realize stealing from my own mother doesn't set a great example for you, Maddie, even if it was only customer loyalty points. But she doesn't approve of your dad, Colin, and this is my only chance to help him. I *have* to go.

In my defense, I did try to ask for permission first.

This was last week, almost two months after my return to Seattle from the hospital in Wisconsin and a few days after I saw the *Arctic Science* article about Colin's research. Mom and I were eating dinner at her condo, and after so many weeks of near-catatonia, I found myself in the strange position of trying *not* to look excited. I wasn't entirely successful.

"You've got a bit more color today," Mom said, too brightly. Everything she's said to me for the last three months has been too brightly.

"Thanks."

"How was your therapy appointment?" Her tone was cursory; she clearly expected another monosyllabic answer.

But it was the opening I'd been waiting for. I stopped poking my cauliflower and put the fork down. "Actually... Dr. Steinman suggested I take some time to myself somewhere."

My mother's eyebrows lifted. "Oh?"

"She thought my mental health would benefit from a change in scenery." I shrugged, careful to keep my shoulder blades in alignment. "I don't know. I found some cheap flights online, but I don't really want to get on a plane again. Or go anywhere hot."

Mom's eyes dropped to my clothes: compression leggings, a baggy tunic, and a thin, draped cardigan. It was seventy-five degrees outside, but I rarely appeared in less.

I picked up my fork, as though the topic was finished, and poked the cauliflower again. "You know," she said slowly, as if talking to a skittish horse, "I've got *so* many points from the cruise line. They always have trips to Alaska in the summer. You know I've always wanted to bring you along on one of—"

"You'll still be teaching summer school," I reminded her, feeling a stab of guilt as her face fell. She doesn't usually teach during summers, but she'd had to take a leave of absence spring semester after my accident. "Maybe I could go by myself."

"Oh, honey, no one goes on a cruise alone. And you won't know your way around or what to do. But I have more than enough points for two tickets. Is Cherie still in Seattle?"

I almost laughed at the thought. Cherie was my best friend in high school, but now I classify all my "friends" according to when they stopped talking to me. "Everyone has school or work, Mom. Anyway, it might be cool to go on my own."

"Heqet, honey, you almost *died*." She *loves* to say this, loves the taste of drama on her tongue. "The concussion alone –"

I cut in before she really got rolling. "The new doctor cleared me for all activities, remember? I can look at screens and read and everything."

"Still."

8

"I've had nothing to interest me, nothing to look forward to," I pointed out, before going in for the kill. "I just thought maybe I could try to make some new friends."

Mom's face lifted for a moment, and *or meet a new man!* was practically scrolling across her forehead. As though I want anyone to see me naked ever again.

But then she shook her head. "I'm sorry, sweetheart; I just don't think it's a good idea for you to go alone. Maybe we can do something together over winter break."

I tried to push her, but Mom was adamant, and in the end I shrugged and went back to my dinner, no longer needing to fake my disappointment. It would have been much easier if Mom had given me the cruise points willingly.

Instead, I had to steal them.

It wasn't exactly a cinematic heist. I already knew the password for Mom's laptop, and her login info was saved on the cruise website. The next day, after Mom left for campus, I logged into her account, signed Heqet Saville up for an Alaskan cruise, and fiddled with all the notification settings so information about the trip would be sent to me. It was easy.

This morning I told Mom I was taking an Uber to the library. As the ship pulled away from the harbor, I texted her to explain I would be gone for the next week. I said I was sorry, but this was something I had to do.

Then I turned my phone off.

Even now, after the Seattle coast has disappeared into fog, my stomach is churning with guilt and nerves. I've never done anything rebellious in my life. When I was little, Mom had to cajole me to leave her side at the playground. Before this, the most disobedient thing I'd ever done was choosing grad school at the University of Wisconsin instead of at home in Seattle.

But now I'm finally here, alone. My mother had been right about one thing: I really hadn't known where to go or what to do. The process of getting to my cabin turned out to be exhausting: waiting in line after line with my cane in one hand in the suitcase handle in the other. When I finally hobbled onto the ship, I discovered that the most functional spaces – hallways and elevators – are very narrow, and pressed tight with strange bodies and cloying smells. Normally the cane buys me a little bit of space, but today people were too excited about the voyage to be careful with their elbows or bags.

Every time someone bumped into me, a new bolt of pain shot into my legs… or down my back, or through my hips. Then I did wish I'd brought someone along with me, if for no other reason than to be a barrier between me and the world of the ship. In those moments I wished desperately for Col or, at least, a friend.

But I made it to the stateroom. Now I'm trying to focus on hope: after months of trying to reach your dad, I finally have a way to see him.

Col sometimes talks about this expression in French – I can't write it out, but it's basically the idea that if you don't leave yourself any alternatives or safety nets, your huge risk will pay off. You'll succeed because you *have* to succeed.

That's how I need to think now: this is going to work because it *has* to work. I'm going to get your daddy back.

Love, Mommy

TWO

Sunday, Day 2 at sea
Pain scale: 6

Dear Madison,

I woke up early, stiff and aching from all the walking and the unfamiliar bed. I was nervous to venture out of my room again after feeling so jostled last night, so my breakfast was three ibuprofen and a granola bar from my jacket pocket. Today's an 'at-sea' day, meaning we're not stopping at any ports. Other than brief excursions for food and a mandatory safety briefing, I planned to spend as much of the day as possible working on Colin's research.

After the ibuprofen kicked in enough for me to think, I got up and opened the curtains – only to find the ship entombed in fog. It was like finding a wall outside the balcony railing. I propped myself up in bed with *just* the right configuration of pillows and opened my laptop.

It felt good to use my brain again. I haven't been able to work on *anything* since the accident. When we first got back to Seattle, Mom decided I needed to follow every concussion protocol she could find on the internet, which left me with nothing to do but stare at the walls and draw mental maps of my body's pain.

When I was finally allowed to use screens again, Mom went on her big anti-Colin crusade. During the previous week alone, she seemed to magically appear every time I opened my laptop, checking the screen to see if I was trying to contact him.

Now I typed for hours, calling up my memory of Colin's voice and letting the words stream through my fingers into the computer. When I looked up again, the sun was peeking through the clouds, burning away a slice of the fog. I was getting stiff anyway, so I worked my way out of the pillows and went to the sliding door. There was nothing to look at but dark gray ocean and light gray sky. It reminded me of the drab hospital aesthetic. The only pop of color there came from the bright red or green marker used to write the on-duty nurse's name on a whiteboard.

I still remember a bunch of those names: Rafe, Michelle, Angie, Ellen. They scroll through my head whenever I smell disinfectant.

The walls of my little stateroom suddenly seemed way too close.

I checked the clock on the laptop and snapped the computer shut. It was time to get ready anyway.

I showered in my tiny bathroom and laboriously pulled on compression leggings, my sacroiliac belt, and a long tunic to cover it up. I restocked the backpack of emergency supplies that goes everywhere with me and secured the straps over my shoulders and across my chest. Then I ventured into the hall feeling like a very sad excuse for an explorer.

Thankfully, my first expedition out of the room went much better than I'd expected. The hallways were nearly empty at this time of day, and without people obscuring my view, I noticed that many of the ship hallways had subtle railings affixed to the wall in case the ship rocked. If I held the safety rail with one hand, I could use the map on my phone to navigate the decks without having to get my collapsible cane out of the backpack.

Most of the passengers had attended a safety talk the night before on one of the main decks, but this smaller, makeup briefing was recommended for guests with disabilities. It took me less time than I'd expected to make my way to the right ballroom, and then the actual briefing was surprisingly quick and painless, just a speech and a few rules.

Since I was already out of the cabin, and the venture had gone better than I'd planned, I decided to take a detour to one of the restaurants for lunch.

I found the entrance to the buffet on the highest main deck, opposite a big, open-air common space. Cafe tables and beach loungers circled a kids' pool, two hot tubs, and a giant screen that cycled through images of Alaska and the arctic. There weren't many people looking for lunch this early, so I had plenty of space to stump along with my cane, choosing a turkey sandwich and some fruit. I carried the food out to one of the cafe tables, feeling quite pleased with myself. The ship looked so massive and labyrinthine from a distance, but I'd managed to make my way around without too much difficulty. I imagined myself telling Col all about it in a few days.

When I finished the food, I transferred my belongings over to a lounger, where I had an unobtrusive view of the whole deck. I've never considered myself a people-watcher, Maddie, but it had been months since I'd looked at anything other than a hospital room or my mother's house. I found myself drawn to the activity all around me. Porters in track suits moved stacks of chairs around, chatting to each other in languages I didn't recognize. Groups of middle-aged women like my mother bent their heads together as they gossiped, trying to keep their draped silk scarves from blowing into their wineglasses.

Most of all, I watched the children playing at the kids' pool. The temperature was only in the mid-sixties (your father would want me to say, "eighteen degrees Celsius," like the arctic explorers he loves), and the sun had been obscured by fog again. Despite the chill, however, at least ten goose-bumped children in swimsuits jumped in and out of the water as though it were the hottest day of summer.

There was one little girl who reminded me of you, Maddie. She was about four, I think, with the cutest chubby legs and an Ariel swimsuit under her life vest. While the other, older kids were hurling themselves confidently into the water, this girl tiptoed up to the edge of the pool and paused for a long time in the cold air. The older kids teased her from the water, but she paid no attention. After a moment I realized her lips were moving. I couldn't hear what she was saying, but I imagine she was steeling herself, telling herself she could do it. When she was good and ready, the little girl jumped in with wild, joyous abandon, as though she'd never had a second's hesitation.

I was so caught up that I found myself actually clapping. The kids in the water looked up, startled, and then the little girl grinned shyly at me.

A soft voice spoke behind me. "She's adorable."

I turned, surprised, and got a quick impression of dark bun, big sunglasses, and ship uniform. The woman was holding an empty tray to her midsection like a shield. I hadn't even heard her approach, but then, all of the employees here manage a pleasant invisibility. It's a neat trick.

I realized she was talking about the little girl I was watching…or rather, staring at. Embarrassed, I pulled the laptop out of my bag and made a show of opening it.

"She is, but she isn't mine," I explained.

"Oh, I'm sorry." I usually have a good ear for accents, but this one was a bit like French, a bit like English. I was certain I hadn't heard it before. She moved closer, standing next to my lounger. "Which one is yours?"

"None of them," I admitted. "I just miss my baby. She's not traveling with me."

"Ah." After a pause, the woman added, "Is there anything I can get you, miss?"

We weren't in the restaurant area. I craned my neck to look at her properly. She wore a knee-length skirt and tailored uniform blouse with short sleeves, and there was a cheap over-the-counter brace on one wrist. Despite the gloomy weather, the woman had on heavy-duty sunglasses that wrapped all the way around her face like something out of an 80s sci-fi movie. Beneath them, her skin was a golden hue that didn't quite look natural. It took me a few seconds to realize she was also almost supernaturally beautiful. It was as though a pre-Raphaelite model had wandered into the twenty-first century and gotten a bad spray tan.

"No, thank you," I said, making a point to look at my computer.

"I work in the adults-only bar just through there," she said politely, and I had to look up to see where she was pointing, to the hallway past the pool. "Can I bring you a drink? It's on me."

I shrunk into myself, confused by the offer. Before I met your dad, I had relationships with both women and men, but I couldn't imagine someone so beautiful having any interest in me. For one paranoid moment I wondered if Mom had called the ship and asked someone to hunt me down and offer me mimosas.

Then I realized the woman must be looking at my cane, which lay folded just under the chaise. I'm still not used to having a physical cue that there's something wrong with me. "No thanks. I'm fine."

"If you need anything at all, my name is Caroline," she added, tapping the silver name tag pinned to her breast. "I hope you have a pleasant stay, Miss…"

"Oh. Um, I'm Heck."

Her pleasant mask didn't waver. "It's lovely to meet you. Is Heck short for something?"

I've had this particular conversation thousands of times, Maddie, with nearly every new person I meet. "Heqet. She was the Egyptian –"

"– Goddess of fertility," Caroline finished. "Likely a precursor to the Greek goddess Hecate."

"Yeah. Jeez, you're like the third person I've ever met who knew that."

For the first time, her smile looked genuine, rather than a professional tool she plastered to her face.

"I've never met a Heqet," Caroline said. "It's a lovely name. And an interesting choice."

At best, "Heqet" sounds like a hacking cough, but I just recited my usual speech. "My father was a classics professor. My mom teaches literature, but she wrote a paper on Heqet in grad school, so…"

I ended, as I usually do, with a shrug, a sort of *what are you going to do?* gesture.

This is usually where the new person suggests I could always change my name. I don't even blame then, really: Heqet could only work for a glamorous, mysterious person, and other than my scars, I am forgettably pleasant-looking. You need have *presence* to pull off an exotic name, and I've never had that. Actually, I thought, life would make more sense if this woman and I traded identities.

Caroline pursed her lips. "Names can be slippery," she said by way of consolation. "Are you an academic as well?"

"I was getting my masters in linguistics until I had my baby. I don't think I'll go back." To push past any follow-up questions, I added, "I was actually just wondering where *you're* from. Your accent is similar to French, but I don't think I recognize it."

Caroline's professional smile turned brittle. "I traveled a lot. Excuse me, I should really get back to my duties." With a little bob of her head, she turned and walked off.

Huh.

As I watched her disappear into the restaurant, I wished so strongly for your father, Maddie, so I could get his take on her. Colin has this gift for glancing at someone once and describing them for entire intricate paragraphs. It's his superpower, like me and my weird memory.

Anyway. I'm back in my room, and now that I'm no longer moving my various joints are reminding me why I shouldn't do so much walking and sitting up. I feel a headache coming on, a bad one, so it's time for ibuprofen and an ice pack. I shouldn't have let myself forget how far my body is from normal. More later.

Love, Mommy

Three

Pain scale: 3

Dear Madison,

I've just had the strangest conversation of my entire life. I can hardly think; I keep triple-checking that my cabin door is locked and bolted. I'm going to write until I can't stay awake anymore.

I think I may have accidentally taken Advil PM this afternoon instead of Advil, because I slept through most of the afternoon. I hadn't remembered to set an alarm, so I woke up at 9pm feeling fragile from the migraine and weak with hunger. There was nothing to do but strap on my SI belt and venture back out for food.

The ship has plenty of restaurants, but I returned to the buffet on the pool deck, simply because I already knew the way. This time I needed both my cane and the railings to work my way to the elevator.

It was quite cool on the pool deck, and so overcast that I could hardly find the setting sun. In the restaurant, I reached for the closest things that I liked: fruit, grilled cheese, some rice. There were plenty more stations farther in, but it was hard to hobble around collecting food with only one free hand – buffets aren't made for canes.

Plate in hand, I gravitated back out to the pool area to sit, partly because it was familiar, and partly because more people-watching seemed gentler on my eggshell brain than trying to work or read. I ate in a daze, still disoriented from the extra sleep and the absence of hurt. My doctor in Wisconsin had told me EDS patients referred to this as "brain fog," a term I've always found too cutesy. I had to admit, though, my thoughts seemed as clouded as the atmosphere around the ship.

A soft voice spoke up behind me. "Hello, Heck. How is your evening?"

I turned my head with great care, because a muscle spasm is the last thing I need. It was the same employee from earlier, Caroline. Despite the near-darkness, she wore the same huge sunglasses as earlier, along with the short-sleeved uniform and wrist brace. I was wrapped in my thickest, longest wool cardigan, but Caroline didn't seem to notice the chill. She had a glass of water in her hand, which she set down in front of my plate. "So you don't have to make another trip," she said simply.

I looked from her to the glass, torn between feeling patronized and weeping with gratitude. "Thank you," I mumbled. "I was asleep all day."

Her professional smile-mask wavered for a moment, then recovered. "Sometimes people have a hard time adjusting to the time zone."

"I live in this time zone. Well, I do now. Since May." Why was I talking so much? I wished I could get my bearings.

Caroline glanced around her once and then pulled out the chair across from me, moving with a sturdy grace. She sat down and leaned forward. "Are you all right, Heck? You look…" she had to search for a word. "Unsettled." Her eyes dropped to the cane. "We have medical –"

"No!"

A couple several tables away turned to look at us, and I swallowed and forced myself to lower my voice. "I'm sorry," I said to Caroline. "I'm not injured; I have a…a disability."

I hate that word so much, Maddie. It's weighted with so many expectations and prejudices, and in every sense I don't feel that I've *earned* it. Usually I just mention an ailment people understand – migraine, sprain, muscle pull, allergic reaction. All the easily digestible things I was treated for before the doctors realized my problems were connected.

Tonight, though, I found myself still talking. "It's called Ehlers-Danlos Syndrome, EDS. My body doesn't produce a certain protein correctly, so my joints are hyper-flexible." It wasn't the first time I've had to explain my stupid, capricious disorder, but it always sounds so ridiculous out loud.

"I think I'll go back to my room now." It took three tries to scoot my chair far enough from the table to stand up, and then I tangled my cane in the chair legs. I made a reflexive attempt to catch it and fell back onto the chair again. Thanks to my stupid perfect memory, one of the doctor's voices echoed in my mind. "EDS often means poor proprioception. Your body doesn't know where it is in space."

Maddie, it seems so unfair that I can have pain in all the tiny parts that connect my limbs together, but I can't feel where I am in a room.

Caroline sprang to retrieve the cane, which she gently placed in my hand. I just sat there for a moment, trying not to cry. "Heck," she said gently. "Is there someone else on the ship with you? Someone I can page?" I shook my head. "I can get you an outside line if you want to call someone," she offered. "A family member, maybe?"

I let out a sob of not-quite-laughter at the thought of calling my mother. "I'm on my way to Juneau to surprise my boyfriend," I told Caroline. "He's a professor at the University of Alaska. He just started their new arctic science program."

"So you're on a cruise… to visit him?" Her brow furrowed – it *is* weird to use a cruise ship as transportation – but before she could say anything else there was a crackle over the ship's loudspeaker. An annoyingly soothing male voice followed. "Good evening, folks; this is Captain Mike speaking. Sorry for the late announcement, but we're about to hit a patch of rough water. The ship may sway a bit in the storm, so please make sure any breakables are in a safe place. If you'd like some medicine for nausea, just inform your deck valet. Thank you for joining us on this adventure!"

The word "nausea" triggered something primal in my brain. My body remembered the weeks of round-the-clock morning sickness, the emergency room visits for IV fluids so I wouldn't die of dehydration like some tragic Victorian poet. I'm not blaming you, Maddie; of course it wasn't your fault. But though there's not much for me to be afraid of anymore, I do fear being nauseous again.

I was hugging my arms to my stomach like I might ward it off. I asked Caroline, "Is that normal? The swaying?"

She gave me her mask-smile. "It doesn't happen often because of the ship's stabilizers, but it's perfectly normal and we're in no danger. Think of it like turbulence on an airplane."

That didn't help – my last airplane ride had been right after the hospital, when I was swathed in compression bandages that covered all the Vaseline-coated stitches. *Colin*, think of *Colin*, I told myself. My hands were shaking, but I managed to pick up my glass of water and take a sip.

Caroline stood up. "There are things I should tend to before the end of my shift. Are you sure there's –"

She broke off as the whole ship listed to my right – I mean, to starboard. The empty chairs and dishes made a loud scraping sound as they slid sideways, and all around us people let out bursts of awkward laughter as they stumbled. Caroline seemed completely unaffected, but she must be used to this sort of thing.

I was still seated, but my arms automatically flailed as I tried to compensate for the change in balance, and icy water splashed over the rim of the glass in my hand. I tried to hold onto it, but the water made it slippery – and then the ship listed back the other way.

I slapped the glass down into the metal tabletop with much more force than if I'd simply dropped it. With a wet crack, it splintered into large, jagged pieces.

"Shoot!" The ship tipped the other way, and I clutched the edges of the table to steady myself.

Caroline had started to turn away, but now she returned to my table, reaching for the broken glass. "Here, I can get this for you."

"I'm really sorry." I reached for a piece of glass, wanting to clean up my own mess, but Caroline waved me off.

"It's not your fault. All the dishes are supposedly made of safety glass, but this isn't the first time one of them has broken during rough water." She said this in a sort of good-natured grumble, depositing one shard in her free hand and reaching for another. "It's something to do with the angle –"

She broke off as the ship listed starboard again, much more sharply this time. I shot out an arm and just managed to brace myself against the plate-glass window.

Caroline was thrown forward toward the table, and she reflexively slammed her hands down to catch herself – and the upturned shards of broken glass disappeared beneath her right palm.

Our eyes locked. Mnemonic memory or not, I stopped hearing anything from the passengers or objects around us. Caroline didn't recoil or jerk away or scream. She just went very, very still.

I forced myself to look down – and it was impossible to miss the half inch of blue-tinted glass jutting from the back of her hand. My stomach rolled over.

With her uninjured hand, Caroline snatched up the bundled cloth napkin on the table across from me, causing the silverware to tumble loose and breaking the spell between us.

As she draped the napkin loosely over her injury, I scrabbled at the pocket of my cardigan to reach my cell phone, babbling. "I'm so sorry, I have the ship app thing; I'll call for help–"

"That won't be necessary," Caroline said in her usual calm, professional tone. Under the circumstances, it sounded absurd. "I'll be fine."

Shock. She was in shock, that must be why she seemed calm. I frantically scrolled through the screen, looking for the ship icon.

The phone was plucked from my hands.

Stunned, I looked up at Caroline, who dropped my phone in her skirt pocket with her uninjured hand. The wound on her right hand was still hidden under the cloth. She reached under the napkin, gave a quick tug. There was a revolting *squelch*, and then she tossed a glass shard onto the table. It was even bigger than it had looked before, but strangely clean. Why wasn't there blood? Shouldn't Caroline's hand be gushing red, staining through the napkin?

Why had she taken my phone?

Seeing my confusion, Caroline gave me a reassuring smile, wrapping the napkin around her palm with unhurried carelessness. "I'm fine, Heck. It was nothing, really."

"I know I look fragile, but I'm not afraid of blood," I told her, scanning the deck for the handle of my cane. "We need to get you help."

I picked up the cane and used it to push myself to my feet. "Give me my phone. I'll call the medical department and tell them we're coming."

"Look, it's not even bleeding." She showed me the white napkin, and it was true. There was no blood.

I stood with my mouth open, my brain fluttering weakly against the problem, finding no way through. How was she not bleeding? The shard of glass had poked right through her skin; I *knew* it had.

(Why had she taken my phone?)

Caroline took a step back, turning to move away. "Thank you for your concern, Heck, but I'm fine." Her voice had taken on an air of desperation. "I need to return to duty –"

It was so unlike me to reach out and grab the corner of the white napkin, tugging it away like a magician with a tablecloth. I think the movement surprised us both, and Caroline didn't react in time to stop me. The napkin slithered free, exposing three enormous, ragged tears in her hand. The largest of them went all the way through.

Caroline jerked her hand to her chest, hiding the injuries again, but it was too late: I'd already seen the gray, bloodless flesh exposed by the torn skin, and the gleaming floor of the deck, shining up at me through the biggest wound.

Four

Remembering that wound now makes me feel sick all over again. In the moment, though, my thoughts just sort of stuttered, not quite connecting to each other. Then three words overrode everything else, the phrase on repeat in my head: *There's no blood.*

There's no blood there's no blood there's no blood there's no blood there's no —

"What — what is that?" I blurted. "What's wrong with you?"

Caroline glanced around, and I followed her gaze. Most people had recovered from the ship's lurch, and several were starting to look our way.

Rewrapping the napkin, Caroline reversed direction and stepped toward me, lowering her voice. "We're going to your cabin."

I can't really explain why I didn't refuse, Maddie, except to say that my thoughts were flitting around like moths in a lantern. In seconds Caroline had put a hand under my elbow, collected my cane, and was helping me across the deck with a strength that would have astonished me if I wasn't already dazed.

There's no blood there's no blood there's no blood —

She steered me toward the elevators, supporting more of my weight than I would have thought possible. I could see flashes of lightning embedded in the fog, and I realized the ship was heading into the storm. The deck pitched and tilted beneath our feet; the fog seemed to tighten around the ship. Most of the passengers were headed in the same direction, all of them focused on keeping their balance. Caroline nodded at a few crew members along the way, but they just took in my cane and gave us both pleasant nods.

She was so *strong*. It felt like my feet were barely touching the floor.

I'm not sure why I didn't fight her. Why didn't I scream? If Caroline had been a man, or produced a weapon, or said anything about hurting me, I'd like to think I would have. But I was just too disoriented in too many ways. The fog, the swaying ship, the shocking, bloodless sight of Caroline's right hand. It took the fight out of me.

When we reached the door to my cabin, Caroline plucked the key card from my shaking fingers and opened it herself, leaving the key card in a slot just inside. By the time I realized she wasn't going to deposit me in the room and leave, she had closed and bolted the door behind us. And it was too late.

I cringed away from her, rubbing my arm where she'd held it. It was obvious that if she decided to hurt me, she could *really* hurt me. My body was a pathetic bundle of floppy joints and flaccid muscles in a too-large bag of skin.

And she was so much stronger than she looked.

I staggered to the small desk on the opposite wall of the cabin, as far away from her as I could get. Sometime between leaving the main deck and arriving in my cabin, the skies had opened, and rain spattered against the sliding door to the balcony. I was trapped.

Fear crawled up my spine, but I made myself sit down in the small desk chair. What were you supposed to do if you were taken hostage? Act normal? Make friends?

Caroline looked around, taking in the various braces on the floor and medications in an open bag on the desk. "You have half a drugstore in here," she noted. She hadn't turned on any lights besides the one at the door, which was behind her now. Her night vision must have been excellent.

I couldn't even see her face, but I had the strange sensation of an *unmasking*. "Do you want a bandage?" I asked nervously. "I might even have some gauze…"

"No." Caroline sat down gracefully on the end of the bed, folding her hands in her lap. The light from the entrance lit about half of her face now, but I couldn't read her expression. Silence stretched between us.

My eyes dropped to her injured hand, which was still loosely wrapped in the napkin. I stared, feeling like I was waking up from a hazy dream. Caroline wasn't holding herself like someone nursing a wound. There was no clenched jaw, panting, wincing, checking the wound. It was like she'd forgotten about it.

Holy shit.

I looked up at her face, trying again to make out her expression in the dim light. "It doesn't hurt, does it?"

Caroline's frozen hesitation reminded me of a little kid who really hadn't expected to get caught in a lie. "It *doesn't*," I marveled. "How did you do it?"

"I see," she said wryly. "You wonder if I have something you can use."

I felt myself reddening, embarrassed that I'd been so transparent. I'd guessed that Caroline had undergone some experimental procedure, a new drug or genetic modification that had side effects for her skin. Of *course* I wondered if it could change me as well.

"I'll leave you out of it," I told her, trying to keep the eagerness from my voice. "Just give me the name of the clinic, or the treatment, whatever it was. I won't say I got it from you."

Between the sunglasses and the inscrutable body language, I couldn't read her at all. It was maddening. "Heqet, even if I *could* give this to you, you wouldn't want it," she said, not unkindly.

The words were like a gnat buzzing past my ear. "Were you born like this? You've had it your whole life?"

She shook her head. "Then *someone* made you like this," I reasoned.

"Yes." For the first time, her voice was sharp. "And then he murdered me."

I could feel her watching my reaction, but I've seen enough crime TV to know people can drown or be electrocuted or whatever and come back. I myself had died in an operating room four months earlier.

I waved my hand in a circle to say go on, but Caroline's lips were pressed together, as though she'd already said more than she wanted to. "And someone gave you CPR or..." I prompted.

Caroline gave me a wry smile. "I'm afraid this predated CPR."

That wasn't right. Caroline couldn't be much older than me. "When did you die?"

"The summer of 1816," she said. "I was born a few days later."

My heart sank. Even in just those few seconds, I'd got my hopes up. But Caroline's mind had obviously been distorted, likely by the treatment.

I still wanted to know about it, though. Maybe it had been in the early stages when Caroline received it. Maybe it was more refined now.

I stared at her in silence for a moment, weighing my options. Dealing with delusional people is like dealing with a bear attack: I can never remember if you're supposed to fight back or go along. "I see," I said carefully. "Will you tell me more about it?"

She sighed. "I suppose it's the only way to convince you not to pursue it."

Caroline began to talk then, in fits and starts that sometimes seemed to shock her, as if she'd never heard the story out loud and she couldn't believe how it sounded. Every now and then she paused, her eyes lost, and I waited, afraid to yank her from her memories.

She doesn't know about these letters to you, or my mnemonic memory. I am copying down as much of her story as I can here, both for insurance, and... well.

You'll see, I'm afraid.

Five

Caroline

I was twenty-four on my wedding day, the day I died. It sounds young by today's standards, but I had known for nearly twenty years that I was going to marry my foster cousin, Victor.

My birth parents died when I was a baby, and I spent my earliest years as an interloper in the cottage of overworked Italian peasants, an extra mouth they couldn't afford to feed. I barely remember that time, although I have an impression of lots of tumbling and laughing with my foster siblings – and of hunger so sharp that it cramped my stomach. I slept in a bed with three other girls, and often fell asleep not knowing where my body ended and theirs began.

When I was four, Victor's mother came to our village in Italy as part of a charitable excursion. She saw me from a distance and, she told me much later, was instantly captivated by my auburn curls and cherubic features, so unlike those of my "swarthy" companions. She decided on the spot that I would make a wonderful gift for her unsociable only son.

I never asked how much she paid the villagers to take me home with her. There is no answer that would feel good. But I never felt that hunger again while I lived.

From then on, Victor's parents raised me as their "niece," with much love and praise. We traveled a lot in the first few years, but when Victor and I were six or seven, my uncle and aunt settled us in Geneva, purchasing both a house in the city and a villa in Bellrive, which was where we spent most of our time. The villa was called *Maison de Creux Gris*, House of the Gray Hollow. It was named for the slate-colored lichen that covered the decorative boulders lining the drive.

It was a charmed childhood in many ways. I never wanted for anything, was protected from the dangers and risks of the world. From the beginning, though, it was understood that I would belong to Victor.

This was communicated to me in a hundred small ways, but the most obvious was gentle isolation. My aunt and uncle always kept my community small. If I showed interest in spending time with the village girls or spoke too long to a male classmate, I was gently redirected back to Victor's side. Aside from him, my only friends were his two younger brothers, Ernest and William; Justine Moritz, who served the Frankenstein family and was the sister of my heart, and of course, Henry Clerval, Victor's closest friend since we were seven. They were my little world, and it was a very happy one for quite some time.

By June of my twenty-third year, Henry, William, and Justine were all dead.

William had been first, murdered nearly two years earlier just outside Gray Hollow at the age of only six. Justine was wrongly convicted of the crime and executed at the gallows. And sixteen months later, Henry was murdered in Scotland.

Henry's killer, like William's, was never found, but his death devastated Victor's mind and body. For some time, I had been terrified that I would lose him, too. After months of recovery in Scotland, he was finally able to travel home to Gray Hallow, and we stood at the altar a month later.

The wedding took place at a tiny chapel near the shore of Le Rhone. It would have been far too small for the wedding I had planned almost two years ago, but we had lost too much to enjoy the revelry of a large party. Still, the tiny chapel was beautiful, and my uncle and Ernest were the only witnesses I could bear to include anyway. They knew the pain of Victor's and my loss; only they could understand the tremulous hope that balanced precariously on this union.

I remember sitting in front of a mirror in the chapel's antechamber that day, tying a wide white ribbon into my hair and studying my appearance. I wasn't a beaming bride. My eyes were haunted, my face hollowed out from months without an appetite. I had put my hair up in a simple bun with tendrils of dark curls spilling loose to my shoulders. It was a style I wore often, but anything more elaborate would have required the aid of another woman. In my stubbornness I had decided that if I couldn't have my aunt or Justine, whom I had considered my sister, I didn't want anyone to help me.

I put on the brightest smile I could muster and went out to claim my place at the altar, in front of the same clergyman who had laid poor little William into the ground months earlier. I did not want to look at the minister, or I would be swallowed by the horrible memory of that day and what followed. Instead, I concentrated on Victor.

He was handsome and pale, as always, but that day he looked even more drawn and hollowed-out than I. He had been very ill in Ireland, and not yet regained the weight or color he'd lost, but it wasn't just a physical malady. I remember thinking a darkness hovered over him, blotting out the ambient light.

Looking back, of course this should have been cause for alarm – my future husband was visibly floundering at the altar. But I assumed he was thinking, as I was, of our dear friends and brother who weren't there. I was arrogant, confident that I knew all of Victor's secrets, even the one that visibly weighed on him.

Only a few weeks earlier, while he was still recovering in Scotland, Victor had sent me a letter to assure me of his desire for our marriage. He had claimed that his recent distress was not due to the press of his grief, but because of a burden he'd been carrying alone, a private matter he did not wish to share until after our wedding. He hadn't spoken of it once after he returned, but I thought I already knew what he would tell me.

Since we were children, I had been aware of the way Victor's eyes drifted after other men. We had never spoken of it, not once, but it didn't trouble me – partly because I was always used to it, and partly because at the time, many such men married women and raised families. Victor was brilliant and kind, in his distracted way, and all I really cared about was that he would take care of me and give me a child. Considering the circumstances of my early life, a pleasant marriage to a good man seemed more than adequate.

Most importantly, our union would make me an official member of the family, in name as well as situation. I believed that was all I could hope for in this world.

This was why, during the hurried wedding plans, I never asked Victor about the secret he'd mentioned in the letter. Not once. I assumed he would tell me on our wedding night that he preferred men, I would assure him that I understood, and our lives would proceed as planned.

As the minister droned on, Victor made an effort to smile at me. I tried to smile back, reminding myself that our marriage was a way to clamber back onto the pre-determined path of our lives. It might feel empty, after so much loss, but it would be a life I could understand. One that could grow instead of decay.

At last, the minister finished his monologue, and Ernest handed the rings to Victor, who accepted them with shaking fingers. He slid the thin gold band onto my finger. When the minister prompted us to recite our vows, a trick of the acoustics caused our words to echo around the near-empty stone chapel, sending an involuntary shiver through me. I don't remember my vows, but I remember how cold Victor's hands were. I clutched them for a moment as I put the ring on his finger, as though I could ease the chill with my warmth alone.

That was it. We had eschewed any additional frivolities, preferring to keep the ceremony as simple as possible out of respect for the dead. As I exchanged a chaste kiss with my fretful now-husband, I prayed that our union – and my soon-to-be acceptance of him – would alleviate his suffering.

How often I have counted up all the tragedies that followed that day, and wished that for once, I had prayed for myself rather than for him.

In fairness, I had been raised with the singular purpose of caring for Victor. I played with him when he was lonely, teased and chattered when he was gloomy. When he wished to talk to someone about his research, I always listened with encouraging attention, though my own schooling had ended too soon to follow the constant grind of his brain. I was his nanny, his cheerleader, his confidant, his Madonna. As with so many other things in my short, sheltered life, it never occurred to me to resist.

Instead, when we stepped out of the cool stone chapel and into the warm sun, I felt true hope lift in my chest for the first time since poor William had been taken from us.

My uncle was throwing a party for some well-meaning friends and relatives who dearly wished to celebrate our union, but Victor and I had demurred, deciding to travel straight to the riverbank. We boarded a small craft that would ferry us toward Austria, stopping overnight at Evian. As we settled on the boat, however, my exhaustion caught up with me. Victor squeezed my hand, and I closed my eyes and leaned my head on his shoulder, savoring what would be my last living moments of peace.

I did appreciate this moment of amnesty, brief as it was. I think of that sometimes. At least I enjoyed it.

The little boat docked in Evian at sunset, and then Victor, who had seemed so content during the journey, transformed before my eyes. He ceased his pleasant commentary on the day and grew silent and troubled. Eventually, he withdrew from me completely, barely speaking or glancing my way.

To cheer him up, I suggested a walk along the shore to stretch our legs. After only a few minutes, though, the rain began and darkness fell, driving us inside the modest inn where we had secured lodgings.

In the lamplit entryway, I finally saw the extent of my new husband's anxiety. Victor's eyes darted around the simple room and halls, his head ticking around like broken clockwork. He seemed almost ill with fear, leaning against walls or in door frames as though he were too frightened to hold himself upright.

This change in his demeanor surprised me. I had tried to tease out his troubles several times throughout the day, but now I asked as firmly as I dared. "What is it that agitates you, my dear Victor? What is it you fear?"

In the many years since, I have very often wondered what might have happened if Victor had chosen the truth. Granted, he had already ignored years' worth of such opportunities, but in that moment I gave him a final chance to change the course of our fates. If he had taken it, perhaps I would have died a plump, happy grandmother, surrounded by the souvenirs of a full and fulfilling life.

Instead, of course, Victor brushed off my queries once again, sending me to bed with a kiss on my forehead, a quick brush of cool lips. He was determined to stay awake, he claimed, until he had settled himself enough to provide me with a restful bedmate.

It did not even occur to me to press him. I had been carefully conditioned to go along with Victor's strange whims. I just smiled prettily and bade him goodnight before retiring to our chamber. It was my first, and final, farewell as his wife.

I remember it was cool in the room, cooler than the rest of the inn had been. When I walked in I checked the window for a draft, but it was closed firmly, and I was too tired to wonder if it had been open before. I had brought along a white satin gown for my wedding night, but given Victor's strange mood and the cold room, I changed into a heavy flannel nightgown instead. I unpinned my hair and crawled beneath the heavy quilt, paying little mind to the rest of the room.

I did not check the closet, or beneath the bed.

I'll never know how much time passed between my climbing into that unfamiliar bed and the moment I was killed. I never saw him slither out from his hiding place, nor heard the footfalls on the carpet. All I know it that I woke up with enormous, powerful fingers wrapped around my neck.

My eyelids snapped up. I had left a lamp on for Victor, and in its dim light I could make out a great hulking figure leaning over the bed. He reeked of unwashed flesh and forest rot. I opened my mouth to scream, but he leaped on top of me with alarming nimbleness, squeezing my throat until no air could come out.

I fought him, my fists pounding his arms, but he was so strong and so massive that it felt like striking an angry bull. I tried to peel his fingers away from my neck one at a time instead, but they were iron bars pressing down into my skin.

Then he bent forward, his face coming into the light, and fresh terror shocked me into stillness. My attacker was hideous, with black lips, yellowed eyes, and bizarrely twisted features. His mottled gray skin was a patchwork of scars.

After the first shock passed, I was far more frightened of his expression than his looks. He was gleeful, his whole bearing rigid with buoyant satisfaction. He panted with excitement, enjoying this moment.

My vision began to fade around the edges, and I knew I would die. Everything that was me was dissolving like grains in an hourglass.

Then, to my shock, he released my neck.

As I gasped for air, he leaned forward, his noxious breath damp on my cheek. "Scream," he whispered. "Scream for Victor."

My vision was clearing and I felt solid again, a thinking being. This monster wanted to use me as bait for my new husband. I may have forfeited hope, but I would not add Victor's death to my own. I shook my head back and forth in the pillow.

"Scream," the creature commanded again, and again I refused.

He glowered at me, then gave a disgusted shake of his head. "Remember," he said harshly. "You could have spared yourself this pain."

He grabbed the fingers of my left hand, including my shining wedding band, and twisted them with a careless strength that would have terrified me in and of itself, if I weren't rocked by agony. I screamed then, my vision exploding into white-hot pain as the bones of my hand were pulverized in his fist.

I don't remember how many times I cried out. I just know I kept screaming until he released my crumpled fingers and his hands wrapped back around my throat.

And then I died.

Six

Heck

"Stop," I said. "Geneva, Victor, little William, an attacker with black lips – I already know this story. My mother is a literature professor. I've probably read *Frankenstein* a dozen times since I was eleven."

Caroline stared at me for a second, and then her lips twisted into a rueful smile. "I admit, that surprises me. Most people your age have only seen one of the films, if that." She shrugged. "Still, you only know what Mary wrote down. It's not the same as knowing the story."

I let out a snort. "*Mary*? You mean Mary fucking Shelley, the woman who published one of the most famous novels in history when she was eighteen? That Mary?"

"Eighteen when she wrote it, twenty when it was published," Caroline corrected. "Do you think I'm lying?"

"Not lying, just…" I put my hands on the desk, trying to balance myself to stand. I needed to get Colin's researched typed up and get it to him so I could jump-start our life. What was I doing listening to this crazy person?

"Look," I said, "if I tell anyone I met Victor Frankenstein's undead widow, they wouldn't believe me in a million years. I'm not a threat to you."

That brought her up short for a moment. "I never thought you were a threat to me, Heck."

I blinked. "Then why did you drag me back to my cabin?"

"I… I suppose I panicked," she admitted. "I'm not used to interacting with people as… as I really am." Caroline reached for her sunglasses and carefully pulled them off her face, squinting and blinking as though the two dim lamps in my cabin were the sun itself. When she tilted her head up and met my eyes, I heard myself gasp.

Her eyes were a startling, robin's-egg-blue. But all around the blue, the whites of her eyes were… yellow. There's no other word for it. I couldn't think of a thing to say.

"I have special contacts that cover the full eye," she said, folding the glasses in her hand. "But they itch when I work long shifts – and anyway, I'm very sensitive to light. I paid a doctor in Glasgow to write a letter prescribing my sunglasses."

I found my voice. "If you're trying to prove you're really Elizabeth Frankenstein, looking vaguely jaundiced doesn't really –"

Caroline lifted her injured hand, letting the napkin fall into her lap.

My mouth snapped shut. A pinprick of light from the lamp on the desk shone through the hole in her hand. Around it, the torn, loose edges of gray flesh had smoothed down as if glued.

When I didn't move, Caroline slowly turned her palm and held it up for my inspection, like a crossing guard giving the sign to stop. On this side, the wound's edges had begun to knit back together, little ropes of living tissue stretched across the red-slimed expanse of gray flesh. Even as I watched, I thought I could see the little ropes thickening, getting pinker.

"The world is bigger than you think it is, Heck," Caroline said softly.

I've never thought of myself as squeamish, especially after childbirth. But now I practically threw myself off the bed and lurched into the bathroom, where I dropped to my knees in front of the toilet.

I threw up over and over, as though direction had been reversed in my body. I couldn't stop. Vomiting is never fun, but the reminder that I had absolutely no authority over my body was almost worse.

When I finally finished, I flushed the toilet and used the counter to pull myself to my feet to rinse out my mouth. The woman in the mirror startled me: I looked so pale and clammy, like the slightest sway of the ship might knock me over. The scar tissue across my abdomen throbbed, indignant about the rough treatment. My body had grown accustomed to infinite care and slowness, and then I'd slammed it around the little cabin.

In the mirror, I looked at the bathroom door, which was still open a crack. If I went through it and turned left, the cabin door was only a step or two away. I could probably make it out of the stateroom before she could stop me.

But then what? There was nowhere to go. We were on a ship, and she was crew. I might evade her for a little while, but if she wanted to hurt me, she could probably get a key to my cabin anytime she wanted.

Besides… she was delusional, yes, but she was *healing*. She'd just proved that her hand was repairing itself rapidly, even if the process looked raw and horrifying.

I wanted to know how. It wasn't just about replicating the process for myself, although I had to admit I still had hopes for that particular long shot. But I wanted to *know*. She'd said it herself: the world was bigger than I thought. Some part of me was interested in that.

I left the bathroom. Caroline hadn't moved from her perch on the edge of the bed, and she made no move when I edged past her and wedged myself against the headboard, hugging a pillow to my chest.

I looked at Caroline. "Okay. Tell me the rest."

Seven

Caroline

I came awake – or rather, came to life –gasping with the need for breath. My torso flew upward, my head whiplashing behind it, and I gulped air down in great heaving breaths that were thoroughly unsatisfying, like someone who wakes from a nightmare only to find themselves drowning.

It was, like all births, fiercely violent.

I don't know how long I sat there huffing and wheezing, my panic and need for oxygen playing tug-of-war over my lungs. When I calmed enough to take in my surroundings, I saw that I was in a small, nearly bare room, sitting upright on a long wooden table. In the center of the room, a gas lamp gave off dim light, enough for me to see that I now wore the short-sleeved white satin gown I had packed for my wedding night. I was certain I hadn't taken out of my valise.

Someone had dressed me. Perhaps the same man who'd attacked me at the inn.

As I remembered his massive size and gruesome face, I had the *feeling* of shuddering, but my body did not execute the movement.

I allowed this odd disconnection between my mind and body to distract from my last memory. Was I injured? Had I been ill? I looked down at myself, taking inventory. My arms were bare, the thin fabric of the gown providing little warmth, yet I felt neither chill nor warmth. I couldn't sense the temperature at all.

In fact, I could hardly feel *anything*. The body I inhabited felt leaden and dulled, my limbs strangely heavy. The only sensation I felt was a curious irritation from my eyes when my gaze ventured too close to the gas lamp. The room was very dim, but looking toward the light bothered me.

With effort, I lifted one of my heavy arms and clumsily probed my neck, expecting the pain of deep bruising. I felt nothing.

Had I been drugged? Perhaps I had been in a coma, my muscles growing weak from disuse.

I tested my legs, bending at the knees and ankles. My limbs sluggishly obeyed, slow but strong. Meanwhile, though, I heard a strange metallic clinking with each movement.

Drawing up the hem of the gown until it was just below my knees, I squinted down to find an enormous metal band circling one of my ankles. This shackle connected to a thick chain that dangled off the table and snaked along the floor, out of sight.

I knew this was wrong, and that it meant something, but I was too discombobulated to follow those thoughts just yet. Instead, I lifted my hands until they were just in front of my face, studying them closely. There was the small freckle on my right thumb, and the tiny scar on my right wrist where I'd fallen onto a sharp rock as a child.

I looked at my left hand – and gasped with fresh shock. The hand was very similar in size and appearance to the right, but a fresh line of ugly raw stitches circled the left wrist like a hideous bracelet. When I looked closely, I saw minute differences in the shape of the fingernails and knuckles.

That's not my hand.

Because I had died.

The knowledge crashed into me like a great wave. I could not tell myself I'd been asleep, or comatose, nor was I hallucinating the changes in my body.

I had felt my life seep away through that monster's fingers, and I had *known* what was happening to me. Now my death was as present and obvious in the room as that huge iron shackle.

My sudden and inexplicable consciousness suddenly frightened me, like a ghost story told to a specter. *I should not be awake. I should not be here.* This was all wrong.

I thought that I would cry, but the tears would not come. I suspect now that my tear ducts, like many of my body's physiological responses, were not yet aligned.

I was dead, I was dead, I was dead. This impossible thought repeated over and over until I began to hyperventilate.

Just as I felt I might faint, a voice spoke from the darkness. "Your left hand was crushed beyond saving. I'm pleased to have found such a near match."

I froze, my brain requiring a few extra seconds to translate the words. I could not make out the speaker —they were well past the outer rim of the lamplight —but I knew the voice. Yet I could no more place it than I could pull a dream out of my own head and touch it.

I opened my mouth to ask who was there, but the words tangled in my throat.

"There, there," soothed the voice, in the same singsong tone one uses for babies and helpless animals. "I know you cannot understand me yet, but soon your mind will make the necessary connections. You shall be able to speak, as I am."

The shadows moved as he stepped slowly into the light: first his legs, one and then the other, great trunks holding up the astonishing mass of him. My eyes passed the point where a man's head should be and continued to travel up, until at last he stepped fully into view. He had to be eight feet tall, or near it. I recognized the black lips and misshapen features of my murderer.

"You!" I cried, terrified. "What have you done to me?!"

That is what I meant to say. But all that came out of my mouth was a garbled whimper. As he moved, he held out his hands placatingly, as if to show himself harmless. I knew better. Those hands had been the death of me.

I shrunk back as he stepped closer, but he angled his movements toward the other end of the table, where a chair had been set out.

"You are safe here," my murderer said as he settled his bulk into the chair. He still spoke in that mollifying tone. "I know this is difficult: your senses are unaligned, and will require some days to recalibrate. You need fear no trespass from me in the meantime. Please, rest."

I stared at him, my incomprehension now total. I understood the meaning of his words, but of what worth was a promise of safety from the very creature who had murdered me?

And why was he speaking to me like this, as though I hadn't witnessed his elation as he squeezed my life out of my body?

Something broke in my newly reconstituted awareness. My vision blurred, and all the new strength left my arms, my torso, my stomach. Each new bodily betrayal built to a defeat, and I sank back into merciful unconsciousness.

I awoke lying on my left side with my head pillowed on one arm. Without moving, I cast my eyes around for my attacker, and found him sitting a chair on the other side of the room. A second lamp had been lit on the floor next to him. Though my sight was still slightly blurred, I could make out that he was examining a sheaf of papers, holding them up to catch the light.

I didn't want to attract his attention, so I studied my surroundings without moving. We were in a single large room with doors at either end, likely a small cottage. There was an air of long neglect, as though the space wasn't used for many years, although a cursory attempt had been made to swipe away the dust and grime. There was very little furniture, but well-used scientific objects were piled against one wall. I recognized some of them from Victor's lab: beakers and tubes and tiny devices

for measurement and analysis. The only items in the room that looked new were the thick, dark curtains that my attacker had drawn over the two sets of windows.

My stomach chose that moment to complain loudly, and my opponent looked up and saw that I was awake.

He stood up slowly, moving closer like a hunter approaching an injured doe. Now that I had grown used to his countenance, I did not find him quite so hideous as at first. But I could not forget how his black lips had twisted with glee when he had been squeezing the breath from my throat.

He sat down in the chair at the foot of my bed, though it looked like children's furniture compared to his massive size. "You should eat," he said softly, lifting a bowl that had been hidden beneath the table edge and setting it on the table. I instinctively curled away from him, pulling my legs to my chest and wrapping my arms around them, the chain moving with me. He blinked with surprise. Later I came to understand that he had not expected such a fluid movement from me so quickly.

"Our bodies don't require as much variety as humans," he explained, "but we must still eat to maintain our strength." He tipped the bowl slightly so I could see the contents: raisins, dried apricots, some almonds and chestnuts. My stomach spoke up again, but I made no move toward the food. How could I trust it?

He seemed to understand my hesitance. "The food is safe, I assure you. See?" He picked up a few nuts and thrust them into his enormous mouth, chewing with exaggeration as if I might not know how. Then he set the bowl on the table between us and leaned back in the chair to show he would not interfere.

My resolve broke, and I plunged my hands into the bowl to snatch up the food. My fingers, particularly those on my left hand, were awkward and stiff, and it took me a few moments to pinch the food between them. Even then, much of it fell away during the journey from the bowl to my mouth. This frustrated and angered me – had he chosen such tiny morsels intentionally, to embarrass me with my clumsiness? I picked up the bowl between my palms and lifted the whole thing to my mouth. I poured in the nuts and dried fruit, barely bothering to chew.

As the edge of my hunger was finally sated, my attention was drawn to the taste of the food. I had always enjoyed chestnuts, almonds, and raisins, though I'd never been fond of apricots in any form. Now, though, I could hardly discern any difference between them. It wasn't that they all tasted the same, exactly, but their flavors were dulled and colorless. If my tormentor had thrown in spices from India or handfuls of salt, I doubted the extremes would even register.

A few crumbs spilled down my chest, tumbling uncomfortably under my nightgown. I lifted the neckline to look – and discovered a whole series of fine pink scars covering my chest, much like the branches of a tree. I let out a squeal of shock.

"I believe they are called Lichtenberg figures," my captor explained, watching me with great interest. "From the procedure."

The scars looked raw and swollen, but I felt no pain. I dropped my neckline and pointed to my captor's chest, my fingers not quite curling.

"Woooooo," I managed to say, and he clapped his hands with something like delight on his misshapen features.

"Very good!" he said, as a proud father compliments an infant's gurgles. "It has only been two days since the procedure. I am impressed."

I extended my finger toward his bulk once again. "Of course," he said, seeming to understand. "You want to know who I am." He smiled sadly. "I have no name, I'm afraid. My father never gave me one, and I never took one for myself. Perhaps you and I can name each other. We shall be blank slates, starting fresh as one."

I frowned at that. At least, I tried to frown. My body was no longer reliably responsive to my commands. It was like being placed inside a machine filled with levers I didn't understand.

Through all of that, however, I knew that I had a name: Elizabeth Lavenza Frankenstein. I had, after all, waited my whole life to be a Frankenstein by name as well as by association. I had paid far too steep a price for the privilege.

Did this creature not know my name? Why was he speaking to me as though I was an infant?

My confusion must have shown on my face, though my attacker misunderstood it. "It is all right," he assured me. "I know you don't understand me yet. I will teach you language and speech, as well as how to use your new body. You have much to learn, but we have all the time in the world." He smiled benevolently, though his words were chilling. "You and I shall live forever; that is my gift to you. And you, my dear," he added happily, "are my gift to myself."

He stood awkwardly, hunching a little so as not to loom over me, and edged away from my table. "I shall let you rest now. Tomorrow morning, your education begins."

He shuffled back into the shadows, making an obvious effort to appear harmless and nonthreatening.

It was a wasted effort. Hideous or not, I saw in him what I had so many times before: a man who was as certain of my purpose as he was confident in my obedience.

For the first time since my death, my thoughts felt clear. Whatever I was now, whatever this creature had done to me, he had not expected me to retain any memories or sense of myself. He thought I was like a child, uncomprehending and trusting. And he was a ruthless killer.

I would need to play along.

Eight

Caroline

Convincing my captor that I was the blank slate he had expected was easiest in those first few days, when I could think of nothing else but adjusting to my new form. My body felt like it had tripled in density, and its requirements had changed. I no longer needed to relieve myself, for example: any food or water I consumed was immediately turned into energy. I required very little sleep, although I often pretended I needed rest just so I could lie on my table facing the wall. I was incredibly sensitive to lights.

After a few days, however, my eyesight and hearing began to acclimate. Seeing this, my captor decided I was past the worst of the metamorphosis, and he began his efforts to "educate" me.

Our time soon took on a dreadful uniformity. Each morning, my captor tried to teach me language, while in the afternoons he coaxed me to exercise my body. Every day he left the cabin just after sundown, returning a few hours later with food that he'd gathered or stolen. We ate, and then my kidnapper read aloud from his favorite works, constantly checking my face to see how much I might be retaining.

The nightly reading sessions were the most difficult part of the day, because I was restricted to my table and closely watched by my captor. He read and lectured from *Paradise Lost*, *The Sorrows of Werther*, Plutarch's *Parallel Lives* – texts that Victor had also read aloud or summarized to me. The similar context made me queasy with disgust, and I had to fight to keep these emotions off my face.

Keeping my feelings hidden was more difficult than I had expected, partly because *I* was different. My new form was slower to move, but my temper seemed to have sharpened. It was hard not to react, for example, to my captor's occasional cruel commentary on the texts he read. When I slipped up, I had to compensate by reacting to other, innocuous statements as well, a balancing act that exhausted me even before I came to understand my captor's true intentions.

Perhaps a week after I awoke in the cottage, I noticed his eyes lingering on my breasts beneath the thin gown. I finally had the realization which now seems so obvious: I was more than an experiment, or even a victim. He was training me to be his mate.

The idea terrified me so much I had to feign sudden exhaustion and turn toward the wall.

In life, I had been almost completely ignorant of human sexuality. It wasn't just that I was inexperienced – I was also unenlightened. Young people today are casual about discussing intercourse, but it was different then, especially for someone as sheltered as I had been. I'm sure many young women discussed their wedding night with mothers or aunts, but Victor's mother had died when we were young, and my isolation prevented me from forming other connections. I had never learned even the mechanics of sexual intercourse.

I'd always felt safe with Victor, whom I had known all my life and who had never been predatory about my body. Victor had admired men. We both assumed we would have intercourse eventually, but for the purposes of pregnancy. The first time would be awkward and embarrassing, but we would find our way together.

Instead, I was trapped in this small space with an enormous, powerful murderer, one who soon looked at me with greedy impatience.

From the beginning, he found excuses to brush against me in small, almost innocent ways. When he insisted that I move around the cabin to test my new body, for example, he took great pleasure in guiding me with a hand on my lower back. He brushed my hair each night, using the opportunity to caress my shoulders. I was glad for my dulled reflexes, which prevented me from betraying myself with a shudder.

The small intimacies escalated alongside my "studies." I came to understand that despite the horrors he'd inflicted, my captor had some sense of himself as civilized. I did not think he would force himself on me, at least not while he thought me childlike and helpless. But the more intelligent and capable I became to him, the faster his physical contact developed.

Every waking moment was fraught with this tension between maintaining the illusion of childlike blankness and my desperation for rescue – or at the very least, answers. Hiding my self-awareness from my attacker was difficult, but it was even harder to suppress the thousand questions I wanted to ask the man who had killed me.

I wondered how he had resurrected me, of course, but at the time I was much more concerned with the *why* than the *how*. Why had he chosen me as his victim? Could there be a connection between this monster and the death of little William, or perhaps Victor's beloved Henry? Those murders were months and countries apart, but it seemed unlikely that the three of us, whose young lives had been so tangled together, were each randomly targeted for death.

The question that *most* tormented me was, however, what had happened to Victor after I died. It seemed likely that my captor had murdered Victor shortly after he killed me, but I couldn't stop myself from wondering if my husband and closest friend might have somehow escaped. If my killer had stolen my body from the room that night, Victor might yet believe me to be alive. In that case, surely he was searching for me.

I tried to think about this idea as little as possible. I was terrified that my captor would see the hope on my face.

Hard as I tried to "learn" slowly, to never react, to obscure my feelings, every day felt like walking a high wire after I'd already plummeted to my death. And the more his eyes lingered on my body, the more tiny liberties he took with his touch, the more I realized I was running out of time.

Six weeks after my resurrection, I decided I could not wait for Victor to find me. I would need to find a way to escape by myself.

But how? It was obvious that I would never win a physical altercation with my captor. My only real chance, then, was to escape during his evening jaunts into the forest.

In those early weeks I had spent those hours collapsed on my table in exhaustion, relieved for a break from my constant performance. Now, however, I began by searching for a key to my shackle. The chain was only about four meters long, but if I laid down on the ground and stretched my limbs as far as possible, I found I could extend that range even farther.

Still, it didn't take long to examine every millimeter of the cottage. I had to conclude that my captor kept the key on his person.

I had no clock at my disposal, but I was mindful of the amount of fuel spent in the gas lamp. When my attacker returned I was sitting patiently at the edge of my table with my hands folded in my lap.

The following night, when he went out to gather food, I began to test my bonds.

The chain that anchored my shackle to the wall was immense, almost comically out of proportion to my own size. It looked like something one would find in a circus, used to chain up bull elephants before their forced performance. I checked each link, one by one, for any weaknesses in the metal. My fingers were clumsy and stiff, especially the fingers on my left hand, the one that had been harvested from another dead woman. I did my best to avoid looking at it.

As I worked, I talked to myself, putting real effort into my speech for the first time. I recited simple nursery rhymes, ignoring my clumsy pronunciation.

I tried again the next evening, and the one after that. Soon I had switched from nursery rhymes to the poetry I had memorized during my limited schooling.

I made my discovery on the eighth night of my efforts, as I went over the chain for what felt like the hundredth time. The chain itself was impossible to damage, but there was a weakness in the component that attached it to the wall: this loop of metal was thinner than the others, and by wrapping my fist around it I could twist it back and forth. The metal warmed in my hand, and my hope was that with enough repetition I could make it snap.

But my captor had already been gone for well over an hour, and I dared not continue that evening. When he returned I was standing next to my table, stretching my arms over my head and rolling my head as though I'd been loosening my body, one of the exercises he'd recommended.

The next night I worked at the metal component again, and the night after that. My hands were clumsy, but they never seemed to tire, no matter how long I twisted the metal.

On the tenth day after I resolved to escape, I found an angle that allowed me to twist the metal back and forth quickly, so it grew warmer and warmer in my hand. Excited, I redoubled my efforts, trying to increase the warmth and soften the metal enough to pull it apart. I was so focused on twisting the chain that I forgot to check the progress of gas in the lamp. I never heard the gentle rain begin outside the window. I didn't even look up until the cabin door swung inward, revealing my captor.

Nine

Caroline

He stood framed in the doorway, rain pelting against his wet back. "What is this?" he roared, crossing the room in four impossibly fast strides. There was no time to bend the metal back into place or disguise my actions; he was on me in seconds, one meaty hand wrapping around my neck and lifting, lifting, until my feet left the floor. He pinned me to the wall with one hand, so we were eye-to-eye.

Lightning struck somewhere outside the open door, briefly illuminating his mottled skin and twisted, enraged features. "You are trying to *abandon* me?" he shouted, his hot stinking of decay. "After all I've done for you?!"

In life, this moment would have terrified me well beyond reason or function. To my astonishment, however, my own temper flared. I batted his hand away from my neck, making him drop me and step back with surprise.

Though I barely reached his shoulder, I glared up at him and screamed. "All you've done for me? *You killed me!*"

"You can speak?" He stepped back farther. "And you... you..."

"Remember?" I spat. "I remember everything. You murdered me!" His face twisted up with doubt and chagrin.

I pressed my advantage. "You wanted me to scream for my husband. Did you kill him as well?"

Strangely, this question seemed to settle him, his expression returning to livid malice. "No. Victor yet lives. I wanted him to suffer your loss before I end his life." His black lips twisted up in a smirk even as he grabbed my upper arm, pinning me in place. "You should have seen his face as your empty coffin was lowered into the ground."

"But *why?*" I burst out. The Frankensteins had money, but not the kind of ostentatious wealth or political connections that would inspire such terrible vengeance. "Why target us? Who *are* you?"

My captor's face went slack, though his grip on me did not loosen. "Victor did not explain?"

"Victor…" His pitying tone unnerved me. I had no reason to believe anything he said, but doubt began to squirm within me. I struggled to pull my arm free from his grasp, but I may as well have been pushing against stone. "Explain what?"

"Just as I am your maker, Victor was mine."

I stared at my captor, bewildered. He was hideous, yes, but it had never occurred to me that he had undergone a similar procedure to my own.

Vainly, my first thought was for my appearance. I had not seen a mirror since my rebirth–did I look as horrifying as he? Then his accusation caught up with me. "You're suggesting my husband resurrected a strange dead man?"

His face hardened again. "Your husband collected the limbs and organs of the dead, merging them into this." He gestured contemptuously at his massive body and twisted facial features. "Then he abandoned me at the very moment of my birth."

I cringed, dropping my eyes from his glare. He shook me violently by the arm until I looked back at him. "I stole his formulas to create you," my attacker continued. "Victor is the architect of us both."

"You're lying," I whispered. The man he described could not be my awkward, distracted, amiable Victor. Surely he wouldn't create this abomination.

My attacker snorted, releasing me with a shake. "I'll prove it then." He stalked across the room to the far end of the cottage, where a stack of papers and novels leaned against the wall.

Numbly, I sank down to the floor, pulling my knees to my body. The heavy chain clinked with my movements. I watched as he sifted through the paper with quick, determined motions.
Finally, my captor yanked a sheaf of papers from his collection and stormed back across the room to me.

"There," he spat, throwing them in my lap, "there is my formation, in Victor's own hand."

He crossed his arms over his chest and loomed over me as I unfolded the papers with my clumsy fingers. I recognized Victor's handwriting immediately, of course—I knew it as well as I knew my own. But these were not the pensive letters or fretting journal entries I had seen so often.

Instead, each page was filled with diagrams, notes, and chemical formulas. Leafing through them, I could only pick out a few recognizable terms: "animation" and "vivisection," and references to specimens from charnel houses and graveyards.

What struck me most, however, were two words scribbled at the bottom of the last page, underlined several times for emphasis:

New species.

My tormentor thrust his finger at the words. "You see?" he said triumphantly. "Your beloved Victor sought to create a new species. I am the result, and I used my father's methods to create you."

I shook my head, overwhelmed to the point of light-headedness. In my previous life I might have fainted, but this body was too sturdy to provide even those few seconds of precious ignorance.

My own, sweet husband had gone against every law of nature and man, creating the abomination that now stood before me.

This hadn't just happened, either: the pages describing his experiment were dated from over a year ago. Victor had kept it from me for months and months.

Years.

The pieces that had been missing so long finally began to link in my mind.

"It *was* you," My eyes met my captor's again. "William? Henry?"

He shrugged. "One to bring him home, one to regain his attention when it waned."

I flinched at his careless dismissal of lives, especially those who had been so beloved to me. "William was a little boy!" I cried, earning a scowl from my captor. "How could you– but no, you didn't stop at murdering him. You made Justine hang for the crime!"

Justine. The sister of my heart.

I remembered the night of her sentencing, when Victor and I had sat with her in her gaol cell. She'd been terrified of her execution, of course, but she was also anguished by the idea that she'd be remembered forever as a child killer. I had clutched her hand until my fingers ached, trying to reassure her as she begged us to believe she'd never hurt William.

And Victor had been right there holding her other hand, weeping alongside us. He'd been nearly green, I remembered now. Victor had always been sensitive; I assumed he was as heartsick over Justine's fate as I was. I had never questioned that he shared my anguish and confusion. But his sorrow hadn't been for Justine's fate.

It had been guilt. Because he knew full well the real killer was the abomination he had created.

As the understanding sank in, time seemed to stop, and I forgot to breathe. Victor had always known who killed William and had not a word, to me or Justine or the courts. He'd watched her die – he'd *let* her die – for his mistakes.

I didn't want to know this. I didn't want to lift the terrible burden of this knowledge, much less carry it with me. This creature had taken my life weeks earlier. That moment of realization in the cottage, however – that was when Elizabeth Frankenstein died.

My own expression must have given away my resignation, because my attacker's face suddenly lit up with triumph. "Now you see my creator's true nature," he crowed.

Then, to my absolute astonishment, my killer dropped effortlessly to his knees, gazing up at me with beseeching eyes. "But I am superior to Victor. He never trained me, never cared for me, never loved me as I have loved you."

"*Love?*" I whispered incredulously, watching him take my hand – no, the hand that was not mine.

My captor misunderstood my meaning and smiled broadly. "Yes. Join with me willingly; become my mate. We shall name each other. Together, we can far surpass Frankenstein's work." His eyes lowered to my midsection, then gazed back at me expectantly.

I was already reeling from the sudden turns of his mood, so it took me a moment to comprehend his meaning.

Children. He wanted me to have his children.

I could not speak. My chest felt crushed by horror and hopelessness. As a living woman, I had been the property of the Frankenstein family, in the eyes of man and God. They had made me into a pet, trotted out to mind the children and organize the household in my pretty dresses. Now was I to spend my remaining years subservient to this creature?

I felt a strange moisture on my cheeks. I pulled my hands away from my captor's and lifted my fingers to my face, examining what I found. Tears. Ordinary, watery tears, indistinguishable from those I shed throughout my lifetime.

Whatever I now was, I could still weep. It was strangely fortifying.

I lowered my hand and looked my captor in the eyes. "No," I said simply. "I already have a name; it is Elizabeth Lavenza. I shall never be your mate, and I shall *never* love you."

He was on his feet instantly, looking over me. I expected his face to purple with rage again, and backed away, bracing myself for the blows that were surely coming.

Instead, however, he examined me with icy frankness. "Clearly, I have erred in your creation."

I took another step away, nearly sliding as my foot found a length of my chain. I was just above the spot where it attached to the wall. "On that we can agree," I said warily.

"Frankenstein constructed me of many parts, man and animal, that I might have my own soul and create my own new memories," he continued. "I previously considered this a curse. Perhaps that was short-sighted."

The same strong fingers that had ended my life reached toward my neck again – but he only collected a springy curl of my hair, like capturing a fragile insect.

"You were so beautiful, and I was hasty," he said thoughtfully. "I used too much of you. Perhaps I need to begin again with less."

He meant to destroy me again, I realized, and use pieces of me to construct a new, soulless creation like himself. I wanted to vomit, to evacuate the poison of that idea from my entire being, but my new body was indifferent to this longing.

The monster stared down at my body with cold assessment, like he was measuring furniture to fit in an alcove.

The fear drained out of me, replaced by wrathful self-righteousness. No. I would not be a pretty present for another. Whatever I had become, I would claim for myself.

But he was so much bigger than me, and I did not know his weaknesses. Would he succumb to the same physical threats as a man?

I dropped my face into my hands, doubling over as if to weep. "Please, you mustn't," I moaned, hoping this creature did not know enough of human behavior to see through the deception. I bent into a crouch, pretending to weep, though my right hand lowered to the chain still shackled to my ankle.

"I shall ensure it is painless this time. Come now." He bent toward me, reaching to pull me up under my arms like a toddler.

I drove myself upward with all my new, leaden power, clutching the slack of my chain in one hand. As quickly as I could, I looped it around the creature's neck and yanked downward.

Surprise overcame his features, and his arms pinwheeled as he lost his balance. We both toppled sideways, thudding onto the floor next to my table. I recovered faster, climbing to my hands and knees and crawling to the table, where I wrapped the final loop of chain around a table leg. I clung to the loop with both hands as he pulled at the other end of the chain. He was trying to loosen that end of it, but his position was awkward, twisted half sideways, and I stretched out my manacled ankle, tightening the noose.

His eyes blazed with a wrath that terrified me even as they began to bulge. I clung to my loop of chain with all my strength as he alternately tugged the chain and flailed his arms, trying to reach behind himself to strike at me. My new body was too sturdy to be affected, and the metal table was held down with four sturdy bolts; the steel groaned but did not give. Then my attacker yanked hard at the other end of the chain – and to our mutual shock, the metal I had worked so hard to weaken tore free from the wall.

He began to scramble toward me, and I scrambled clumsily to get away. My churning feet kicked his head, which bounced wetly off one steel table leg – a lucky strike.

My murderer lay still.

I suspected he was dead, but I didn't wait to find out. I patted his pockets and found what I hoped for: a small silver key. With trembling fingers, I unlocked the manacle on my ankle and snatched up the sheaf of paper with the instructions for reanimation. Then I half-crawled, half-staggered toward the door.

As I threw myself into the cool, impossibly fresh night air, I thought I heard a groan behind me. I ran for the cover of the trees, praying that my attacker would not follow.

Ten

Heck

Maddie, most of the women I know have at least one story about being physically threatened of a man. Mine isn't that bad, luckily: a guy cornered me in the stairwell when I was a freshman at the University of Washington Seattle. I was coming back from the library, where I'd been cramming for a biology midterm the next morning. By the time I got back to my dorm it was nearly midnight, and my brain was so stuffed with information that I thought it might leak out if I stopped thinking about it for two minutes. All I wanted was to fall into my bed.

The only working elevator in the building took forever, and my room was on the second floor, so I'd automatically gone to the stairwell to trudge up the stairs. This was long before I knew anything about Ehlers-Danlos Syndrome, and I could handle most physical demands back then, thanks to lots of walking and yoga.

As I climbed, I barely registered the door opening again below me, or the person who started to ascend the stairs after me. I wasn't think about anything but biology until I was on the landing and a male voice said, "You're that freshman with the weird name, right?"

I turned and finally noticed him: a tall sophomore I'd seen around the building. That night he was dressed in jeans and a

Seahawks jersey, and I remember thinking he would have been cute if he took better care of his skin.

"Heck," I'd said.

"I'm James." His breath stank of beer. I automatically stepped back as he advanced, and then I was backed against the wall. "You smell really good."

"Thanks." I tried to sidestep, keeping my voice light. "Sorry, I have an early midterm tomorrow. I'm just headed to bed."

He put a hand up against the wall, trapping me. That was the moment when I realized I might need the pepper spray I kept in my backpack…which was now pressed firmly into the wall, out of reach.

He put his other hand on my waist. "Maybe I could join you." He loomed over me.

This went on for a few more minutes – I made polite excuses to get away, he told me not to be such a bitch, that I should give him a chance, he was a really good guy. All the while he was touching me, his hands sliding to the small of my back.

I still remember the strength in his arms, and the horrible realization that to this person, I was nothing more than a body he wanted to borrow for his own use. When he bent his head down to kiss me, ignoring my stammering protests, I thought my racing pulse alone was going to kill me.

Then the door opened on the floor above us. Three people came laughing and stumbling into the stairwell, talking about a party, and James was distracted. I pushed away one of his arms and fled.

I never told anyone about James and the stairwell – after all, I'd escaped. I rode the slow elevator for the rest of the year, always with my pepper spray in hand, but I'd come through the moment unscathed. More or less.

It a very specific flavor of fear, though: being trapped by someone bigger and more powerful who wants to fuck you.

After Caroline described her escape from her captor, she didn't say anything else for a long time. Her head was turned downward, and with her strange skin and unnatural stillness, she looked like a store mannequin.

I tried to choose my words carefully. "It sounds like you went through something really scary," I said. "I'm sorry."

Her eyes lifted, narrowing at me. "You still don't believe me."

I shrugged. "Lots of people go through trauma and tell themselves a different story to hide from the truth. Plenty of them even believe the new story. I haven't heard 'I'm the bride of Frankenstein' before, but it's not that different from 'I made him do it.'"

To my surprise, Caroline laughed. It wasn't a happy noise. "You really don't see it, do you?"

"See what?"

Caroline took a slow, pointed look all the way around the stateroom, her eyes lingering on the medications and braces scattered around. "You're not on a cruise to have fun, Heck. Are you really going to Juneau to see your boyfriend?"

Ah. She could tell there was something I wasn't telling her, and that made me look hypocritical. Fair enough.

"Yes, but he's not expecting me." I told her. "We broke up four months ago. I'm trying to win him back."

"Why not just call him?"

I took a deep breath. "I had an accident, a concussion. I was in the hospital for a long time. By the time I got out, his number had changed."

"And he moved to Juneau while you were in the hospital?"

It was the lack of emotion in her voice that got me, I think. I could have fought off condescension or pity, but she sounded so… mild. Like my therapist. It made me feel crazy.

No – it made me feel like she'd exposed my crazy. "You don't get to judge me," I snapped. "I'm not the one who thinks I'm a fucking literary character."

She regarded me for a moment, then asked a question that was soft but sharp, a blade thrust into the space between words. "Where's your daughter, Heck?"

My mouth dropped open slightly, and I felt the paranoia bubble up. "How do you know about my daughter?"

"You told me your daughter's not traveling with you."

I *had* said that. I relaxed an inch.

"So where is she? With her father?" Caroline persisted, blade pushing deeper. "Did he take her to Juneau to get away from you?"

"That's enough." Dropping the pillow, I carefully swung my legs over the side and stood up from the bed. I was done being curious about this woman, done humoring her. "You told me your story, and I listened. Now I'd like you to leave."

Caroline stood and took a tiny step sideways, blocking the hallway. We stood there looking warily at each other like two gunfighters in front of a saloon. I felt out of control and weak, wishing I could dig my nails into my torso and scratch the itchy mess below the skin. My doctor in Seattle had sworn all the dissolvable stitches would have been absorbed by my body by now, but I could still feel them.

Finally, she shook her head, turning toward the door. "We'll talk again soon." She slipped into the hallway and disappeared.

I stared there, gaping. It seemed... too easy. After a moment I went to the cabin door and checked through the peephole, pressing my ear against the cool laminate surface until I was certain the hallway was empty. I tested the lock and bolted the door.

Now my brain is full of fog and horror – the image of Caroline's skin worming itself back together seems to appear on the back of my eyelids whenever I blink. *We'll talk again soon.* What could she want from me? We have nothing to offer each other.

The idea that she could come back at *any* moment and intrude on my space scares me more than the idea of physical pain. I gathered up this journal and my pen, along with some blankets and pillows, and made myself a nest on the floor in front of the door. Now my hand is cramped and aching from hours of writing, and I'm no calmer than I was when Caroline left.

There is someone *wrong* on this ship, Maddie, and I'm trapped here with her. If anything happens to me, if I don't email your grandmother tomorrow, hopefully someone will find this journal.

All my love to you and Colin, Mommy

Eleven

Tuesday, Day 4 at sea
Pain scale: 6

Dear Madison,

I slept fitfully in my blanket nest, my dreams an unsettling tangle of memory and nightmare. I kept seeing the sickly strings of Caroline's flesh reattaching themselves in her hand, mixed with Colin's face the last time I saw him, and all that blood in the hospital.

I woke up aching and stiff and feeling... well, extremely silly. Especially after I re-read all the dramatic stuff I wrote last night. I bought this journal so I could write about Colin's and my love story. Dr. Steinmen said it would help to frame it as letters to you, even if you can't read them. Now I feel as though Caroline, or Elizabeth, or whatever she wants to call herself, has hijacked this lovely diary. Frankly, I'm halfway to tossing it over my balcony railing and straight into the ocean – but there's a tiny little voice telling me... not yet. Not until I get safely to Juneau. Caroline is still out there.

This morning, I crept out of my cabin to retrieve breakfast from the Starbucks on my floor. When I got back to the room, I took my medications and some Advil and spent some time just staring through the sliding glass doors into the gray fog and thinking.

There is an employee on this ship with me who cannot be trusted. She's either a two-hundred-year-old monster from

Regency-era literature, or, *much* more likely, a regular person suffering from a number of physical and psychological illnesses that make her potentially dangerous. And she wants something from me.

I could go to the ship authorities, but what would I say? There are video cameras on the pool deck and in the hallways, but they'll only show an employee being injured by glass and then escorting a disabled woman back to her cabin while the ship was unsteady. If I try to tell them Caroline is delusional, it'll be my word against hers. Given how crazy it all sounds, the staff might take a closer look at my ticket. It wouldn't long to realize that the points I used came from someone else's account. Would they call my mother? If they did, would she mention that she hadn't given me permission to use her points?

I'm almost certain Mom wouldn't have me arrested… almost. But there was a moment back at the hospital when she threatened to have me committed, and *that,* she might still do.

I need to forget about last night and stay away from Caroline. Focus on getting to Colin.

But why did she say we'd speak again soon?

The ship is docked in Ketchikan this morning – we're already there; although I can't see much through the damned fog. My original plan was to stay in my room all day, but I'm too unnerved by the idea that Caroline could turn up at my door at any moment. If your dad was here, I know he'd be kissing my hands and pulling me gently toward the door, teasing me until I laughed and agreed to follow him anywhere. Without him I feel trapped by my shyness and fears. But I've decided to load up on ibuprofen and knee braces and go ashore. I'll find a library or coffee shop and work on Colin's research. Wish me luck, sweetheart.

Love, Mommy

Twelve

Wednesday, day 5 at sea
Pain scale: 5

Dear Madison,

I did go into Ketchikan yesterday, as I promised, but that's where my plans fell apart.

Getting off the ship in the morning took ages – I had to wait in a long line to have the security people scan my ship ID badge, and then I had to cross an enormous gangplank to get to shore through the fog. I grew up in Seattle, a city famous for its wet climate, but after only a year in Wisconsin this weather feels strange to me. Since we left Seattle, I've only seen opaque, monotonous fog.

Ketchikan was no exception. When I walked into the "downtown" area I could only make out two or three storefronts at a time. It didn't take long for me to need a rest, so I sat down on a bench and pulled out my cell phone.

I didn't get service on the ship, so it had been off for the last few days. I took a few breaths and powered it back on, watching as it linked up to the local cellular towers and the notifications came in.

There were thirty-nine missed calls and twenty voicemails from my mother.

I didn't have it in me to listen to them. She wouldn't say anything that I wanted to have recorded verbatim in my memory

66

forever. But my phone had the option to turn voicemails into text, so I scrolled through, skimming the text.

Don't know what you were thinking

Half a mind to call the police

And my least favorite: *Thank God your father's not alive to see you like this*

I wrote her a quick text that simply said, "Ship is docked in Ketchikan and everything's going great. Let's talk after the cruise." Then I turned the phone off again and stowed it in my backpack. She was furious and hurt, but it didn't sound like she was going to call the police. And hopefully the next time I talked to her I'd be calling from Juneau, asking her to send my things. Or maybe Colin would want to do long distance for a little while first, to make sure he and I could get back to how things used to be. I could handle that. I could be flexible.

The moisture in the air coagulated into misty rain, the kind that seems to come from every direction at once. I'd worn a rain jacket, but my leggings and orthopedic shoes were soaked through almost immediately. I got up from the bench and began walking further into town, looking for a café where I could spend a few hours working on Colin's notes.

While I waited at a crosswalk for the light to change, I scanned the nearby businesses, still hoping for a coffee shop. Instead, two words jumped out at me: Parnassus Books.

Maddie, when you grow up with history and literature professors and then study linguistics, certain words just snap out for attention, especially anything related to Greek or Egyptian mythology. Mount Parnassus is a mountain above Delphi. It was the home of the Muses… and sacred to the sun god Apollo.

Suddenly I was back at the University of Wisconsin campus a year and a half earlier, walking into Weeks Hall for a job interview with a geologist named A. Colin Carson. I was in grad school on scholarship, but I needed a part-time job if I was going to avoid taking out student loans to cover my food and housing.

Early December in Wisconsin was freezing. A blizzard had deposited eight inches of snow two days earlier, so I paused inside the entrance to the geology building to stomp off my boots and unzip my lumpy quilted parka, an early Christmas gift from my mom.

Dr. Carson's email had instructed me to meet him at "the big globe," which made more sense when I saw the small museum just inside the building. The space was divided by a wall of clear glass, giving me a good view of the massive globe suspended from the ceiling just inside the entrance. It was anchored by a small pedestal, but even if had been set on the ground, it would have been taller than me. I headed towards the museum.

I didn't see them until I paused inside the door: a dozen elementary school children were laying on the floor under the globe, the tops of their heads crowded around the pedestal. There was an adult under there, too, although from that angle all I could see were a set of adult-sized legs in jeans and black Chuck Taylor sneakers. "Most people visit Antarctica by this route here," he was saying. "There are lots of penguins and seals, just like in the book we read. There's also a *lot* of permafrost, which is what I study. "

A pile of colorful children's coats was heaped on the floor next the only other person in the room: a nervous-looking woman who watched the kids with her arms wrapped around a thin stack of picture books. She was clearly the teacher in charge.

Awkwardly, I edged around the globe toward her, taking care not to step on any tiny legs. Every step revealed a little bit more of the man under the globe: first the shirttail of a black canvas button-down, then a right hand with four small casts on the fingers, which rested on the man's stomach. A broad chest, trim goatee, and there: a man's face. I stood near the teacher, watching him interact with the kids.

She leaned in to whisper to me. "Are you here for Dr. Carson? I'm afraid our field trip is running a little late."

"I'm early," I assured her, still looking at him.

I'd thought Dr. A. Colin Carson was handsome when I saw his photo on the department website, but the picture hadn't captured his vibrancy. Even just lying on the floor, he was animated and charming, with a kinetic Midwestern energy, as though he was about to pop up and offer to help milk cows.

"No, I've been to the North Pole, not Antarctica," he said to a little boy, answering a question I hadn't heard. "It's on the top of this big globe. I wish I could show you, but the nice lady who runs the museum says I'm not allowed to roll the Earth around on the floor."

The children giggled. One particularly eager boy used the moment of distraction to stretch a hand up toward the model. Before I even fully registered his intention, his teacher was stepping forward.

"Felix," she began, but Colin was ahead of her, gently catching the boy's sleeve.

"Hey, buddy, remember I said we were only going to look with our eyes?"

"I just want to know how the water feels," the boy protested.

"It's *very* cold. *Brrr.*" Colin gave a dramatic shudder, which had a couple of the kids giggling again. "And if you really want to know what the south pole feels like, you can study geology like me. When you're a grownup, we'll go to Antarctica and touch anything we want."

"Penguins!" one little girl declared.

"A big seal!" said another.

Colin nodded solemnly, beginning to slide away from the model so he could sit up. "These are good ideas; we'll touch all of those. What else will we touch in Antarctica?"

The kids crawled away from the globe and stood up, naming everything they could think of that lived in Antarctica – which was a fairly short list, so the suggestions quickly escalated to "Yeti" and "mermaids" and something called Octonauts. Colin made a show of considering each idea as he and the teacher helped sort out the big pile of coats.

I hung back shyly, admiring his easy way with them. I wasn't easy with anyone.

As the students and their teacher departed, Colin turned to me and lifted his left hand to smooth down his hair, grinning. "I've got dust all over my back, don't I?" he said, turning sideways to show me. The black shirt and jeans were streaked with white.

"Um… yes."

"Awesome." He pumped his fist. "I'll tell the janitor she doesn't have to clean under the globe again this week."

I smiled hesitantly, not sure if he was kidding.

"You must be Heck Saville. Thanks for meeting me here. I do technically have an office, but I'm just an assistant professor, so even calling it a 'cubicle' would be aspirational."

"Do you do a lot of field trips?"

"Whenever I can. It's a volunteer thing, a few of us take turns on our lunch breaks. I love kids." He looked around him suddenly, scanning the floor and exhibits. "Let's see, I had a… there it is."

He speed-walked to a display of geodes, reaching behind it to retrieve a messenger bag. With the strap over his shoulder, he gestured to a nearby bench. "Shall we sit?"

"Sure." I followed him to the bench, settling down at one end so he had plenty of room. Colin set the bag on the bench between us and blew out a breath. "Okay, so, over the summer I led a research trip to the north pole – the magnetic north pole, not the geographic one. Do you know anything about the poles?"

"No," I admitted.

"That's okay; I just didn't want to assume. The *geographic* north pole is the northernmost point on the planet. But the magnetic north pole…" he reached awkwardly into the breast pocket of his shirt with his good hand and pulled out a chunk of metal about two inches long. "I had this for the kids. Can I see your hand?"

He held out his injured hand to me, and without a second's hesitation I laid my own hand over it. By then I was already lost.

Colin put the magnet in the center of my palm and sort of spun it slightly back and forth. "The forces that generate Earth's magnetic field shift, which means that the north pole and south pole wander around a bit." He touched his left pointer finger to several spots on my palm as he spoke, sliding the magnet to point to them.

"Okay..." I said, trying not to blush. I really didn't want him to take his hand away.

"We know it moves, but we don't know why it's started to move faster the last few years," Colin said, looking up to meet my eyes. "But I've got a theory that it's connected to the melting permafrost."

"Uh-huh."

He picked up the magnet and slipped it back into his breast pocket, releasing my hand. I took it back with more than a little disappointment. "Last summer I took a bunch of readings and notes while I was on a research expedition. Because my fingers were too cold to write, I recorded my notes in a digital recorder. I've been trying to transcribe everything this semester, but then I went rock-climbing over Thanksgiving break." He held up his injured hand and ruefully waved the little casts at me. "The department scraped up a budget for me to get someone to transcribe the notes and help with some other stuff: organizing the research for my paper, typing up my lectures, that sort of thing. Your application said you've done transcription work before?"

"In high school I had a part-time job transcribing school board meetings."

He nodded, and I saw a flash of curiosity in his eyes. "Under 'skills,' your resume says you have a mnemonic memory."

"Yes." I fought not to squirm. This was another conversation I'd had a thousand times.

"There was a kid in my neighborhood who had a photographic memory, but I didn't know there was an audio version until I read your resume."

"It's not a magic superpower or anything," I warned. "I can recall things word-for-word when I hear them out loud, that's all. It's a party trick."

"For how long?" He held up a hand and sort of waved it, looking for words. "I mean, for how long can you recall something you hear?"

I shrugged. "A year? Two? I've never tested it like that."

He looked disappointed with that answer. I took a breath and recited, "Most people visit Antarctica by this route here. There are lots of penguins and seals, just like in the book we read. There's also a lot of permafrost, which is what I study."

Colin beamed, actually clapping his hands – well, his palms – together. "You're wrong, Heck, that *is* a superpower." He paused, tilting his head to think. "Is Heck short for something?"

"Heqet," I admitted. "She was the –"

"Egyptian goddess of fertility," he supplied.

"Well done," I told him. "Most people outside the History department haven't heard of her."

"I went through a mythology phase when I was trying to decide between geology and archeology." He repeated the name slowly, as if tasting it. "Heqet. Hmm."

"I know. It sounds like a cat coughing up a hairball."

He chuckled. "It's not *that* bad. But you could always take a page out of my book and go by your middle name."

"I don't have one."

He widened his eyes dramatically. "Wow, your parents *really* committed to their plan. At least mine gave me Colin as an escape hatch."

"Why, what does the 'A' stand for?"

He lowered his voice and leaned toward me, holding up one hand to dramatically cover his mouth as he whispered, "Apollo."

Now, eighteen months later and three thousand miles away, I stared at Parnassus Books. I suddenly had a crazy impulse to go inside and look for a copy of –

"It's not there," said a familiar voice over my shoulder.

I jerked around to find Caroline standing on the sidewalk right behind me, holding a wide umbrella. I automatically took a step back.

Today she wore a shapeless gray dress instead of her uniform, her eyes still hidden behind the sunglasses. When I recoiled, she made a little noise of impatience and inched closer, and I realized she was trying to shelter me under the umbrella. "I'm not going to hurt you, Heck." She smiled dryly. "Especially not out here on a public street."

I made myself hold still. "That's not funny."

"My apologizes." Waving at the door to the bookstore, she added, "I saw you standing here and thought you might be looking for Mary's book. This place mostly sells airport thrillers and adult coloring books."

"What are you doing here?" My heart felt like it was about to bounce right out of my chest. The whole point of leaving the ship was to avoid bumping into Caroline, and now she was close enough for me to smell her lilac perfume. "Did you follow me?"

"Of course not. I come here whenever I'm in Ketchikan," Caroline said matter-of-factly. "We don't get a lot of free time on the ship, but I spend most of it reading."

I started to edge away again. The fog was too close, and I was still unnerved by the night before. Caroline's presence disrupted my quiet little world. I realize, of course, that insanity and delusions aren't actually contagious, but I also know being around crazy people can make you feel crazier yourself.

"If you're going back to the ship, I could –" Caroline began to say, but just then a little girl of around six came sprinting down the block to my left, headed in our direction. She wore a denim jacket, fairy wings, and an enormous, impish grin.

There was a woman behind her, huffing to catch up. "Lila! I said stop!" the woman yelled, but the little girl ignored her. "Don't run into the street!"

As the girl raced toward us, Caroline leaned against the brick building, as though making way for the girl to run by. Reflexively, I planted my feet and held my arms open as the girl approached. Lila ran straight into me, throwing her arms around me, causing me to drop my cane and stagger backward.

Pain ran up my spine, but I couldn't help but laugh as Lila giggled into my waist. "Hi-hi!" she sang to me, as though we'd planned this game in advance and she'd just won.

The woman, red-faced and distraught, caught up to us and took the girl by the arm. "Lila! You scared Mommy!" she panted. "You could have been hurt!"

Lila tilted her head up to look at me, still giggling, to see if I agreed. "She's right, sweetheart," I said, trying to make my face solemn. "You might have fallen. I'm so glad you're okay."

Intrigued by this possible future in which she had fallen, Lila released me and turned to her mother. The woman was already thanking me, in the apologetic babble of the recently terrified. "She's not usually this hyper, but the time change is messing with her and I think she just had all this pent-up energy –"

I stopped listening. I'd glanced sideways, and seen Caroline still pressed up against the side of the brick building. Her gaze was fixed on the little girl, her lips pressed together in a trembling line as she stared at the little girl.

She was *afraid* of her.

The mother took Lila firmly by the hand and led her toward the bookstore, still tossing apologies over her shoulder.

When the door closed behind them I turned on Caroline, emboldened. Something had shifted now that I'd seen her cringe in terror of a little girl. "What was *that*?" I asked. "You want me to think you're the bride of Frankenstein, but you're scared of a six-year-old?"

Her lips tightened, but she said nothing.

"Never mind." I shook my head and started back in the direction of the ship. I'd wanted to find a coffee shop, but now that Caroline had found me anyway I might as well go back to my stateroom.

I heard Caroline's soft voice behind me. "I stay away from children."

The words were full of sadness. I turned around. Even with the sunglasses, her face was turned downward.

"Why?"

"It's a long story."

I studied her, trying to glean some kind of clue from that opaque expression. Did she avoid kids because she couldn't have them, because of whatever had been done to her body?

Did she *have* kids somewhere, but she couldn't remember them?

I knew what it was to miss your baby. The rain was in my eyes now, but I pulled the hood of my jacket up and squinted back at her. "Do you know anywhere around here with good tea?"

Thirteen

Caroline

After my escape, when I was certain that I was well clear of the creature, I began traipsing back toward the place I still thought of as home: the Frankenstein estate in Geneva.

It may seem like a foolish decision now, but at the time, nothing else even occurred to me. Victor had betrayed me, yes, but I knew no other city than Geneva, no other family than the Frankensteins. Where else could I go but back to where I started?

Before I set off, however, I spent several moments destroying the papers I had stolen with Victor's formulas. This was not a difficult decision. In my mind, at that time, it was hardly a decision at all. I was certain that what Victor had done went against all that was right and good. Of course I needed to prevent this knowledge from spreading like a virus.

Over two hundred years, I have altered my perspective on many things, but never this.

I shredded the pages into the tiniest bits my clumsy fingers could manage, watching the confetti float away on the breeze, and started out for home.

Of course, it wasn't quite so simple as a long walk home. I have since worked out that the cabin where my murderer had imprisoned me was located some thirty miles south of Geneva. Had I gone directly home in a straight line, I could have made the journey in a matter of hours. But I was disoriented, and besides, I still didn't know what I looked like now. My captor had often spoken of the public being horrified by his appearance, even attacking him for it. There had been no reflective surfaces in the cottage; I suspected my appearance was equally as revolting.

For the first part of my journey, I simply wandered, trying to adjust to the changes in my body. In the cottage I had been like a parakeet in a cage, my movements limited and my habitat controlled. When forced to spread my wings, however, I quickly realized the severity of my body's alterations. Any amount of sunlight caused me physical pain, and even the mild summer heat was intensely uncomfortable. I still felt leaden, and my equilibrium and balance were now foreign to me. As I stumbled through forests, I often had to lean against one tree before lurching toward another, trying to hurtle my body in the correct direction, not knowing if I would succeed until my hands struck bark.

To protect myself from heat and sun – and to conceal myself from people – I traveled mostly at night, tramping along the sides of the roads. Whenever I heard the approach of hooves or feet, I would retreat into the trees or crops. Near dawn, I'd find a ditch or ravine with sufficient foliage and burrow myself in until I was blanketed by cool darkness, hiding until the sun went away again.

These miserable days and nights soon became a blur. My flimsy nightdress was quickly shredded and soiled, and my long hair, in which I had once taken such pride, caught on so many brambles that I soon longed for a knife to cut off the bulk of it. Though my balance did eventually recalibrate, navigation still eluded me. I searched for signs to towns I might recognize, but as I traveled mostly at night, they were difficult to spot.

After some days of this – I don't know how many – I was walking along a road just after dawn, searching for a place to nest for the day, when I came upon a sign for Les Clefs, a French town that I knew.

I froze in mid-step, stunned. For the first time since my death, I understood where I was.

Encouraged by this discovery, and the overcast skies, I did not curl up to rest during the daylight hours. I continued walking throughout the morning and into the early afternoon, winding north through the forest, trying to keep the road in sight through the tree line.

It wasn't easy, trying to operate my changed extremities with my eyes squinted and my thoughts racing with my discovery. Near midday, I took a step away from the trees, intending to dart through a small clearing, when I suddenly came upon a child, carving her name into the thick gray bark of a tree. She had been so quiet, and I had been so lost in my thoughts, that I was practically on top of her before the two of us looked up and spotted each other at the same moment.

Our eyes met, and we both yelped. She was about twelve, dressed in simple, handmade clothes, clumsily stitched together. Behind her, through a tangle of trees, I could see a small cabin, where she had surely originated.

I instantly shrank away, terrified for her. What must I look like, after weeks in the wild? How frightening it must be for a young child to come across such deformities! I staggered backward, turning to run, and I heard her clear voice behind me calling in French, "Wait! Don't go!"

I paused, looking over my shoulder. The girl's expression was eager. I had obviously startled her, but she did not seem horrified by my appearance. Seeing me about to flee, she had even taken a few steps closer.

I turned around slowly, and the little girl wrung her hands. "Oh, miss, what has happened to you?" she cried. I looked down at my shredded clothes and dirt-caked skin, not sure how to reply. "Your eyes... are they sick?"

"I do not know," I said, truthfully.

My gaze was drawn to her knife, still stuck in the tree. I was thinking how such a tool could help me gather food, but she misinterpreted it as fear for my safety. She stepped away from the weapon, holding up her hands as though to pacify me. "Please," she said earnestly, "let me help you. I am Alice Roussel; what is your name?"

I hadn't been practicing my speech as I stumbled through the woods, and my voice came out in a slur. "Lisbeth."

"I'm so pleased to make your acquaintance, Miss Lisbeth," she said. "You must be so cold! Please, won't you come in by the fire?"

"Where are your parents?" I asked. This little girl did not seem troubled by my appearance, but children were forgiving in that way. An adult might not react so kindly.

"My mother is dead, and my father is helping our neighbor with his sheep today," Alice explained.

"Are there any other people here?"

She shook her head. "I am the only child left living at home, but I am twelve and quite capable. May I offer you some food and shelter?" She pointed behind her shoulder, toward the cabin, and then added delicately, "and perhaps a chance to bathe?"

My instincts told me to run – now that I knew the way home, I wanted no further delays – but my longing for real food and a bath, the comforts of civility, was overpowering. I allowed the girl to lead me toward her abode. She kept a good six feet between us as we walked. It may have been to keep me placated, though I suspect it may have had to do with my odor.

During this short journey, she kept up a stream of one-sided conversation, though I had asked her no questions. "My sister is married and lives away from here," she chattered, "and my brother has joined the military. I am often alone and glad to see a friendly face!"

It seemed strange that the girl wasn't asking more questions of me, given my current state, but in the moment I assumed it was just the novelty of my sudden appearance and the natural self-involvement of the young.

79

The cabin was a small, spartan affair, not unlike the one from which I had escaped. Alice had left the front door open, and as we approached I saw a single large room with one doorway in the back, which probably led to a bedroom. I paused at the threshold, bending forward to scrape the clumps of mud off my limbs and bare feet. Alice bounced on the balls of her feet as she waited for me, chattering about her older sister, who had married and moved away, and a dog she used to own.

When I'd gotten the worst of the debris off my skin, Alice ushered me into the cabin with great excitement, pointing out the wooden ladder and small loft which served as her bedroom. I noticed how little effort had been made to decorate the cabin's rough-hewn walls. There were no rugs or needlework of the kind I was used to, nor were there any books. I wondered how the girl spent so much time here, alone. No wonder she was glad to see another person.

My eyes were caught by the modest bathtub sitting next to the fireplace. Alice saw me looking and said, "My apologies, Miss Lisbeth, but it takes some time to fill, and then more time for the water to warm. Our well water is quite cold." She wrung her hands, looking anxious, as though she half-expected the water temperature to make me flee.

It occurred to me, for the first time, that although I had been wandering the wilderness for weeks, filthy and miserable, I had not once been cold, though the autumn was well upon us. If air temperature no longer affected me, why should water temperature be any different?

"Can I tell you a secret, Alice?" I said, and the girl looked positively delighted at the prospect. "I do not feel the cold."

She clapped her hands, as though I had just demonstrated juggling or archery. "Oh, what a wonderful talent! I wish I never felt cold. Here, let me get you some bread and cheese, and while you eat I can fetch the water for the bath."

I wanted to help, but at Alice's insistence I sat down at the modest table and eagerly consumed a small loaf of bread and wedge of cheese. As before, the flavors were disappointingly muted, but I was just happy to have different fare. Alice may have winced as she saw how quickly I devoured the food, but she tactfully turned away and began hauling in buckets of water, two at a time. As soon as I had finished eating, I began to help.

Until that moment, I had viewed the changes in my body as purely negative: the initial loss of balance and clumsiness, the aversion to light, the heaviness in my limbs. But as Alice began to hand me buckets of well water, I realized that they weighed nothing to me. It was easy to carry four. I could have carried many more if there were additional buckets.

"You're strong!" Alice said admiringly. I dumped the new buckets into the tub, and she handed me a thick wedge of soap and a towel. She cast a nervous look at the water, which was indeed cold. "Are you certain the chill will not bother you?"

"Let us find out."

"Shall I turn around?"

This took me aback, at least momentarily. In my life I had been drilled on modesty and propriety, but sometime between my murder and the arduous trek through the wilderness, I no longer cared. This odd body did not feel like mine; what difference would it make if someone looked at it? But I felt Alice might be more comfortable, so I nodded.

When her back was turned, I dropped the tattered shreds of my nightgown and lowered one foot into the water. I held it there for a long moment, assessing my own reaction.

I could tell the water temperature was different from the air, and my mind provided the supplementary information to indicate that this difference was called *cold*. But it caused no discomfort.

Intrigued, I quickly brought the rest of my body into the water. "I am fine," I told Alice. "I can tolerate it."

She turned around, her expression changing from excitement to dismay. "What has happened to you?" she cried, pointing at my chest. I glanced down. I had forgotten about the tree-shaped scars. I had no idea what had caused them, nor did I know how to explain them to a young girl.

"I was in an accident," I said at last.

"Is that how you came to be lost?"

"No." It was obvious that she expected me to elaborate, so I lied. "The scars are from a different accident, when I was small. I became lost while traveling home to Geneva, when my horse threw me."

She nodded thoughtfully. "Is that how your wrist was injured too?"

I struggled not to wince, though I couldn't stop myself from clapping my right hand over the stitches that still wound around my wrist. They were enormous, black, and crude; of course Alice had noticed them. Why hadn't I prepared a story? "Yes, I was wearing a bracelet when I fell," I improvised, hoping she hadn't had a close look, "and landed right on it. I'm afraid it cut me. But I'll be just fine."

"You don't have to leave right away, though, do you? You'll stay and recover awhile?"

This, too surprised me. "I must continue, tonight or first thing in the morning," I said gently. The girl's face fell. She must struggle with loneliness, I thought.

To change the subject, I asked, "Do you have clothes I can borrow, Alice? I have no money with me, but I can send some when I reach my home."

Alice clapped her hands again, looking relieved to have a task. "Of course! I will be back in a moment."

She disappeared into the small bedroom, and I set to work scrubbing my arms and legs with the rough soap. The water quickly became filthy. When my skin was at last clean, I began pulling twigs and thorns out of my long dark hair, until Alice returned with a folded stack of clothing. "These belonged to my mother," she said with reverence.

"Oh, Alice. Are you certain I can use them?"

The girl nodded. "Mamá believed in helping those in need. She would want you to have them." She eyed me for a moment. "Do you want me to help with your hair? Your arms must be getting tired."

They were not, but another person would be able to see what I couldn't. "Please."

Alice set the clothes near the fire to warm and came around behind me. Patiently, she began disentangling the many souvenirs of the forest.

"When did you lose your mother?" I asked.

"Five... no, six years ago now. She drowned."

"I'm very sorry. That must have been very difficult."

There was a long silence, and I grasped about for an easier topic for the girl. "Do you ever go into town, Alice?" I asked, and the girl was off again, chattering away about a friend in town. Alice didn't go to school anymore, she said, because her papa needed her, but sometimes she still saw her friend Bernadette at church on Sundays. I felt a pang of sorrow at the mention of church, considering my current condition, but I let Alice talk. I remembered how Ernest and then William had often prattled on to me about their latest woes.

At last, Alice declared my hair free of forest debris, and I moved it aside to wash with the soap. Alice gasped.

"What is it?" I asked, looking around in panic. I half expected my attacker to burst through the cabin door.

"Your back... you have the same scars."

"I do?" In vain, I tried peering over my own shoulder.

"You didn't know?"

I tried to think of a good lie. "The accident happened when I was a baby," I explained. "I rarely think about it."

"Oh." She seemed uncertain, but said nothing as I finished washing my hair. That left me with a new conundrum: I was ready to get out, but I didn't want her to see any more of my body, in case it held further surprises. "The fire is getting a bit low, Alice," I said. "Perhaps you could retrieve some of the firewood you were cutting earlier?"

"Of course!"

While the girl was gone I quickly dried off and dressed, grateful that Alice had brought me a dress with long sleeves. We emptied the bathtub together, and then Alice asked if she could comb my hair. "My sister always used to comb mine," she said, blushing a little. "But now I am old enough to do it, and she is gone."

I sat down at the hearth, though I did not like the heat, and she retrieved a comb and a hand mirror from a little shelf of her things. She handed me the mirror. "So you can see what I'm doing."

I had relaxed into the small routines of civilized life, but now fear gripped me. I accepted the mirror but kept it angled away from me. What if I no longer looked like Elizabeth? What if I *did* look like Elizabeth? Would that mean I was still myself, despite what the creature had done? How, then, could I feel so completely different?

What was I?

I felt a small tug at my hair, and Alice yelped. "I'm so sorry," she said fervently. "That must have hurt!"

"No, no. You're doing wonderfully."

Enough of this. Holding my breath, I angled the mirror to see my reflection.

The woman who stared back at me was both familiar and unfamiliar. I had all of Elizabeth's features, but my skin was a different shade: slightly more yellowed, and uniform in color, as though I had been dipped in paint. The circles under my eyes that I'd seen on my wedding day were gone, but my eyes themselves had altered: The irises were a tawny yellow, and the rest of each eye now bore an eerie yellowish tint. No wonder it had surprised Alice.

Overall, though, my appearance was not nearly as bad as I had feared, to my great relief. I had seen people wearing tinted glasses in Geneva. If I could secure a pair of those, and carefully apply some cosmetics, I could pass for normal. A knot of worry finally loosened within me. My attacker may not have been able to pass among humans, but I could. It was the first true advantage I had over him.

"Thank you, Alice, you've been a great help," I said, lowering the mirror. Alice began chattering away about her sister, Jeanette. I learned that Jeanette had married a young tailor, Luc, and she was expecting their first child. They had moved to Chambéry, a town of some twelve thousand people back then, and Alice only saw her sister at Christmas.

As Alice finished brushing, there was a soft pounding just outside the door, as of one stomping dirt or snow off their shoes. The girl let out a small intake of breath, and before I could ask, she whispered, "Papa is home!" She scrambled to her feet, dropping the comb.

I stood up as well, uncertain how to present myself. Should I say I was Elizabeth Lavenza? Elizabeth Frankenstein? She was dead, and presumably had been mourned. Oh, why hadn't I prepared a story? I'd had weeks to prepare for this moment.

The man who entered the cabin was quite tall and well-muscled, with a rough beard and soot smeared on his neck. He wore heavy wool clothes that looked homemade but aged, probably from when Alice's mother was alive. A dead rabbit dangled from one beefy hand by its ears.

His gaze was on a piece of wet leaf attached to his boot, so it was a moment before he looked up. "Alice, girl, why haven't you – oh!" His eyes widened as he took me in. I wondered how I must look – a strange woman some twenty years his junior, with long damp hair, yellow eyes, and dressed in his wife's clothes.

"Papa, this is Miss Lisbeth, she was thrown from her horse and got lost in the woods!" Alice said in a voice that was so enthusiastic it bordered on hysteria. I expected her to run to her father, but she stood next to me and a little behind my shoulder. "Can she stay the night?"

The man looked at me, his heavy brow furrowed. "It's a pleasure to meet you," I said formally. "Alice was kind enough to help me after my accident, but I'm happy to be on my way. I'll send money for the clothes, if that's all right."

There was a long, pregnant moment while Alice and I both waited for the verdict. Slowly, the confusion faded from his expression, and he cleared his throat. "I'm Charles Roussel," he said at last. "Of course you are welcome to spend the night. It's beginning to rain now, and I'd prefer not to have you catch your death."

For one terrible moment I thought a hiccup of laughter would escape through my lips, but I swallowed it down and nodded, dipping a curtsy. As much as I wanted to get back on the road to Geneva, I was reluctant to give up my new cleanliness. "Thank you, monsieur."

Beside me, Alice sighed with relief, the tension broken. "Are you well?" Charles asked, gesturing toward my eyes with great curiosity.

I could think of no truthful answer to that question, but I replied that I was in good health, that my strange-colored eyes were a birth defect. Satisfied, he handed Alice the rabbit and retreated to the bedroom to change his damp clothes. I told Alice I would help her prepare dinner.

Fourteen

"Have you ever baked before?" Alice whispered a while later, eyeing my attempts to shape dough for a loaf of bread. Much of the dough was adhered to my clumsy fingers. I was glad her father had not reappeared from the bedroom to see my clumsy efforts.

"I never had much of a knack for it," I admitted, which was true enough. I had been in charge of the Frankenstein household since I was sixteen, but they had a cook and several maids.

"Because you're a lady," Alice supplied, her voice awed.

"I suppose so." I was acutely aware of the silliness of that term. Whatever it meant to be a lady, surely I was one no longer. Alice showed me how to coat my fingers in flour to keep the dough from sticking, and I tried again to shape it into a loaf. Giggling, she took the lump of bread from me and began to knead it with nimble fingers.

While the bread baked, Alice demonstrated how to skin and prepare the rabbit, and we both sliced potatoes, though my fine motor skills made mine lopsided and uneven. As we worked on dinner, the girl's chattiness waned, and she focused on each task in front of her with careful concentration, as though deeply concerned about getting any detail wrong. The whole time, she kept very close to me, so I had to take care not to bump her with my elbow.

When the meal was ready Roussel appeared, dressed in clean clothes, to preside over the dinner table. It was a pleasant enough meal, though Alice was much quieter than I would have expected, and Roussel had many questions for me. I told him my surname was Moritz, which I borrowed from my dear Justine, and I said I had lived with my uncle's family in Geneva until very recently. When it transpired that Charles had traveled there several times, I did my best to steer the conversation toward harmless observations about the city and its inhabitants. Roussel was quite disparaging about city life, praising a simple rural existence instead.

"What is it you do, Monsieur Roussel?" I asked politely.

"Call me Charles," he said gruffly. "I work on house and ship interiors, do some cabinetry. We keep a couple of cows and some chickens as well." He gestured at my plate. "You don't like the rabbit?"

I looked down at my plate, and realized that although I'd devoured the potatoes, my portion of rabbit was untouched. Alice gave me an anxious look. "I've yet to try it," I said, as gaily as I could manage.

The smell of the meat cooking hadn't bothered me, and in my human life, I'd enjoyed rabbit stew. As I cut off a piece of the meat and held it to my lips, however, my gorge rose. I put the bite in my mouth and chewed, trying to make appreciative noises, but the taste was abhorrent to me. As soon as Charles and Alice were looking away, I spat the bite into my napkin and resolved not to take another. I spent the rest of the meal pushing a few bites of rabbit off my plate and into my lap. I have never since been able to stand the taste of flesh.

Eventually Charles asked how I had come to be lost in the woods, alone, and I had to elaborate on my story. I said that I had been on my way to Lyon with a traveling companion and her maid, but we had been separated during a storm, and I had been thrown from my horse shortly thereafter. Charles seemed to accept this explanation, though he did mutter about the foolishness of girls traveling alone.

After dinner Charles went outside to look after the animals, and Alice clutched my hand. "Won't you share my bed, please?" she said in a pleading voice.

"Of course." The cabin was small, and my only other option would have been to stretch out in front of the fire. As cozy as that sounded, I didn't care to get too close to the heat. I was happy to please Alice.

She looked like she wanted to say something else, but just then Charles returned and announced it was time for Alice to go to bed.

"And Lisbeth, too?" she said tentatively.

"Miss Lisbeth is an adult and can decide for herself," he told his daughter sternly.

I looked between the two and elected to turn in with Alice. As we climbed the short ladder to her loft I caught Charles giving us a peculiar look, but I could not interpret its meaning.

The cramped loft space looked far more welcoming than anything below, and I smiled as I saw that Alice had turned it into a nest, with rough blankets twisted about the center space like the walls of a fortress. Ernest had done the same thing as a boy, when he'd gone through a phase of frequent nightmares.

And suddenly I missed him, missed them all, a longing that pressed down on me and took my breath away. I didn't hear Alice's next words.

The loft barely had room for my body and hers, but the girl huddled close, and I allowed her to stretch one arm over my chest, as if to reassure herself that I was real.

"I'm glad you're here," Alice whispered to me, her eyes already closing. "I wish you'd never leave."

I stroked her hair and wondered how long it had been since she had seen her sister. I thought of how desperately chatty she had been throughout the day, until we began dinner. Despite recent events, I had loved growing up in a busy, bustling household, with my three male cousins and Justine as my daily companions. Now, after my escape from captivity, I'd had more than long enough to feel the ache of loneliness.

It must be terribly difficult for Alice, I concluded, certain I had diagnosed the problem. She was still so young, with many years until she was of marriageable age. She shouldn't be spending her days alone and friendless, waiting for a taciturn father to come home.

Beside me, Alice's breathing became regular, her eyes closed tightly. I could hear Charles moving around a bit on the lower level, doing something with papers. Writing to his adult daughter, perhaps. That settled it: I decided to go down and offer to escort Alice to Bonneville to visit her sister the next morning. It was close to the route I'd take to return to Geneva, and it would do Alice good, even if Charles would have to go without her help with cooking and chores.

In my naïveté, it didn't occur to me that he might have other reasons for keeping his youngest daughter close.

Quietly, so as not to wake Alice, I climbed down the ladder. The light from the hearth was dim, but I found my vision clearer than it ever was during the day. Charles was at the dining table, with an open jug of wine by his elbow. He had been fiddling with some small machine parts I didn't recognize, but as I approach he stood.

"I appreciate your hospitality, Monsieur," I began in a low voice. "I'm already quite fond of your daughter."

"Alice?" He sounded dubious.

"Yes. She's a lovely girl."

He blinked very slowly. "She's very useful to me," he said after a moment's pause.

I looked for a way into the topic. "I am concerned, though, about her isolation. She seems lonely –"

Roussel interrupted me with a snort, seeming to rally his wits. "Perhaps she needs more chores."

His harsh tone took me aback, but I tried to recover. "I wondered if she might benefit from some time with her sister. I would be pleased to chaperone –"

"You?" he sneered, tossing down the parts and stepping away from the table. "A girl who gets lost in the woods with no clothes?"

A spark of cold fire ignited in my belly, but I tried to keep my words measured. "Monsieur Roussel, I was merely suggesting that a young girl such as Alice might benefit from time with female relatives."

"How charitable of you, my lady, but Alice is my business, and she stays right where she is."

I had little experience with alcohol, so it wasn't until that moment, when he began to weave slightly on his feet, that I realized Charles Roussel was drunk. Why had I opened my foolish mouth? Better to revisit this topic in the morning.

I lowered my eyes. "I understand, monsieur."

I turned to go back to the ladder, but quick as a snake, his fingers darted out and grabbed my wrist. I looked back with surprise. "While you are here, however, perhaps you'd like to express your gratitude," he whispered.

"Excuse me?" I said politely.

He stepped closer still, so we were nearly toe to toe. "Fancy accent or no, your story reeks of lies. You are very fortunate that I have been so generous with my home."

The anger I'd felt for my captor had been complex – layered with the emotions of my own transformation, my discovery of Victor's actions, the *unrealness* of my situation. This was different. The rage I felt in Charles Roussel's cabin was a cold blue flame that began to climb out of my heart and lick through the cracks of my ribs, threatening.

"Release me," I said tightly.

But Charles Roussel did not listen. His fingers locked on my wrist as he loomed over me. "You're very pretty, despite those freakish eyes," he slurred, his stinking breath enveloping me.

"Let me guess. You were a rich man's plaything, but he discarded you on a journey."

I wrenched my hand free, more easily than I'd expected, and stepped back. "Please —"

But he pushed me backward, his foot already hooked behind my ankles to trip me. I fell hard on the stone floor, the back of my head striking first. Roussel's clumsy fingers were fumbling at my skirt. One meaty paw rose to anchor itself over my mouth, pressing my bruised skull into the floor, as his heavy upper body pinned my arms. I felt as though I were being pressed to death, and panic and fear made me dizzy.

For a moment.

Then the cold fire in my chest banked into a tempest. Scarcely aware of myself, I folded myself forward and sat up. Roussel let out a grunt of surprise as he was forcibly displaced, but he recovered quickly, throwing his weight forward again. We grappled on the floor for a few seconds, he trying to get a grip on my clothes, me fumbling and awkward. I could not get the leverage to properly push him away, and then he was on his feet, his fingers wrapped around my throat as I knelt.

Then a plaintive voice floated down from the loft. "Papá?"

I froze, and Roussel tilted his head back to look up at her. "Go to sleep, Alice! I'll deal with you later."

Until then my attempts to fight him off had been unfocused; I was too stunned to gather my wits. But hearing Alice's frightened inquiry stirred me, and I felt my arm drawing back, my fingers balling together. I had never punched anything in my life, but I propelled myself up and jabbed my fist into Roussel's face.

The blow fractured his cheekbone, and blood spurted from his mouth where he'd bitten his tongue. I lost my balance, and bloody drops rained down on my face for a moment before Roussel staggered backward with a rivulet of red running down his chin. I got my legs under me for real this time, and though I could see Roussel spitting curses at me, I heard nothing over the roaring in my ears.

I could have walked away then. There was nothing to stop me from turning and leaving the cabin at that moment – except that the woman who would have done that was dead. The creature I am now moved forward, advancing on him. The whole cabin was suddenly white and hazy, nothing clear except the confused, bloodied face of another man who wanted to hurt me.

I lunged forward, my arms pressing against his chest and pushing out with everything I had. Roussel went flying backward as if pulled by a rope – and straight into Alice.

I hadn't even heard her climb down the ladder, or seen her rush toward us. Father and daughter collided, but the force of my shove sent them hurtling across the room. Alice's small body hit a stacked pile of firewood and everything became very still.

"No!" I cried, scrambling to Alice's side. The cold fire in my chest had snuffed out so quickly that it stunned me. Alice's eyes were wide open, her expression confused. "Are you hurt?" I asked, but she didn't answer. Her pupils slowly rolled over to fix on me, and she touched her chest, her lips moving wordlessly. For one blissful moment I thought she was simply stunned, but I gently rolled her over and saw that a protruding branch, as thick as my thumb and five inches long, had punctured her back at an angle. "No," I whispered. "No."

"Al'ss!" Roussel slurred from his hands and knees. His trajectory toward the wall had been softened by her poor little body, but blood still ran from the back of his head, pooling forward to drip off his chin. His daughter looked at him, and an expression of hatred came over her too-young face. Her lips trembled a final time, and then her eyes fluttered closed.

"What have you done?" he screamed at me, crawling brokenly toward his daughter. "You've killed her!"

"She… I'm…" Speechless, I carefully lowered Alice's lifeless body to the floor. No words could express the depth of my horror and remorse. I backed away.

But Charles Roussel wasn't finished. He looked around the room like a hunted animal, his eyes alighting on the wine jug. He staggered to his feet and fetched the bottle, his arm lifting it like a club.

"You murderous whore," he cried, raising the bottle above his head and stumbling toward me.

Suddenly, without thought, I was on my feet, rushing to meet him. As the jug whistled down toward me I easily leaned aside, catching his arm and swinging it, my other hand grabbing his waist as I used his own momentum to fling his body. It was as easy as throwing a doll.

I was not aiming in any particular direction, but Roussel flew straight into the fireplace, where he too lay still. Shocked at my own action, dazed by the swiftness of events, I ran over to him, reaching for his ankles to drag him out of the fire. The moment I touched his legs, though, my eyes found his face, and I could tell he was dead. His head had caved in against the stone mantle. Horrified, I let go, and the body dropped onto the hearth, one arm flopping into the coals.

In seconds his rough clothes began smoking.

I looked at the gruesome scene: the two corpses, the splashes of blood dripping from the wall and the woodpile. Blood on my clothes, my face. Then I turned and fled, weeping, back into the woods where I belonged.

Fifteen

Heck

"It wasn't your fault," I said.

We were in a small coffee shop in Ketchikan, only two blocks from the bookstore. Like every other business I'd seen in town, this was a tourist-friendly place, with glowing wood paneling on the walls and quirky "Alaskan" names for every beverage. But there were booths along the side wall and low lighting. We could talk in relative privacy, and Caroline had even taken off her sunglasses.

Her eyes were fixed on the mug of tea in front of her.

"I killed a child," she said in a quiet, maddeningly even voice. "A child who had wanted my protection."

The dignified, devastated way Caroline said it made something tug in my stomach. It was as though she said this sentence to herself a hundred times every day.

"You weren't *trying* to hurt her," I pointed out. "It was an accident."

She met my eyes. Caroline was wearing her contacts today, and in the dim room I would never have thought her anything but a very beautiful woman. "She's dead because I lost control," she said flatly.

"Of a body you barely understood how to use!" I argued.

Caroline gave me a funny look, then shook her head.

I took a sip of the tea, knowing I shouldn't ask my next question. "He wasn't just an asshole, was he?" I said. "Roussel. He was…" I couldn't say it.

But Caroline caught my meaning. "Molesting Alice?" she said flatly.

"Well, yeah. You said she wanted your help, and she stuck so close to you while you were there, and he sounds…I don't know."

Caroline sighed. "In hindsight…I suspect that he was. But I'll never know for sure, and Alice will never have a chance to tell me." She stared down into her tea, as if there were terrible answers at the bottom of the mug. "That's part of what I took from her."

"You didn't *take* anything–"

"Of course I did," she snapped, her eyes flashing as she looked up at me. That look had the strangest effect: I didn't *feel* afraid, but my stomach rolled over with alarm. It was like coming across a big canine in the woods, and your body recognizes the threat long before you know you're seeing a wolf, not a dog.

I closed my mouth.

"That little girl never got a chance to leave her father, do you understand that?" she said, her palms flat on the table in front of her, pressing down. "She never got to grow up, to leave, to experience the world as more than chores and darkness and abuse. Because *I took that from her.*"

"Okay," I murmured. "I'm sorry."

We sat without speaking for a few minutes, letting the coffee shop's mild background chatter wash over us and cleanse away Caroline's memory.

Caroline had folded her hands neatly on the table, and I envied her stillness. My own fingers were wrapped around a latte made with Earl Grey tea and lavender, partly for warmth, and partly so they wouldn't shake.

She was the first to break the silence. "I looked up Ehlers-Danlos last night. It sounds very difficult," Caroline said. "When were you diagnosed?"

I was a little taken aback by the change in subject – and the question. I'd told almost no one about my health problems, but the few people who'd heard had been polite and careful, so wary of hurting my feelings that they hadn't asked many questions. It was sort of refreshing to have someone just ask what they wanted to know. "A few months ago."

"So late?" Caroline sounded surprised. "It's genetic, isn't it? You're what, twenty-three? Twenty-four?"

"Twenty-five. I've had it my whole life, but the changes that come with pregnancy were the tipping point for figuring out the connection. Before that, I always saw different specialists for different symptoms – allergies, migraines, dislocations, joint pain... My mother used to tell people I was 'sickly,' like a tragic Victorian heroine." I eyed her. "Um. No offense."

Caroline gave me a tiny smile. "None taken. Queen Victoria was after my time."

She turned her mug of tea around idly for a moment, then added, "I also looked you up in the passenger manifest. "Your ticket was purchased by a Margaret Saville, with her loyalty points. Your mother?"

I think I nodded, but the latte in my stomach had turned to ice and my thoughts spun out. Why was she bringing up my mom? I'd assumed Mom wouldn't get me in trouble with the police, but had she called the cruise line?

"I have to ask," Caroline picked up her mug and held it in front of her for a moment. "Why do this trip alone? Why not bring your mom or a friend?"

I swallowed hard. "My mom is teaching summer classes."

"And your friends?" Caroline pressed.

"They're..." I was about to say "busy," but my voice faltered. I suddenly felt too tired to lie to her. "I don't spend much time with friends."

"By choice?"

I shrugged miserably. How long had it been since I'd talked to Cherie or Diana? Before the accident I'd spent all my time with Colin. Occasionally we went on easy hikes or to a movie, sometimes with his friends and their wives. But most of our time was spent on his work.

We finished the paper I'd been hired to help him with in record time. After it was published, Colin received a research grant to study magnetic fields in Greenland. By then we were a couple, and he convinced the university to send me along as his research assistant.

Colin put so much faith in me on that trip – he'd cut back on taking notes himself, dictating them straight to me so I could type them up later. We spent three frenetic weeks traveling around Greenland taking measurements. I went through three bottles of Advil, pushing myself hard in order to keep up. We were so busy, but I was also so happy. I think you were even conceived on our last night in Greenland, Maddie.

When we returned to Madison, I cut back on my Linguistics classes so I could transcribe and organize data for his new paper. Colin and I spent most of every day together, so at night when he went out with his friends, I usually begged off. I was too exhausted to do anything but crash and try to catch up on my classwork.

If I was being honest with myself, during all that time, nearly a year, I'd hardly missed my own friends. Colin just *needed* me so much more than they did. He'd often call me in the middle of the night to fret about the research or the wording of a particular paragraph. It was a side of Colin that almost no one got to see: the worrier, the perfectionist. I was touched when he called me to ask, again and again, if I thought the new paper would be any good. If it would be *important*.

Then it was October, and I took a pregnancy test.

I didn't want to think about that, though. I cast about for a change in topic. "You know what I don't get?" I asked Caroline.

"If you're so scared to be near kids, why do you work on a family cruise ship?"

"I work in the adults-only bar," she replied, primly smoothing her skirt on her lap. "And normally, I work on the adults-only cruise line. This is my first time aboard the *Mariner*."

"Why'd you change ships, or lines or whatever?"

"This ship was headed north." Her shrug was like every one of her movements, artful, poised, and efficient, like a ballerina. "I only work the cold weather routes."

"Because it's easier on your zombie body?"

I was rewarded with an actual smile, one that didn't look like it was plastered over a hole. "I don't eat meat, much less human brains, Heck. And I so rarely shamble."

It was quite possibly the first joke I'd heard from her. "Colin loves zombie movies. He got me to watch a bunch of them."

I felt myself smiling, remembering one of his film rants during a movie at his apartment. He'd got so into making a case for why the social commentary of a certain film was more relevant today than ever; he had to stand up and pace while he talked. I hadn't been invested in the subject, but I loved watching him make his arguments.

In academia, everyone is always trying to out-think everyone else: to outdo someone else's analysis, to have the loudest and strongest voice in the crowd. Being Colin's girlfriend had made life so simple, so clear. I didn't have to out-think anyone. I could listen and laugh and agree, and that was all it took to please him.

"Are you all right, Heck?" Caroline asked.

I shrugged at her, willing myself not to tear up. "I just really miss him."

"Can I ask why you two broke up?"

"He wants more kids." Dammit, why had I told her that?

"Oh." Caroline looked surprised. "And you don't?"

I looked away. "My doctor doesn't advise it."

Caroline reached across the table and rested her hand on mine for a moment. Her hand was neither cold nor warm, but there was a comfortable pressure to it. She looked at me with something close to pity, but there was an element of commiseration, too. I had the wild urge to turn my hand over and grasp hers. Tell her everything that had happened, before and after the hospital. Hold her hand as long as she'd let me.

"But if your doctor said –" she began.

I snatched my hand back. "I should get back to the *Mariner*." I scooted sideways along the booth, awkwardly bending to pick up my cane, which had fallen onto the floor on my right.

Caroline hadn't moved. "Heck, wait. I'm sorry if I –"

"It's fine." I reached for my backpack without looking at her. All I wanted was to be back in my room on the ship, typing up Colin's words. "But I need to focus on what I came to do. I think we should stay away from each other."

Pulling the backpack along the booth seat, I looped the straps over my shoulders, then pushed down on the cane and raised my body, feeling off-balance. In that moment I hated myself for sitting in the booth, and hated Caroline for sitting there watching me struggle – although I would have been furious if she'd tried to help. I turned to walk away, but the toe of my left shoe caught on the foot of the table.

There was an audible *pop* as my left kneecap dislocated, and I went down.

Sixteen

Heck

For the next few minutes I was dimly aware of a lot of noise and movement, though none of it reached me. My eyes were screwed closed, my breath coming in ragged pants through my teeth. I lay on my back with my hands wrapped around my knee, squeezing, squeezing, as though I could simply hold the kneecap back in place forever, as though that would erase the pain.

Involuntary tears streamed down my face. The same word kept echoing around my head, lancing through the clouds of pain. *Stupid, stupid, stupid.* I had forgotten to be careful, to navigate slowly. For a moment I had simply assumed I was normal, and agony was the cost.

Finally, I heard Caroline's voice over the screaming of my body. "Step back please, she'll be all right. She just twisted her knee."

Caroline crouched down next to me so she could look into my eyes. "What can I do?" she asked in a low voice. "Hospital?"

I shook my head. By then the first wave of pain had receded enough for me to form words. "Kneecap…went back in. Just get me out of here."

Caroline insisted on paying for a cab, though I have no idea how she got one to arrive so quickly. On the way back to the pier I slipped the emergency pill case out of my backpack and grudgingly chewed up one of the hydrocodone, trying not to make a face at the sharp bitterness. I hate taking the pills – not because they don't work, but because they work so well. They smooth everything into an easy blur, and then you have to come back to reality later. I know better than anyone how dangerous that particular tug-of-war can get.

While I waited for it to kick in I sucked on a mint and cursed myself for being so careless. The whole point of this fucking trip was to show Colin that I'm recovered, and I can hardly do that if I can't walk.

But there was nothing to do now except follow the usual steps: ice, elevation, rotating over-the-counter pain meds every four hours. Tomorrow, after the swelling went down, I'd put on the hinged knee brace. Hopefully I wouldn't need crutches, which would mean a trip to the ER or at least the ship's health facilities. "Fuck," I mumbled.

"Did you say something?" Caroline's voice came from somewhere very far away. I opened my eyes. Right, the cab. We were in the backseat of a cab. She'd put her sunglasses back on, but her mouth looked worried. "Daze," I blurted, feeling helpless to explain myself. "Daze of pain, then a daze of meds. It's always a daze."

Caroline just nodded as though this made perfect sense. "I'll get you back to your cabin as fast as I can."

Caroline kept her word. Forty minutes after the fall, I was lying on the bed in my cabin with pillows propped under my swollen knee and a plastic bag of ice balanced on top of it.

"Can I get you something from the buffet? Or any of the other restaurants?" Caroline asked, drying her hands with a towel from the bathroom. She'd brought me the bag of ice.

I looked at her. Under the sunglasses, she looked guilty-anxious in a way that reminded me of my mother. She wanted to do something to help, to make up for the fact that she hadn't prevented this from happening.

"It wasn't your fault," I told Caroline wearily. "I'm the idiot who wasn't careful about getting up. I know better."

"I chose the booth," she pointed out. "And I upset you, so you were distracted."

I shook my head. "You sound like my mom. 'I should have asked the doctors more questions.' Like she could have personally reversed the zebra mentality with a couple of follow-up emails."

Caroline sat down slowly on the edge of the bed, being careful to stay several feet away from my leg. "Zebra mentality?"

Right. This happened sometimes on the drugs; I got chatty. "In med school, baby doctors are taught this saying – 'if you hear hoofbeats, look for horses, not zebras.' It means they should look for the most statistically likely possibility."

"And that's bad?"

"It's limiting. If a sports doctor sees a hundred patients who have stretched-out knee ligaments, they assume all hundred are athletes who put repeated stress on their knees playing sports. But what about the one or two patients who *haven't* been doing that? No one questions why their joints hurt."

I sighed, suddenly exhausted with all of it. The stupid system, the doctors who miss things, the gaslighting. "No one looks for zebras, meaning no one looks for an unusual diagnosis. That's probably what happened with my dad."

"What happened to your father? You've hardly mentioned him."

I winced. I hadn't meant to start this particular conversation. "He died when I was in sixth grade," I said brusquely. "He had a lot of health problems."

"Were they like yours?"

I studied the pattern of cracks between the ceiling tiles for a moment. They looked a little bit like a big yellow bus. I'd never ridden the school bus again after that day in sixth grade. "I don't want to talk about that," I said.

There was a pause, then Caroline said lightly, "Tell me something you love about him."

I didn't realize I'd been tensing until I felt my body relax. No one in my life ever asked about the best parts of my dad. "He was really involved. Always at every parent-teacher conference or soccer game, no matter how he was feeling. He could be a little intense, wanting my team to win, but he never minded when we didn't, as long as I'd done my best."

Saying it out loud felt surprisingly good. The only person who ever tried to discuss my dad with me was my therapist, and she only brought him up as part of an insidious therapist trap. I'd be talking about something else and she'd slip in a question like, "Is it possible that your father's unexpected death contributed to how strongly you attached yourself to Colin?"

This was better. I kind of liked talking about the good stuff. "He was the one who figured out about my memory. He was so excited."

"Your memory?"

Right; I wasn't supposed to tell Caroline about that. But I couldn't remember why, and at the moment I couldn't see how it would matter. Caroline had confirmed that she didn't see me as a threat. "I have a mnemonic memory. I can recall anything I hear out loud… at least for a while. It's similar to eidetic memory, when people can recall images or words they see."

"Interesting," Caroline said, though she didn't sound particularly interested. "That must come in handy."

I shrugged. "Everyone says that. It can help me with exams, sure, but most people don't like knowing that you can throw their words back at them anytime you want. It makes people careful."

"It sounds like your father valued your memory," she ventured.

"He had big plans for how I would use it someday. It's why he wanted me to study linguistics – he thought I was going to be an interpreter for the United Nations, or translate great literary works into other languages to share them with the world."

I heard my own words and thought of what my mother had said in her voicemail. *Thank God your father's not alive to see you like this.* "She was right," I muttered.

I didn't realize I'd said it out loud until Caroline asked, "Who was right?"

"Nothing, I just mean… my dad wouldn't be very impressed with me now."

"I'm sure that's not true."

Through the fog of medication, I felt the old sting of guilt and resentment, followed by grief. Caroline had stamped on the thin ice that covered this particular pond: my depthless inadequacy as an adult. Long before I met Colin, I struggled to keep up with classes and bills and laundry, all the minutiae of daily life that exhausted me. Then I met Colin, and that other future felt like someone else's dream. Because it was. Colin was my dream.

Lying in the bed, I could almost hear the ice cracking underneath my back, my legs, threatening to suck me down. I forced myself to sit up a little bit and look, *really* look, at Caroline. She was as composed as ever. "Why are you here?" I asked, not caring that there hadn't exactly been a conversational transition. Hydrocodone reduces the number of things you care about by like eighty percent.

"What do you mean? On the ship?"

"No, here in my stateroom. You said you aren't going to hurt me, and we both know I'm not going to try to reveal your big secret. I'd just end up looking like a nutcase. So why are you still here?"

She studied me for a minute. "You said you've read *Frankenstein*," she said finally. "What was Victor's fatal flaw?"

"Hubris," I said immediately.

She smiled. "Very good. Mary once told me if I wasn't careful, apathy would be mine."

105

Something about that was interesting, but by the time I pushed my thoughts into the right shape to ask more, I'd forgotten. "So you're helping a complete stranger because you want to care about *someone?*"

"Is there a better reason?"

Well, I was definitely too stoned to answer that. I could sort of feel, though, that Caroline was trying to get at something, to push the conversation in a certain direction – asking about my mother, bringing up fatal flaws. I had no interest in letting her dig her fingernails into the seams of my walls, trying to worm her way into my brain.

But for some reason, I didn't want her to leave.

"What happened after Alice?" I asked abruptly. I had almost said, after you killed Alice, but even stoned, even wanting to lash out, I couldn't be that cruel. "I'm assuming you didn't spend the next two hundred years as a forest goblin."

"No, I suppose I didn't."

"So what happened?"

Seventeen

Caroline

When I left the burning cabin, I ran for hours, paying no attention to the direction. The rain had ceased, but the leaves and twigs were damp and slippery under my bare feet, and more than once I lost my footing and tumbled to the ground, filling my nose with the scent of wet rot. I'll never forget that smell.

I kept running, half-blind with tears, until nearly dawn, when I came upon the remains of an old stone bridge that probably once crossed a creek. I crawled beneath it and collapsed in the decomposing foliage, certain I would never get up again.

Drawing my knees to my chest, I wept, first for Alice, and then at my own stupidity. That poor girl would still be alive if I hadn't allowed myself to pretend I were still a normal human being, still Elizabeth Lavenza of Gray Hollow and the Frankensteins. Elizabeth would never hurt a child or kill a man who attacked her. Yes, I knew that Charles Roussel had been a terrible man, but as much as he'd taken from Alice, I was the one who'd taken her life. In that moment I realized that I was even more dangerous, in some ways, than the monster who had made me. My benign appearance had been an entrance ticket into the Roussel's lives, and I had destroyed them as thoughtlessly as crumpling paper between my fingers.

If my actions in Les Clefs had taught me anything, it was that I was Elizabeth Lavenza no longer. Alice was dead because I'd pretended I could still be that murdered girl.

But if I wasn't Elizabeth, who was I? What was I?

As I lay in the rotting leaves on that long, dreary day, my heart pulled me back to my Sunday School teachings, the years and years of prayer that had sustained me through every minor injury and perceived injustice of my school years – and later, through the death of my aunt and young William. When I was a captive, I had thought of Victor's creation as a foul monster, even a demon. Entirely self-absorbed in my own pain and self-pity, I had been arrogant enough to believe I was not like him.

Now, though, I could see my hubris. Had I not just killed a child and a grown man, the same as my murderer? Did I not now possess a terrifying anger that could blind me to reason, just as his had? I hadn't forgotten that blue flame in my chest, and even I wasn't naive enough to think it was gone forever. I'd had an opportunity to walk away from Charles Roussel, and instead I had attacked. Victor and his foul creature may have made me an aberration, but I had made myself a monster.

I didn't look it, though. I had such perfect camouflage.

I spent the day and most of the night curled motionless under the stone, caught in this anguish like a butterfly pinned to a board. I drifted off for a few hours near sunrise, but woke up with the repugnant memory of Alice's caved-in skull fresh behind my eyes.

By the end of the following day, I was in need of water and food, but instead I stayed huddled under the stone remains, unmoving, my heart at war. My hunger and thirst begged me to rise, but why? Why should I fight to live? Would death not be better than this abominable perversion of life? God did not like suicide, but God clearly had no interest in whatever foul monster I had become. He would probably consider it a favor to the world.

I might have lain there forever, letting this body slowly decay along with the rest of the forest's debris. Then a single sentence echoed through my thoughts, a memory of the fiend's words: *Perhaps I need to begin again.*

I opened my eyes and sat up, ignoring the twigs and leaves that stuck to me. No one knew about Victor's creation. No one was looking for him. If my second life, cruel joke that it was, were to end, there was no one left who could prevent him from starting over with a new corpse. Yes, I had stolen Victor's instructions, but I didn't know how much he might have memorized, or whether he'd made copies of the formulas. If he resurrected another woman, she would be trapped as I had been. His plaything.

Or, I realized with fresh horror, he might succeed in combining the pieces of several dead women, as he had said. Without their memories, another creation might be even more dangerous than I was now.

The image of Alice popped into my mind again, but this time it galvanized me. How many more children might die if no one stopped Victor's creature? I needed to convince someone in authority of his existence.

It never occurred to me to turn back and face him alone, even if I could find the way. I'd accepted my monstrosity, you see, but not the idea I might have power. In my mind, I was nothing but the walking corpse of a pretty girl. I needed help.

That decision made, my only possible course became clear. I would return to Geneva as planned, but now with a singular goal: I would confront Victor, if he were alive. I would show him what had been done to me and convince him to find and destroy his abominable creation.

If, however, my captor had lied and Victor was dead, I would enlist my uncle and Ernest as my allies instead. They had loved Elizabeth dearly and were honorable men. Though they would undoubtedly be horrified by my new manifestation, surely they would understand the need to find the monster and prevent future violence.

Either way, after we destroyed Victor's creature, I would ask the Frankensteins to exterminate me as well. They would protest, of course, but I would convince them to do it as a last gesture of their love for Elizabeth. And that would be the end of this odious affair.

I stood, brushed off the leaves and twigs that clung to me, and began to walk toward Geneva. Once again I traveled mainly at night, to avoid the sunlight, but this time I knew the way.

I went straight toward Gray Hollow. Victor and I had planned to live at a modest home in the city after we returned from our honeymoon, but given my death, I wasn't sure Victor would have kept the arrangement, gone back to stay with his father, or some other alternative. But my uncle and Ernest, at least, were sure to be at Gray Hollow.

When I finally stepped onto the carriage path a few nights later, it was very late, hours after even restless Victor would have gone to bed. I prayed that Ernest's dog would be in his bedroom with him, unable to hear my footfalls. The moon was nearly full, lighting my way, but in truth I could have made this walk blindfolded with my hands tied. Every crunch of gravel under my feet felt familiar, and as I rounded the slight bend my breath caught.

The house spread out before me, wide and pale in the moonlight. My breath condensed in the cold night air, adding to the ghostly effect. Guilt wormed in my stomach for what my sudden appearance would do to poor Ernest and my uncle, but I couldn't deny my overwhelming relief. Despite everything, I had made it home.

Eighteen

Caroline

I had formulated my plan during the journey. With the household asleep, I would go first to Victor's room and wake him. I wanted to confront him away from the rest of the household, in case I could not manage to keep the blue flame of my temper in check. I did not truly wish to harm my husband, but I no longer trusted myself after what I'd done to Alice.

If, however, Victor was not at Gray Hollow, I would speak to my uncle first. At just 18, Ernest wasn't old enough to be considered the man of the house. Alphonse was quite elderly, but I hoped if I approached while he was still half asleep, it would lessen the blow of my horrific existence.

This plan lasted only until I climbed the stoop and reached for the doorknob. It stuck in my hand, surprising me. We had never locked the doors, not in all my life. Geneva was safe.

Then again, given that I had been murdered, was it any wonder that my uncle had begun to take precautions?

I did not have a key to the manor, so there was nothing to do but knock. I grasped the big brass knocker and pounded it against the door, knowing it would echo throughout the house. Then I stepped back so I could survey the windows for the flicker of lamplight as someone awoke to greet me. Would it be one of them, or all? What could I possibly say in greeting?

When no answer came, I knocked again. There was still no response, and fear gripped me in a vise, slowly ratcheting up with each second I waited. Had my murderer come to Gray Hollow? Had he killed the last, innocent members of the Frankenstein family?

I ran around the side of the house, guided by weak moonlight and long memory. I broke the large kitchen window and climbed through, although I felt the skin of my left palm tear in the process. The window faced the wrong direction for moonlight, making the room too dark for me even me. I felt for the linen drawer and pulled out a kitchen towel, hastily wrapping it around my hand. "Hello? Ernest? Uncle?" I called.

Silence. I felt for the cupboard where we kept matches and candles. It took several tries with my clumsy fingers, but I struck a match and lit one of the candles, placing it in a pewter candlestick.

The kitchen was disheveled, I saw, with several drawers partly open and dishes scattered about. Perhaps the maids had left after my death? This looked like the kind of mess my uncle and Ernest would create if left to their own devices.

Then I noticed that my breath was still condensing in the air, and realized it was just as cold inside the house as it was outside.

There was no one here.

Crestfallen, I left the kitchen to search the rest of the house, holding the light in front of me. As soon as I stepped into the sitting room, however, I saw that the house was altered. Books and small items of furniture were missing, along with treasured heirlooms. Sheets had been hastily tossed over the remaining furniture, with little care taken to straighten them.

They must have fled.

But why? Had my captor threatened them? Had Victor returned and persuaded them to run?

Needing answers, I broadened my search, going room by room. Ernest's bedroom had been packed up, but hastily, with all but his most treasured belongings still in their usual places. I expected the same in my uncles' room, but was surprised to find it almost exactly as I remembered. A few books were missing from his shelf, and his prized possession, a pocket watch inherited from his own father, was gone, but all his clothes and personal items were still there.

Worried, I kept on down the hall to Victor's bedroom. The chaos here was different from that of the other rooms: every book had been removed from the bookshelf and then tossed onto the stripped bed, and each drawer had been emptied, the clothes in a pile on the floor. This wasn't just packing – someone had been looking for something. I toed the pile of discarded clothing, thinking about Victor's wardrobe. I calculated that several items of clothing were missing, but it was hard to be certain.

I went to Victor's bed and got down on my hands and knees to peer beneath it. For as long as I could remember, Victor had kept diaries, which he filled and stacked beneath the bed. I had no doubt that they would contain everything he had been doing and thinking, both before and after Elizabeth's death.

There was nothing there.

I sat back on my heels. What had happened here?

In my own bedroom, everything was exactly as I'd left it, except for a single addition: my aunt's necklace, the valuable gold pendant the creature had stolen and used to frame Justine for William's murder. The police must have returned it to my uncle after her execution, but someone had left it centered on top of my pillow.

My first response was shock that Ernest hadn't taken the locket with him. Then I realized that to him, the piece must have seemed cursed. What had begun as a cherished heirloom, a keepsake memorializing my beloved aunt, had likely come to symbolize the abrupt loss of William, Justine, and then me.

The unfairness of this struck me, and I resolved not to let my attacker twist another thing I had loved until it felt like a perversion. I picked up the necklace and fastened it around my neck, tucking it into my dress.

That done, I returned to the manor's central staircase and sat down on the top step, the candlestick beside me. Its light only extended a few feet, so I felt as though I were suspended in the dark room, untethered and floating.

At that time and place, women were considered intellectually inferior to men, an idea that had been conditioned into me from a very young age. I felt that the mystery of the disordered house must be beyond my limited powers, but with no one else to talk to, I couldn't help but try to reason through it.

I had seen signs of packing, but also signs of searching. It wasn't always easy to distinguish between the two, but Victor's bedroom had been the most thoroughly searched, which led me to surmise that my captor had already visited Gray Hollow.

But had he been here before or after the Frankensteins had packed up and left?

Although there was plenty of mess, I hadn't seen any signs of physical violence or even damage– no drops or smears of blood, no caved-in walls, like the ones in the cottage I'd escaped. The furniture was largely unbroken. It seemed appropriate to theorize that the Frankensteins, or at least some of them, had left Gray Hollow *before* my captor had arrived.

My plan to convince them to help me stop the creature and then help me end my second life could remain intact, but only if I could find them.

I checked on my wrapped hand, suddenly concerned that *I* might have left new bloodstains behind, which could confuse things for the authorities. But I saw with surprise that the thin kitchen towel around my palm was unbloodied. There was no pain either, I realized. Had I imagined the cut? Was I going mad, too?

Cautiously, I unwrapped the towel. There was indeed a deep cut in the meaty part of my palm, but only a tiny, blackish-red imprint on the towel opposite it.

Repulsed, but fascinated, I held the hand in front of the light so I could examine the cut closely. On my travels through the forest I had received many small scratches from branches and brambles, but none of these injuries had been deep enough to draw more than a thin line of blood anyway. This cut, on the other hand, should have bled enough to soak through the towel.

Quickly, before I could think too much about it, I prodded the wound with a finger. And then again. When I pushed on it quite hard, I felt a flare of muted pain, and a bit of watery black fluid oozed out.

Elizabeth, I was certain, would have fainted or even vomited at the sight, but despite my disgust I felt no visceral reaction. This disquieted me even further. Would the cut heal, or would I spend what I hoped would be a short life with this raw wound?

I watched it carefully, and after several minutes it seemed to me that something was happening, a sort of sped-up closing of the wound, similar to what you've seen yourself. I wrapped the towel back around my hand and tucked it under my arm. I couldn't bear to think about yet another sign of my transformation, especially at that moment, when I felt so disheartened.

I decided that I would get no additional answers in the dead of night, and even my bizarre body needed to get some sleep. I thought about returning to my own bedroom, but I found the idea of my old bed disturbing. I did not want to be surrounded by reminders of my former life. Instead, I returned to the front parlor and stretched out on the sofa, blowing out the candle and leaving it on the floor next to me.

The comfortable old couch should have been heaven after weeks of sleeping on the ground, but it seemed to make no difference to my new body what was underneath it. I stared at the darkness and waited for sleep.

My new form did not dream during repose, which was likely a blessing. The next morning, however, I woke to the familiar scents of the house, and for just a moment I imagined I heard Ernest and William, laughing as they chased the dog.

Instead, of course, when I opened my eyes, everything was just as I'd left it the night before. The little bit of cloudy daylight that filtered through dusty curtains only emphasized the house's disarray.

Sitting up, I checked the cut on my hand and saw that it had closed overnight, leaving only a pale red line.

My stomach growled, the noise loud in the silent house. Later, I would come to realize that these two conditions were related: whatever had been done to Elizabeth Lavenza's body involved re-prioritizing energy so that fuel, in the form of food and water, was used more efficiently and with no waste. Victor really had been trying to create a new species, and he'd experimented with making improvements on the base model. I went to the kitchen and scrounged through the familiar cupboards until I located some barley and nuts.

As I ate, I considered my new situation. The thought of confronting Victor and seeking help from Ernest and my uncle had kept me moving, but now I'd been denied whatever reckoning or reunion I'd expected to find at Gray Hollow. It was clear that I needed information in order to proceed in any direction, but how could I find out what had happened here without revealing myself? Elizabeth Lavenza could not be alive, not publicly. It would lead to many questions, and though I was furious with Victor, I did not want to ruin the Frankenstein name. I know how silly that sounds now, but this was long before Mary's book. I was still in the habit of protecting my family's reputation, especially because I was certain my uncle and Ernest were innocent in all this. My uncle would never have let Victor experiment the way he had, and Ernest was a gentle, shy young man whose greatest aspiration was to own his own farm. I had helped raise him, and I believed in him still.

But if Elizabeth Frankenstein stayed dead, how would I find out what had happened?

Eventually, an idea struck me: my uncle had a solicitor, Mr. Albin, who handled his financial affairs. I had only spoken to the man a few times, but I remembered the way to the lawyer's office. Surely Albin would know what had happened to the remaining Frankensteins.

I looked down at myself. I was still wearing the dress, now soiled and torn, that I'd borrowed from poor Alice. Visiting town would definitely require fresh clothes.

There were clothes in my bedroom, but once again, I found myself shying away from my own quarters. Instead, I traipsed up to the attic, where my uncle had kept several trunks of my aunt's things after her death. I found an old-fashioned black dress fairly quickly, but kept looking until I at last unearthed a Mary Stuart cap with veil, wrapped in protective paper. If I was going to interact with the outside world, I would need a way to hide my eyes until I could get some tinted glasses.

I would also need money. After I dressed, I went to Victor's chamber and pried up the loose floorboard just below his bed. I smiled as I saw the small, dusty pouches filled with coins. When we were children, Victor always hoarded money for books and sweets. In his typical distracted fashion, he'd forgotten all about the money after he left for school in Ingolstadt.

I felt my smile fade. Perhaps he'd forgotten about his pocket money not because he'd been distracted by school, but because he'd been distracted by what he'd made. By his secrets.

My eyes traveled around the familiar room, where I'd spent many rainy afternoons as a child. How often I'd visited Victor here in our adolescence. Yet it was really the home of a stranger.

Or was it? Had some part of me known that Victor was rejecting everything I understood to be moral and right? Had I simply chosen not to see it? Many times, I'd started to ask him questions about his work, but stopped myself before getting any details. Hadn't there always been questions that I didn't want answered?

The pain and betrayal rose within me again, and I wrapped my arms around myself to keep the cold, furious pressure from igniting. The books, the discarded scientific instruments, the piles and piles of notebooks filled with notes and scientific calculations... it was all right here, if I'd only paid attention. But I'd let myself be absorbed in my silly schedules and domestic responsibilities. I'd embraced credulity, tried to maintain the childlike innocence others seemed to value in me. And because I had, William and Justine and Henry had died.

In this, I was complicit.

Nineteen

Caroline

That afternoon, veil over my face, I walked nearly ten kilometers into the center of Geneva. Even with the veil the bright sunshine seemed to affect my eyes, and so before visiting Albin's office I stopped in a shop and purchased tinted glasses with some of Victor's pocket money.

Albin was an old-fashioned solicitor in his mid-sixties, nearly the same age as my uncle. His office was a modest two-room affair in an esteemed part of Geneva, because Albin was the type of man to value age and prestige over size. I introduced myself to his secretary as Emily Lavenza, Elizabeth's cousin. I said I had received word of Elizabeth's death, and I was seeking the location of her grave, to pay my respects.

The secretary spoke briefly with Mr. Albin, and within minutes I was being ushered into his office, a small, stately room decorated with his hunting trophies. Albin was a compact man with white hair and a fussy manner, his face more lined and tired than I remembered. He led me to a chair beneath a massive stuffed deer head, which he seemed to view as a place of honor.

"I'm pleased to meet you, Miss Lavenza, though of course the circumstances are simply too tragic," he said. "My condolences for your great loss." He looked closely at my face, and I struggled not to recoil or hide my eyes. I had checked my appearance carefully in the mirror to be sure that the veil protected me. "I do see a resemblance to our Miss Lavenza –

Mrs. Frankenstein, I suppose – but of course her eyes were different, and the way she carried herself." He shook his head. "Such a tragedy. Had the two of you been in contact long?"

"No," I said, having prepared for this question on the walk into town. It was common knowledge that Elizabeth had been adopted, but to family acquaintances, there had always been an air of mystery around the circumstances. "Our fathers were half-brothers; we had only began writing to each other last year, after I learned about her," I explained. "We were supposed to meet in person in Vienna after her wedding."

He made a small clucking noise of sympathy. "Of course, of course."

"I would like to pay my respects to her husband and uncle, but there was no answer at their estate. Would you be so kind as to give me their location?"

"Ah." Albin smoothed at his flawless shirt. "Yes, well, I'm afraid tragedy has continued to befall the family. The shock of Miss Elizabeth's death, so soon after William, was too much for my old friend, Alphonse." Albin's sorrow seemed genuine. "His heart gave out."

I gripped the edge of the desk to steady myself. Despite the untouched state of his bedroom, I had held out hope that my uncle still lived. "That's terrible," I murmured.

Then I remembered my captor's murderous expression when he spoke of Victor and his family. Was it possible that the creature had come for the Frankensteins after all? Tentatively, I added, "I do hope he didn't suffer, poor man."

"No, no, my dear," Albin said reassuringly. "Ernest found him in bed the morning after Elizabeth's funeral. He had passed peacefully in the night."

I nodded, comforted. My captor might have been able to sneak into a house unnoticed, but I couldn't picture him killing a single member of the household and exiting without disturbing anything.

He would have killed them all, said an unpleasant voice in the back of my mind.

"As for Victor," Albin continued, "his health was always poor, particularly after the losses he suffered this past year. His mind couldn't take losing his father, too." He coughed delicately. "I'm afraid he has been institutionalized, for his own safety."

Victor. I'd prepared myself to hear of his murder, or even that he had run away to escape the consequences of his creation. I hadn't thought of a lunatic asylum, as they were called then. Somehow, though, it didn't surprise me to learn that his body had followed his mind into darkness.

I checked my emotions and felt nothing more than a simmering anger. I would not be able to confront Victor for his crimes.

"What is the institution?" I asked, my thoughts racing.

But Albin gave me a pompous, pandering smile. "I'm afraid I can't say. But rest assured Victor is physically well and being cared for with every consideration."

I spent several additional minutes employing Elizabeth's most charming tactics to get Mr. Albin to reveal more, but on this matter the little man held firm. He would not give up Victor's location. It angered me to have come so close and have no way of finding my husband. When I felt the spark of cold flame flare in my chest, however, I forced myself to drop the subject.

"And what of Ernest?" I asked instead, prompting Albin to lift his eyes to me. "Elizabeth mentioned him in her letters."

"Yes, well, I'm afraid you just missed him. Ernest left Geneva three days ago."

"Where did he go?"

Albin ruffled the edges of the papers on his desk. "Miss Lavenza... I'm afraid this is rather a delicate subject –" He paused, his eyes suddenly meeting mine with just a shadow of suspicion. "How did you know to come speak to me, if I may ask?"

Another question I had anticipated. "Elizabeth mentioned you were a great friend of the family. She said you were especially close to her uncle, Alphonse."

As I'd expected, this pleased Albin, and he seemed to forget his misgivings. "Well as you are a close family friend, I shall tell you, though I must insist that it stay confidential —"

"Of course."

"Ernest came to see me after Alphonse's death," Albin explained, adjusting the angle of various items on his desk. "The poor boy believed a... presence... was stalking the Frankenstein family. There had been a break-in at Gray Hollow a few days earlier, shortly after the deaths of Miss Elizabeth and my own dear friend. Nothing was taken, mind you, but Ernest seemed to believe he might be... well. Cursed." Albin fell quiet, looking newly uncomfortable.

Of everyone in the family, Ernest was the least superstitious; I wouldn't have expected him to believe in curses. But he was young, and the only Frankenstein left alive and well. I could hardly blame him.

"Cursed?" I prompted.

"Yes, Miss Lavenza. I couldn't make head nor tail of it, I will admit, but one could hardly blame him for being fearful. He made sure Victor was provided for, then cashed out all of Alphonse's accounts and left Geneva."

"And his destination?" I asked immediately.

"He would not say, other than it was abroad." Remembering himself, Albin puffed out his chest with self-importance. "Though if he had, I would have kept his secret as well as Victor's."

"Did he say what he'd be doing?" I asked. My hopes of reaching Ernest, at least, to help me hunt for the monster were slipping away. "Even a hint of the location?"

Mr. Albin gave me a sharp look. He might have been elderly, but there was nothing feeble about his mind. I hastened to add,

"It's just that I did so want to pay my respects to members of the family, and to ask for stories about my cousin."

He relaxed. "I understand. All Ernest said was that he'd be starting a farm."

Disappointment burned in me. Ernest had always loved the land, and his fondest wish had been to either become a soldier or work the soil. Later I would be intensely pleased that he had escaped this grotesque nightmare to pursue his dream...but in that moment I was far too selfish. If my younger cousin was gone for good, that left me without a protector – or even a friend.

A cloud of despair hovered over me like one of Albin's poor dead animals. "What about the house?" I asked out of desperation. "Surely he'll need to come back to deal with a sale?"

Albin coughed. "I am to sell it and put the proceeds in trust for him. The lad is young, and seemed quite frightened." He looked distinctly uncomfortable. "I dare say, Miss Lavenza, I cannot blame him. I have never seen such a streak of terrible luck as has befallen that poor family these last few years. It was almost as though they were being..." He glanced around the room, perhaps realizing the irony of his words, and fell silent.

Before I left, I asked after Elizabeth's grave, and was told that the recently deceased had plots in a nearby churchyard, next to my aunt and uncle. Then Albin cleared his throat, looking uncomfortable. "I'm afraid, however, Miss Elizabeth's grave is yet... er... unoccupied."

"Pardon me?"

"There was some misunderstanding in the transfer of her body from Evian back to Geneva," he explained, squirming. "It is yet to be recovered."

This didn't surprise me, for obvious reasons, but Albin took my silence for shock and rushed to say, "The police are looking into it, of course. I'm sure they will recover her remains shortly."

Twenty

Caroline

There was nothing else Albin could tell me, so I took my leave, stumbling back into the grotesque sunshine, where I fumbled for the tinted glasses. Not knowing where else to go, I made my way back to Gray Hollow, feeling dazed and empty.

For the first time in either of my lives, I was completely at a loss. I had been brought up to nurture and care for Victor and his brothers, and now they were gone. Meanwhile, my murderer roamed free, perhaps looking for another victim. I hadn't the faintest idea how to go about stopping my attacker. I had no experience with deductive reasoning or investigation, and nothing in my ladylike skill set could assist me.

Even if I could locate my attacker, I thought as I let myself back into the manor, no one was left to help me prevail against him. Victor was gone, my uncle was dead, and I could not find Ernest. Everyone I'd ever loved was dead or lost to me, and now I was unable to move either forward or back.

The rest of that day was lost in that daze. Then another day passed, and another.

Time began to pass in a long, languid blur.

My days were spent wandering from room to room in a kind of torpor, my thoughts ticking through images like a second hand around a clock face: the night William died, Justine's trial, my wedding night, Victor's creation, poor Alice. Even the memory of Charles Roussel's broken skull tormented me.

It was ironic, really: though my form was corporeal and solid, I seemed to be a walking ghost, unable to rest until completing my impossible unfinished business.

When I became hungry, I went out at night and searched the orchards and gardens for scraps of fruit and roots. When my clothes become filthy with the dust and grime of an unloved building, I simply scrounged for fresh ones, taking what I could from my aunt's trunks in the attic. Occasionally I would attempt to read a little from my uncle's remaining library, but the books couldn't retain my interest. What use had a monster for modern philosophical theory?

I knew this fraught limbo couldn't last forever, and I lived in fear that a new owner would arrive any day to claim the house. I kept the curtains drawn, and never lit the lamps, preferring the darkness. My altered eyes could see with a fraction of the light I'd once needed, and I took full advantage of that. Meanwhile, my ears were always tuned to the front door, waiting to flee should I hear a key in the lock.

No one ever came. Had I ever stopped to consider it, I would have realized that to anyone else, the house must indeed seem to be cursed, having lost so many of its inhabitants to recent, violent deaths. Outsiders would have no way to know the curse lay with the family, not the building.

With each day that passed, my urge to track down my attacker dulled, and the divide between Elizabeth's life and my existence widened. The memory of my actions in Les Clefs was always in my thoughts, taunting me. Elizabeth had believed in God, had trusted that He would guide her soul to heaven. Instead she had been killed – and I was a killer of children. Was I soulless? What sickness animated me, if not the spark of human spirit?

I was often tempted to return to town to buy a few bottles of laudanum, which would allow me to pass on peacefully. By then, though, my own fugue had conquered me too thoroughly for such a bold action. I was a prisoner once more, held captive by my own indecision and guilt.

Time passed, too much of it. The weather grew cold, and then warmer again, though my body barely recognized the difference. Eventually, though, the wet spring was replaced by a summer even I came to notice.

In two hundred years on earth, that remains the strangest season I've yet encountered: weeks of terrible storms and endless rain and fog. The sun seemed to have completely abandoned Geneva, and when I realized this I did not mind in the least. It suited my mood.

On one rainy morning, there was a knocking at the door. I had been dozing in a chair – I slept only fitfully in those days, and always sitting upright, waiting as I was for someone to arrive and evict me. But the persistent knocking confused me. A new owner would have a key. Surely anyone else would go away after a few minutes with no reply?

Eventually my curiosity rose, and I put on my tinted glasses and went to the door, cracking it just far enough to peer out.

A young woman of about eighteen stood on the stoop, her shoulders thrust back and chin raised, paying no attention to the light rain that spattered her shoulders. She was my height, with inexpensive clothes and tired eyes. Despite her youth, there was a look of determined calculation on her face that unnerved me. "Hello," she said pleasantly, in English. "I'm Mary. I am looking for Elizabeth Frankenstein."

I stared blankly at her, for what felt like several minutes. Considering my appearance and the state of the manor, her friendly, polite tone was surreal, like being confronted by an alien visitor.

When I did not respond, the girl tried again, this time in accented French. "Elizabeth Lavenza Frankenstein? Is that you?" She pointed to my chest.

Why would a young Englishwoman be here looking for my former incarnation? "Elizabeth Frankenstein is dead," I replied. "She was murdered in Evian in August." I closed the door again.

Mary immediately knocked again. I ignored her and returned to my seat, assuming that the young woman would give up soon.

That was the first time I underestimated Mary Godwin, though unfortunately it wouldn't be the last.

I tried to close my eyes again, but the knocking – not forceful, but very determined – continued at a steady pace, with only the occasional pause as she switched hands. It made it impossible to lose myself in my thoughts, or return to sleep. I began to fret that she might contact the authorities, or perhaps break a window and climb in. I had nailed a board over the broken kitchen window on a particularly snowy evening, but there were plenty of others to choose from.

After an hour or so the knocking stopped, and I thought, with great relief, that she'd finally gone home. A moment later, though, the tapping resumed – but the nature of the sound had changed. She was using a stick, to save her knuckles.

More than three hours after Mary's arrival, I stalked back to the door and jerked it open. "What do you want?" I demanded.

With surprising speed, she reached out and snatched the glasses off my face.

I recoiled at the rudeness and the sudden brightness of even an overcast sky, but not before Mary had seen my eyes. "It's you, isn't it?" she said triumphantly, as pleased and excited as if meeting a beloved idol. "He brought you back!"

Stunned at her audacity, I managed to slam the door again. Feeling disoriented, I rested both of my flat palms against it for a moment, eyes still squeezed shut.

How could she know? And if she knew, how could she be so calm?

I had fallen out of the habit of human interaction, and even if I hadn't, this was not a situation I could have prepared for. I had no idea how my aunt would want me to behave, or what my new temper might spur me to do. I resolved that the best option was to hide myself away in one of the upstairs rooms, with their thick walls. The girl could knock all day if she pleased.

But I hadn't taken more than two steps from the door when I heard her clear voice calling from the other side. "I have Victor's journals."

Twenty-One

Caroline

Journals. It was quite possibly the only word that could have seized my attention so strongly.

Whirling around, I opened the front door and squinted past the girl, who still held my tinted glasses. There was a carriage waiting at the end of the drive, but as far as I could tell, no one else was in sight.

I grabbed Mary's upper arm and jerked her inside, practically throwing her into the house ahead of me.

It was more strength than I had intended to use, and though she remained on her feet, Mary yelped as she stumbled to a stop. She rubbed her arm and gave me an injured look. "That was unnecessary."

"Who are you?" I demanded, stepping close enough to snatch my glasses out of her hands. I felt better as soon as they were on my face again.

The girl drew herself up. "I am Mary Wollstonecraft Godwin," she declared, and seemed slightly disappointed when I did not react. "My parents are William Godwin and Mary Wollstonecraft," she added, in a tone that suggested this should mean something.

I shook my head, even more confused than before. "I do not know those names."

She frowned. "My mother was a great writer. My father is a notorious writer and publisher."

That meant nothing to me. I used to read a little poetry, before my aunt died and I became busy with the children and household, but it had been a decade since I'd read anything but what Victor suggested. "How did you get Monsieur Frankenstein's journals?" I said impatiently. Without intending to, I had reverted to Elizabeth's commanding, lady-of-the manor tone. "I want them immediately."

Mary smoothed a strand of hair behind her ear, clearly in no hurry. "Could we have some light? And perhaps sit down? I am quite tired from my journey."

Before I could tell her to leave, she glanced down at herself and sighed. "Oh, dear, I should have thought. Would you happen to have a towel?"

I followed her gaze to the front of her dress, which had darkened with moisture. It had been so long since my aunt had nursed little William that it took me a moment to understand.

"You... you have a baby," I stammered. This unnerved me more than it should have. She was so young, at least five or six years younger than me, and I...

I rested a hand on the back of an armchair, momentarily staggered. I'd worried about my attacker attempting to impregnate me, but somehow, until that moment, I hadn't quite processed the idea that I could never have my own baby. Even if it were physically possible, the child would be even more of an abomination than I was. That miracle was lost to me forever.

Mary didn't seem to notice my sudden comprehension. "Yes, I have a son," she said, smiling proudly. "William. We call him Willmouse."

William.

It was a common name, of course, but it still conjured up a dozen images of the sweet little boy whom I'd lost.

When I didn't move, Mary prompted, "May I have that towel please?"

"Oh. Yes." Dazed, I went into the kitchen and fetched a towel from the drawer, returning to find that Mary had taken a seat on the sofa. She accepted the cloth and began tucking it into her bosom, while I averted my eyes. My aunt would have been scandalized at Mary's frankness.

"There, that's better," she said at last, her voice warming with motherly satisfaction. "My son, he –"

I couldn't bear to hear this. "The journals?" I interrupted, meeting her gaze.

Mary's face set again. "Yes. I have them, though I did not bring them with me."

Irrationally, I felt betrayed. "Then why are you here?"

Her face changed, then, from imperious dignity to something childlike, nearly desperate. "I need a story," she said very seriously. "And I want to use his. Yours. You are Elizabeth Frankenstein?"

"How do you –" I began, but cut myself off. She could be bluffing. Even if she had Victor's journals, she had no way of knowing what his creation had done to me. Who could possibly have told her? I doubted she'd encountered my attacker, Victor's creation; she was far too cheerful and unharmed.

"I do not know what you mean," I said. "That is not my name."

Mary pursed her lips together for a moment, then said, "Let me start again. My lover, the father of my baby, is a poet. His name is Percy Shelley." Her face flushed with pride, though of course I did not know the name. "He and I came to Geneva with a group, which includes my sister and the baby, as well as Percy's friend, Lord Byron, and his personal doctor. Surely you have heard of Byron?"

"I have," I said primly. Byron was an English poet of some renown, though my impression was that his fame had more to do with his many public scandals than any writing talent he may have possessed. As distracted and upset as I had been in the months before my death, even I could not avoid tales of his escapades.

"Last week, Shelley and Byron took a tour of Chillon Castle," Mary said, and looked at me expectantly, as though the statement answered all my questions.

I could only stare at her blankly. I knew of Chillon, of course. Today Chillon would be described as a popular Genevan tourist attraction, but at the time, the castle had been a prison for many decades and had only recently been conquered by the French-speaking Vaud district. They were still in the process of moving in munitions and weapons for storage. But I didn't see what any of that had to do with my own situation.

"Byron talked the local officials into a tour during the transition," Mary went on, "and of course, the two of them just strolled around on their own. In the crypt, they encountered a single prisoner, left in a room all by himself. This man was emaciated and babbling, yet his room was spotless, and he'd been given a number of small comforts that seemed at odds with his environment."

Here Mary paused and gave me another look, but I was still disoriented by what felt like a drastic change in topic. She continued. "The guards told them that the prisoner was quite insane, and really should have been in an asylum, rather than Chillon. The rumor was that one of the castle supervisors had been a friend of the prisoner's late father. The supervisor had agreed to keep this man at Chillon for a time out of respect for the father."

The purpose of her story finally became clear. "*Victor*," I whispered.

My uncle had indeed been a public official during his younger years. I was aware that he had many friends – and was owed many favors – in the Genevese government, but it had not occurred to me to connect them to recent events.

I had to admit, it was a brilliant place to hide Victor. Mr. Albin had indeed kept his promise to keep Alphonse Frankenstein's sons safe.

Mary nodded. "That wasn't the name the guards used, though. Percy asked what the man had done, and the guard said the prisoner claimed responsibility for a number of deaths… though it had been proven that he'd been out of the country for several of them.

"Shelley and Byron told me this story over dinner, and then I dare say the two of them forgot all about the prisoner." Mary's eyes seemed to sharpen. "But I did not."

Then, finally, I understood the intensity of her interest. "You went to see Victor," I surmised. "And that's how you got his journals."

"Yes. He may be listed under an alias, but his journals are all labeled with his full name."

"When was this?"

"Just last month."

That didn't help me. "What month is it now?"

Mary blinked with surprise, but said quite smoothly, "June."

I needed a moment to absorb that. Even taking into account the weeks I had spent with the creature and the lost time wandering the forest, that meant I had been haunting this house for more than six months. Time had simply fallen away from me.

"How was he?" I said, finally allowing myself to ask.

"I'm afraid he's doing quite poorly," Mary said, her face somber. "He is very thin and has a cough from the damp air. They haven't chained him, so he is free to move about the crypt rooms, but he is too weak to move much." She hesitated for a moment, then added, "His mind is also unwell. I stood near his cell for over an hour, asking questions, and though he spoke nearly continuously, I don't think he answered one of them."

"What did he speak of?"

"Someone named Henry, mostly, and Elizabeth, and William. He spoke a great deal about his creation, but I didn't understand any of that until I read his diaries."

"Do you think he knows?" I found myself saying. "About me, that is." It had occurred to me that my attacker may have bragged to him after my death.

But Mary shook her head. "I do not believe so. He gave no sign."

I didn't know what else to say. Despite what he'd done to me and the people I loved, the thought of Victor mad and imprisoned was distressing. My husband had always cherished his own intellect more than anything else in his life – more than Henry, or money, or his family. Being stripped of his mind and abandoned in a locked crypt – I couldn't conceive a more terrible punishment.

So why did I not feel triumphant?

Mary, I noticed, was looking around the sitting room with curiosity. I followed her gaze, trying to see the room as she did. Several pieces of furniture were obviously missing; the rest were covered in sheets. A layer of dust and grime. Stuffy air that smelled of mold and something sour. I felt shame churn inside me, like acid under my skin. My aunt would be appalled to see what had happened to her precious home.

But Mary did not appear to be offended. "This house must have been beautiful, once," she remarked.

It did not escape me that as I was trying to see Gray Hollow through her eyes, she was trying to see it through my memories. "There was always so much activity," I heard myself say.

"I am sorry for what's happened to you, Elizabeth." Why did it still hurt so, to hear that name out loud? She looked at me with anticipation, wanting confirmation of my identity.

"Elizabeth is dead," I replied. "I am not she."

"Perhaps we are both correct," Mary said mildly. "Yet your eyes are yellow and your skin waxy. There is an angry scar that encircles your wrist completely, as though an entire hand was removed and reattached."

I pulled the sleeve of my dress down and did not reply. This young woman unnerved me – not just for her forwardness, so unlike Elizabeth's demure disposition, but because of the casual way in which she discussed such gruesome matters. Why wasn't she repulsed by me, by the circumstances of my presence here? "Elizabeth is dead," I mumbled.

"And you are here in her form?"

God help me, I nodded.

We sat there in silence for a few minutes, before I made myself say, "If Victor does not know of my fate, how did you find me?"

"Reasoning." Mary gave a small smile, unable to hide her pride. "In Victor's diary, he mentions that his progeny stole the instructions for reanimation. Then the creature killed you – Elizabeth. It was easy enough to learn that the body was lost on its return to Geneva for burial."

It was a remarkable bit of inference, but Mary shrugged. "If one accepts Victor's story as fact, it is simple enough to reason that his creature decided to resurrect you as revenge for Victor's abandonment. I retraced your trip to Evian by boat and spoke to the family of the coachman transporting your body. He was killed. Did you know?"

Another death, courtesy of my husband's actions. "No. Nor does it surprise me."

"I suppose if the fiend was capable of killing a young child, one more adult male would not faze him," she agreed.

I felt a fresh pang of guilt and remorse, though I knew she was not referring to Alice.

"Victor mentioned William in his diaries?" I asked.

Mary nodded. "He wrote of feeling terrible guilt over his brother's death, and of his ambivalence about whether or not to come forward. He did speak to the magistrate, after your death – but no one believed his claims."

She hesitated and, for perhaps the first time, looked uncertain. "In fairness, after seeing him in that cell, I do not blame the magistrate for finding Victor's story unreliable."

I opened my mouth to ask for a hundred more details about Victor's state – was he confused? Frightened? Could he perhaps be nursed back to health? – before I reminded myself that Victor's wellbeing was no longer my responsibility.

Then it occurred to me that Mary seemed to be stalling. Out of reflex, if nothing else, I tried extending my hand, the perfect, unmarked one. "I would appreciate if you'd return my husband's belongings and leave me in peace."

Mary ignored my outstretched arm, glancing around the empty, neglected room once more. "This is peace?" she asked, not unkindly. "Being alone in this tomb?"

Disconcerted, I pulled my hand back and used it to rub my left wrist. "What do you want with me? You said something about a story."

Mary smiled, and even gave a little bounce on the sofa, as though the question delighted her. "You see, I'm a writer," she said. "That is, I wish to write, like my mother, but I have been struggling for an idea worthy of my ambition. I..." she paused, considering her words. "Well, Shelley and Byron are both older, more intelligent and more experienced writers. But I wish to impress them. Byron proposed that we all write ghost stories, as a sort of challenge. As he and Shelley tour the mountains, I have been wandering the city in search of such a tale. That is why I asked Victor for his journals."

I could not get used to the casual way she spoke Victor's name, *my* Victor. "He just gave them to you?" I asked in disbelief. "A stranger?"

"With eagerness, yes," Mary replied. "When he finally understood what I wanted, and realized my interest, he seemed hopeful, as though I might go out and continue his research."

"What?" I gave her a sharp look, but Mary's nose was wrinkled in disdain.

"I would never. But I do want to rewrite his journals and publish them as a novel. I decided to find you and ask for your permission." She looked at me expectantly.

My breath caught, and with no warning the cold anger began to build in my chest again. This girl was discussing my family's most shameful tragedies as though they were a new play she'd viewed. "My permission," I repeated coldly.

"And your assistance," she admitted. "I would like to know more about your husband and his upbringing, his desires, his intentions." The enthusiasm in her voice made me sick.

"Let me test my understanding," I said at last, my voice coming out near a growl. "You're holding my husband's journals hostage until I agree to help you reveal his gruesome and criminal activities – not to mention my own wretched existence – so you can impress your husband and his friend?"

Mary lifted her chin. "Shelley is not my husband," she said defiantly. "We are deeply in love but remain unmarried."

I clenched my teeth in annoyance. She was so young. "If he loves you," I countered, "why do you need to show off for him? Why, for that matter, does he leave you alone so he may traipse around a foreign country with an infamous scoundrel?"

Mary stood up then, tossing her head and glowering down at me, hands on her hips. "Do not dare to presume you understand our love. You are not exactly an expert on happy marriages."

"I see, so this Shelley is a good man, then," I said pointedly. "He'd never betray or ignore you?"

It was a catty, unnecessary question, a vestige of my own pain and bitterness, but it hit home. Hurt flared in Mary's eyes, and I regretted my attack immediately. I took a deep breath and said, "My apologies. You're right, I have no business criticizing another's relationship."

Mary nodded coolly. "We have wandered off topic," she said stiffly. "You asked me about Victor's diaries. I am hoping to gain your permission to use them in this book, and your help in rounding out Victor's character. Yes, I hope to impress my love and his peer, but writing is much more to me than that."

She leaned forward. "What happened to you was gruesome, yes, but all the elements are of great interest to me. Death and

137

birth and passion, the creation of life, the careless arrogance of man... I cannot help but feel as if I came upon this story because I am meant to tell it. Please, give me the tools I need to do so."

Mary looked at me again.

"Before I give you permission to publish my husband's most private thoughts," I said, "I should like to see them."

Mary looked bewildered. "There's very little in there other than daily records of his experiments and theories," she said, "and a few notes when he receives a letter or attends a class. Surely the journals contain no unfamiliar information."

I abandoned my efforts at subterfuge. "Do they contain his precise formula for reanimating dead tissue?" I demanded.

She tossed her hair. "Of course not. It would be irresponsible to publish that information."

I fought the urge to sigh with relief. So he had only kept the one copy, and I had destroyed it. Perhaps this freed me of any further obligation to the world. I would consider the idea later, after this pest had departed.

"Do you not see, Mary, that simply by writing this story, you may provoke others to recreate Victor's experiments?" I shook my head. "This entire idea is reckless and foolish."

"Then help me," she said, leaning forward so she was sitting on the edge of the sofa. "Tell me your side, the true events, and I shall write it as a cautionary story of man's hubris. Icarus and the wax feathers! Prometheus and his fire!"

I found myself wanting to strike her and realized that my left hand had already risen. Lowering it, fighting the anger that was beginning to spark, I glared at Mary.

"I will not," I said, my demeanor as hard and brittle as I felt. "You speak of man's arrogance, of stories in which he overreaches and creates disaster. Do you not see that you are threatening to do the same?" Trying to fight the flare of anger, I shook my head with vehemence, tucking my hands under my seat and curling my legs under me to prevent my body from stepping toward her, threatening her. "You will return my husband's belongings to me. They are mine by law."

My voice had become harsh and commanding. William would have burst into tears if he'd heard me speak like that, but Mary only stared at me in silent assessment for a long moment. "By law," she said at last, "you are dead. You have no rights. No possessions."

My mouth dropped open. Before I could respond, Mary stood and said, "Now I have upset you. I apologize. Perhaps we both need some time to digest this meeting, and for you to consider my request." She turned and was striding toward the door before I could reply.

"Where are you going?" I called after her.

"I must feed the baby," she said over her shoulder. "I shall return tomorrow for your answer."

Flummoxed, I could only sit there in the darkened, decaying room, staring after her. I remained on the sofa for what seemed like hours, contemplating how a single conversation could have so complicated my already strange existence.

The silly girl wanted to turn my Victor's actions into a book, one that could potentially give others the secrets of his experiments, or at least send them down a similar path. It would have been laughable, if it weren't so appalling.

As I sat there I could not help but imagine dozens of horrific outcomes, that always ended in me being tortured to death, or an army of unfeeling revenants destroying my city. Or both. It would be another eighty years before the first motion picture was publicly shown in Paris, but it felt like I was watching events unfold right in front of me as I sat there.

No. I would not allow it.

I snapped back to the moment, seeing that the living room had grown dark around me. I jumped to my feet and began pacing through the house, furiously contemplating how I might stop Mary from writing her book as the blue flame in my chest flickered and breathed with me.

139

I am mortified to say that the first course of action I considered was violence. I had learned in Les Clefs that this new body was strong. Mary did not seem like she would frighten easily, but if I hurt her even a little bit, to show what I was capable of doing...

Then I remembered the stains on Mary's dress, and the fond way she'd spoken of her infant, and the fire in my chest was instantly extinguished, replaced by shame. If I tried to intimidate Mary, I wasn't at all sure I could prevent myself from killing her. Even if I was certain that I could keep control — and how could I, after what I'd done to Alice? — I had not sunk so low as to consider threatening a nursing mother. I would not deprive an infant of its parent.

No, I concluded, I could not hope another wrong would make something right. But what options were left to me? I needed to find and obliterate Victor's journals, for a start, just as I had done with his notes after escaping my captor. Mary had claimed the journals didn't contain Victor's formulas, but I couldn't trust her word.

If I did destroy the journals, though, what then? It seemed unlikely that Mary would abandon her book project — she clearly wasn't a girl who would be easily deterred. But without them, Mary would have no details, no proof. And perhaps she could be persuaded in some other way — I had very little money, but I could give her items from the house to sell. It would hurt my heart to lose the little that was left of the Frankensteins, but they weren't things I needed myself.

As soon as I stopped Mary's book, I resolved to let myself die. The creature who had made me would not be able to make another. Someone else would have to find and stop him. I would surrender.

Twenty-Two

Caroline

I spent the remainder of that day planning my strategy: when Mary returned, I would feign compliance with her plan, pretending to have a change of heart about telling my story. I would then persuade Mary that I needed to see the journals in order to spark my memory. All the while, I would try to convince her of the folly of telling such a horrifying, grisly story to the public.

If, after all that, she still planned to publish her novel... well, I would be gone.

The next day, I rose early and fed well off the tiny, unripe apples in the orchard. I put on a clean (though musty-smelling) dress, and tied up my hair. When I was convinced that I was as human-looking as I could be, I swept some of the cobwebs from the corners of the room, pulling the dusty sheets off a couple of pieces of furniture. I even pushed the heavy sofas together to create a new seating arrangement, making the missing pieces less noticeable.

At mid-morning, I heard a carriage approach on the driveway. It was raining again, and I hurried to the door, reaching it just as Mary knocked. I was ready.

Only Mary hadn't come alone. When I opened the door there was a plump, gurgling infant in her arms, tucked under her coat to protect the baby from rain.

I stumbled backward, trying to create as much distance as possible between the child and myself. "No! What were you thinking?"

"That my nursemaid is visiting her mother this afternoon," Mary said pragmatically, entering the house without invitation. "Luckily Byron let me borrow his carriage again, so I did not need to walk the whole way with this hefty boy." Smiling, she gave the child a little bounce in her arms.

I backed away, toward the far side of the room. All my careful planning, my strategies for handling Mary, vanished. I was terrified of what I might do.

"It looks much nicer in here," Mary said, looking around the room. Finally her eyes landed on me, and she noticed my discomfort. "What is it?" she asked, brow furrowed.

"You must get him away from here!" I said shrilly.

She smiled with hesitation, as though she suspected me of playing a joke on her. "What do you mean?"

"He's not safe!"

Her lips pursed. "Elizabeth, the creature who killed your cousins wouldn't come here. The city is so close to this estate; surely he would not risk exposure. We are quite safe." She sat down on the uncovered loveseat, setting the child down between her knees and grasping his little fists, so he could play at standing.

Her indifference to the danger somehow made me more furious still. "You *stupid* girl!" I cursed. I was near the opposite wall, but it didn't seem nearly far enough. The baby gazed at me, pulling one hand free so he could gnaw thoughtfully on his fist. "You think my killer is the only danger?"

"What do you mean?" Mary looked around the house. "Is there someone else here?"

I felt the anger building again, and panic along with it. I pressed my shoulders into the wall, spreading my fingers against it for good measure. "Get out!" I screamed.

The baby's face crumpled and reddened. As he began to wail, Mary picked him up and hugged him, murmuring in his ear. She stood, gave me a wary look, and strode to the door, letting herself out with great calm.

Hugging my arms around myself, I allowed my body to slide down the wall until I hit the floor. I drew my knees to my chest, unconsciously making myself as small as possible.

A baby. The thought of what might have happened, what I could have done to him in a rage –

To my surprise, the unlocked door swung open again, revealing Mary, alone. She stepped inside, closing the door behind her. "The carriage driver will only hold William for a few minutes," she announced, crossing the room to my side. "Thank heavens he's a father."

Without waiting for permission, she lowered herself to the floor facing me. "What happened?"

I did not answer, and she prodded, "Why does a harmless baby frighten you, Elizabeth?"

"I am not Elizabeth."

She smiled, and I realized she'd done this on purpose, to provoke me into answering. How had this gone so wrong? How had all the power shifted to this slip of a girl?

"I... I killed a child." The words had escaped my lips before I could help it. "When I first escaped him, there was a little girl..."

I'm not sure how I expected Mary to react, but at least with horror and revulsion. She was barely more than a child herself.

Instead, though, Mary's face remained composed. "Tell me."

So I told her about my actions in Les Clefs, about the way Alice's body had flown against the woodpile, how flat and lifeless she had been in my arms. When I told her my suspicion that Charles Roussel's had been abusing Alice, Mary paled considerably, but she remained quiet.

Perhaps the confession should have felt like an unburdening, a freeing of my soul. But really, it felt only like debasement of

143

myself. Though I wasn't particularly interested in impressing Mary, I could not stem the shame that flooded me as I spoke the words out loud, detailing my crimes.

"Don't you see?" I concluded. "I deserve to be put to death. I must be put to death."

"Death?" She was incredulous "But it was an accident!"

"Was it? I had more than enough time to flee the house, but I attacked because I could not control my temper." I pushed out a breath. "I must be destroyed, Mary, before I harm another innocent."

Mary stared at me in horror. "You mustn't say that!" she cried.

I almost had to smile at that. How could anyone be so brazen and tactless, yet still so naive? It was strangely endearing.

Still, that did not make her right, nor I wrong. "I am dangerous, Mary," I said softly, carefully enunciating each word. "Just as dangerous as Victor's creation. More so, even, because I am pretty and feminine." I gestured down at myself. "I must make sure no one else can become like this, and then this body must be destroyed."

I went quiet after that, and a long silence followed my confession. My eyes caught movement in the corner, and I watched a long-legged spider bundling up her meal for the day before she devoured it. Spiders used to terrify me, but the thought seemed laughable now. After all, I was the greater monster.

At last, Mary said, "If Alice had stayed in her bed that night, what do you think would have happened?"

This surprised me, but after a moment of consideration, I replied, "I would have still killed Charles, most likely. He was drunk, and ignored my protest. I would not have let him... do what he wanted."

She nodded, a satisfied teacher with a slow pupil. "And then?"

I blinked. The question hadn't occurred to me before, but I found the answer easily enough. "I... I would have escorted Alice to her sister's house." Images from this potential development filled my head: Alice embracing a relieved sister, Alice growing up in a loving household, Alice getting married, becoming a mother. Each new scenario provided its own individual sting.

"And what would have happened to Alice if you had never come into their lives?"

"I... suspect Charles would have continued forcing himself on the girl."

Mary gestured for me to continue, and I thought about Alice's desperation, her clinging despair. "She would likely have become pregnant, or run away."

"Or taken her own life," Mary concluded. "Children die, Elizabeth."

"Do not call me –"

"They die every day," she interrupted, with a look of terrible sorrow, well beyond what should have been possible on such a young face. "And every day, they are beaten and raped. But not every child is avenged."

She gave me an expectant look, but I just shook my head. "I have no idea what you mean."

"You have astounding abilities," Mary pointed out, her face beginning to lighten.

"Deformities, you mean." I looked down at myself in disgust, and saw that I was once again rubbing the ugly scar on my wrist.

"You could do great things," she insisted. "You could be an avenging angel, a phoenix who returns to –"

"Stop," I interrupted, holding out my hands. I wanted to put them over my ears. "You cannot turn me into one of your stories, Mary. I am not a creature of good."

"But you *could* be." Her eyes were suddenly bright and feverish. "I've read Victor's journals; I know of his creature's

145

abilities. If you are the same, you have stamina, strength, and impermeability. Imagine the possibilities!"

"Like Victor did?" I countered. "You sound just like him. Is this – I gestured to the shadowy, moldering room – "the possibility you seek? Death and horror cursing you and everyone you love?" I looked pointedly toward the door.

Mary flinched. "Let's leave William out of this," she said primly.

I nearly choked on a bitter laugh. "Your William, you mean. *My* William is already dead, before his sixth birthday. I raised that little boy, after his mother's death, and now I shall never raise another." I curled myself into a ball, pressing my face into my arms. I expected to feel the anger building again, but only grief and self-loathing raged within me. "You speak of possibilities, but I have lost the possibility of birthing a child. That is what I wanted from my life, and it is gone. You can never understand that."

Mary fell silent for a moment, taken aback. I was certain she was thinking of her own babe, perfect and whole. For a moment I felt sick with envy.

"What about love?" Mary said finally. "You can still fall in love."

I lifted my head then, meeting her desperate eyes. For the first time since she'd introduced herself, Mary seemed like the teenage girl she was. "I will not age, Mary," I said. "Don't speak to me of love. It is not a possibility for monsters."

"You're not a monster!"

"Tell that to Alice Roussel," I said bitterly.

"And what of Alice?" she countered. "If you die now, her death has no meaning."

"You said yourself that children die every day. Do you think any of those deaths have meaning?"

Mary stood up, anger on her face. "They need to," she spat. "They must!"

That drew my attention. I studied her face, momentarily forgetting my own pain. "Who did you lose?"

She glowered at me for a moment, then the words tore out of her. "William is my only child. But he is not my first."

Her shoulders slumped, and I suddenly felt tired. I had made assumptions again, that the daughter of literary celebrities must have an easy life. But Mary herself had said herself that birth and death were of great interest to her.

Would I never learn to look deeper? "You have my condolences, Mary. Truly."

She looked at her hands, as though something might appear in them at any moment. "I still dream of her," she said softly.

I said nothing, and eventually Mary looked over at me. "The coachman will be anxious for me to return for the baby," she said. "So... will you help me with the book? I can return tomorrow and we can get started."

I sighed. I would never make her understand. "Mary. I have told you the truth about who I am. Now do me the courtesy of truth in return. Do Victor's journals include the instructions for reanimation?"

She bit her lip, eyeing me for a moment. "They do not," she admitted. "I do not have the formulas."

"Is there anything I can say that will dissuade you from writing this story?"

"There is not."

That was as I had expected. She was too tenacious, too strong-willed. I could not stop this, any more than I had been able to stop my murder. A great weariness settled over me then.

So be it.

"He may come after you," I warned. "Not Victor, but his creation."

Mary lifted her chin. "You said he was a thinking, intelligent being. If I publish this book as fiction, coming after me would prove his existence. If anything I will be safer once the book is out, because the knowledge will be as well."

I wasn't sure I agreed with that assessment, but there was so little I could do. "Can you publish it anonymously, as a precaution?"

She thought for a moment. "I suppose I could," she allowed, though not without a hint of disappointment. "I was already planning to alter the dates, and change the family name, of course —"

"No," I said, my voice coming out much harsher than intended. "Leave his name." Ernest was in hiding, no doubt under an alias, and there were no other Frankensteins left to be harmed. I wanted my petty little retribution. "Alter the timeline, yes, but keep the name Victor Frankenstein."

Many, many times, since then, I have regretted this hasty, vengeful decision. In the moment it seemed like a fitting – and overdue – retaliation toward my husband, but as often happens with revenge, it proved to hurt me more than anyone else. Every time I walked into a bookstore or passed a movie theater and saw the name Frankenstein, I was back in that wretched cottage with Victor's creation, being treated as his plaything.

"All right," Mary said with a nod. "Victor Frankenstein it shall be."

"Then I shall help you with your book," I said, forcing myself to smile. "We can begin tomorrow."

"I'll leave William at home," she promised.

I went to the window and watched the carriage make its way down the drive, rain pounding down on the roof. I waited until it had disappeared from sight, and then collected my hat and tinted glasses. I left Gray Hollow and made my way into town to buy as much laudanum as I could.

The sun had fallen by the time I returned. I had visited three different shops, recklessly spending the last of Victor's money to secure three full bottles. It seemed fitting that my late husband should contribute to my suicide, having contributed so much to my undoing.

Back in the house, I went first to a drawer in my uncle's office and took out a piece of paper, scribbling a letter. I still remember every word.

Mary,

I know you will not understand, but I can go no farther on this journey with you. I can never restore what was taken from me; nor can I make whole what I have broken. Please do not come into the house. I would consider it a great favor if, instead, you informed my uncle's solicitor that "Elizabeth's cousin" has taken her own life at Gray Hollow. I am sure he can make the necessary arrangements.

His name is Mr. Albin, and he has an office on Water Street. I wish you all the luck in the world with your writing, and your children.

Fond regards

Here I stopped. How should I sign it? If I was Elizabeth no longer, then I had no name. I considered my options for a moment, and then simply put a period after the word "regards." It would be enough.

I slid the note partway under the front door, anchoring it with a heavy book so the wind would not snatch it away. Then I sat down on the same sofa where Mary had perched with her son and unwrapped the packages of laudanum. Each of the chemists had warned me never to swallow more than three drops of the stuff, and each bottle contained twenty times that.

Quietly, I whispered every prayer I remembered. It was pointless, I knew, since murderers and suicides don't go to Heaven, but the instinct was so strong, and I could see no harm in it. Then, before I could sink into any more morose thoughts,

149

I quickly downed each bottle, one after another. I lay down onto the sofa and waited for death to claim me once more.

This time, I accepted it – not with peace, after what I had done – but at least with resignation.

For the first time in my wretched new life, I dreamed.

I was back in the gaol cell on the evening of Justine's trial, sitting with her as she awaited execution.

In life, Victor and I had both been with Justine that night, but now she and I were alone in the dark, moldy cell. It stank of recent vomit and urine, with older, more horrific smells layered beneath that.

Justine had been petite and pale, with strong hands and arms from years of hard work and a tiny crucifix fixed around her neck. "I swear, Lizzie, I would never hurt him," she cried, kneeling at my feet as I sat on the cell's cold bunk, the metal edge digging into the backs of my legs. Justine's hands were wrapped up in my skirts, and now she lowered her forehead to them. "You have to believe me!"

Serene and unworried, I stroked her hair and promised, "Victor is coming home, Justine. He will fix this. He will save you."

Justine recoiled, staring up at me with those terrified, pleading eyes. I saw how young she was, how innocent in every sense. "But, Lizzie," she said, her voice now cold and practical, "It was Victor who put me here. Victor, and you."

"Me?" I glanced down and saw that I now wore the black robes of a judge. Bewildered, I looked back at Justine, but the poor girl had backed away from me, curled up on the cold stone floor of the cell. When she lifted her head, I saw the thick rope of the noose dangling from her neck, trailing down her back like a broken spine.

"You sentenced us to death, Miss Elizabeth," Justine said, her voice cold and hard now.

"I did not –" I began, but fell silent as two figures appeared behind Justine: little William and Alice Roussel. Alice had her arms around William's shoulders to comfort the smaller child, but they were both weeping. William raised his sleeve and dragged it over his face, sniffling, then he pulled free of Alice's embrace and ran toward me, and I opened my arms to embrace him. He smelled of dead things, though, and when he pulled back his white face, tilted so he could look up at me, his eyes were desolate. Black bruises nearly covered his neck, and his eyes were clouded with blue film. "Why didn't you save me, Lizzie?" he sobbed, stepping back. "Why didn't you stop them?"

"Stop who?"

I reached for him again, but he stumbled away from me, hiding behind Alice once more. She didn't speak, but smiled at me with the same open, trusting expression from the moment we met in the forest. Only this time, there was blood in her teeth.

"Don't worry," I assured her, wringing my hands. "I am ending this. I will die, and I can harm no one else."

All three of them, Justine and William and Alice, stopped crying, staring at me with empty eyes. Then Justine said, "If you die, Miss Elizabeth… who will stop him from remaking the world?"

The idea struck me with a flurry of horrifying images, but I shook my head to clear them away. "He can't," I told Justine. "I destroyed the papers with all the instructions, and there's no other copy. He can't ever do it again."

Even as I said it, uncertainty made the words taste sour. I could sense that I was overlooking something, a terrible notion that hid just out of my sight.

In the distance, I heard someone calling my name, but I was distracted as William, Justine, and Alice suddenly backed away from me, spreading out to form a circle with me in the center. "He can make another," Justine whispered. "There's a way."

"She won't be like you," came William's small voice. I whirled to face him. The skin of his face was beginning to decay. "She'll be a blank slate, ready to sponge up his lessons."

I turned toward Alice, expecting her to speak next, but when she opened her mouth, bright red blood spurted from her mouth and ran down her chin.

I turned away, shaking my head. Even if the creature could do these things, I wasn't the person to stop him. I was a silly girl, reborn by aberration. "Mary," I told Justine, my voice desperate. "Mary will go to the authorities, or her wealthy friends. They will stop him."

Justine and William gave me a look of terrible, pitying disappointment, but it was Alice who finally spoke, though a stream of blood gurgled out with her words. "And who shall atone?"

From outside the cell, I heard my name again, but again I paid no mind. I wanted nothing more than to stay here with the three children I had failed.

"Atone?" I repeated, confused. What atonement could she require, aside from the deletion of my malignant existence? "How else can I atone?"

Twenty-Three

Caroline

"Elizabeth!"

A bucket of icy water was dumped on my head.

I woke up drenched and sputtering. "What in heaven's name were you thinking?" Mary Godwin's voice shouted.

I blinked, disoriented beyond words. How could I still be alive? Why hadn't the laudanum killed me?

The damned body, I thought, and laughed wildly at my own phrasing.

This only seemed to upset Mary more. "Elizabeth!" Mary cried. She stood over me looking frightened and enraged – and very pale. "Answer me!"

"I told you not to come in," I mumbled, sitting up and looking myself over. My body desired food, and my dress was soaked, but I felt no pain or sickness. I wasn't immune to the drug, but its effect on me had simply... worn off. I'd been denied even the escape of suicide.

It was almost funny.

Squinting past Mary, I saw the shattered window next to the front door. Beyond it, the air was filled with fog, but discernible light had risen beyond that. It was only a little after dawn. "You're early," I said numbly.

"And you are a coward," she spat. Mary had crossed her arms over her chest, but her lower lip was trembling, and her eyes bright red. "You have no idea how long I tried to wake you, and I could not hear your heartbeat..." Her voice shook, and she snapped her mouth closed, shaking her head and turning away from me.

"Sit down, Mary," I said gently.

To my surprise, she plopped down onto the sofa next to me, arms wrapped around her middle. "Why did you come so early?" I asked. If she hadn't woken me, would I have died? Probably not. But I could have at least made a better try of it.

"The servants," Mary said distractedly. "Byron's servants, that is; I only have William's nursemaid. The servants were upset, and they woke William, who woke me.' She rubbed her eyes with the heels of her hand. "I could not fall back to sleep, so I thought to get started on the book with you. You mustn't do that to me," she added, more subdued. "I had such a fright."

"Why?" I asked, genuinely curious. What was I to Mary? "Because it would affect your book?"

In her lap, Mary's hands clenched into fists. I watched for a long moment as she took a few deep breaths, slowly uncurling her fingers. Her face softened, and she said stiffly, "It seems I owe you an apology, Eliz—" She swallowed the word and started again, her words stiff. "I owe you an apology. I addressed you as a research subject. I lost sight of your humanity."

I made a choking sound, part laugh and part cry. Humanity. Could one have that, when one was no longer human?

"Here." She reached into a dress pocket and pulled out five small notebooks, bound together with string. They were the size and style Victor had always favored.

I made no move to touch them, so Mary deposited them on my lap, avoiding the wet stain. "Read them, burn them, whatever you wish. A book is not worth your life," she said gravely.

Surprised, I picked up the journals, turning them over in my hands. They represented everything Victor had been thinking about during the year leading up to my death. All the lies, the secrets he'd kept from me. The horrors of the thing who had taken my first life.

I was tempted to build a fire in the fireplace right then and there, but instead I set the packet carefully on a side table, as though it might bite me at any moment.

Mary yawned, collapsing backward into the thick sofa. "I could fall asleep right here. I should go back to the villa and check on W—on the baby," she corrected, and I was touched that she'd avoided her son's name out of respect. "And think of a new novel idea, of course."

As frustrated as I was with Mary, now I found that I didn't want her to go. I was afraid to be left alone with the images from my drugged dream. I was even more afraid that with Mary gone, I might try my hand at death again. I grasped about for something to say, a question to ask. "What happened to upset the servants?" I said finally.

"Oh." Mary sat up again, her eyes bright. "Goodness, I nearly forgot! There was a murder in Geneva last night," she confided. "Word is spreading all over the city."

My breath caught in surprise. I had never heard of anyone being murdered in Geneva. "Who was killed?"

"A barrister of some kind," Mary said, not quite shrugging. "He is not one of the men Byron works with, that's all I know."

Even back then, Geneva was a good-sized city; with something like thirty thousand inhabitants, there were naturally many lawyers. And yet I was suddenly gripped with a terrible unease.

Mr. Albin, the solicitor, was a well-known friend of my uncle – I believe he was even the godfather of either William or Victor – and it would take very little work to discover the connection. Albin's name had likely been on some of the papers back at Gray Hollow.

Mary said something else, but I didn't hear the words. *He can make another*, Justine had said. *There is a way.*

But that was just a strange dream, the result of all that laudanum. If my attacker wanted to make a new mate, he would need the instructions, which I had destroyed. And that had to be the only copy, I reasoned, because if there was another set he wouldn't have needed to come to Geneva and search the manor.

I had that irritating sensation again, of missing something. Albin was connected somehow.

I stood up, looking at Mary. "You have a carriage?"

"Yes, though it's not Byron's absurd monstrosity; I have borrowed his post-chaise. Why?"

"We need to go into town," I told her. "I must know the identity of the victim."

Mary eyed me with some curiosity, but she didn't argue. "Perhaps you would like to change out of your wet dress."

I put on a different dress, as well as my veiled hat and tinted glasses. Then Byron's driver, a short, stout man with an enormous mustache, followed Mary's directions into town without a single remark, or even a change in facial expression. I could see how a philandering celebrity despot would find such a man useful.

It was only a little after eight in the morning when we arrived in the esteemed center of the city, but as the carriage turned the corner and Mr. Albin's office came into sight, my breath caught.

There was a crowd of people gathered near Albin's door, and a single policeman in uniform appeared to be calling to them, his hands raised as if to ward off blows.

"Is that –" Mary began, and I nodded.

"I need to be certain." Ignoring Mary's cry of alarm, I opened the carriage door without waiting for it to stop and hurried around the back and over to the throng of people.

Several of them stopped talking and made way, probably noticing the quality of my clothes and the veil over my face. They begin to whisper, and I realized that I must look like the widow or daughter of the deceased. I skirted the onlookers and marched straight up to the policeman, whose eyes widened as he took in my appearance.

"I beg your pardon, my lady –" he began, but I decided to channel my aunt at her most commanding.

"That's quite enough," I said coolly. "I need to know if the deceased man is my husband." Behind me, the crowd murmured in sympathy.

The policeman, who was probably all of twenty, looked from the crowd to my veil, obviously confused. "The doctor is in there with him now, ma'am, but surely they will have informed –"

"What, the public? The newspapers?" piped a voice at my elbow. I glanced sideways and saw Mary, with her worn dress and bright excitement in her eyes. She looked at me, and I inclined my head ever so slightly toward the doorway. Mary blinked, and I almost missed the tiny nod that was her reply.

"Surely you intend to warn the public of an immediate danger," Mary said to the policeman, her accented voice verging on the edge of cheerful.

If anything, the officer looked more confused, and I almost felt sorry for him. He looked back at me, the lady with the well-bred native accent. "Is this your maid, madam?" he asked me.

Mary's eyes almost popped out of her head with feigned outrage. "How dare you," she cried, angling her body to play to the crowd and gesturing wildly. The policeman had no choice but to turn sideways too. "My name is Mary Wollstonecraft Godwin, and I am in this city as a guest of the esteemed Lord Byron," she announced. "We came here in his carriage," she added to the woman next to her, who had to be at least sixty.

"Is it as big as they say?" the old woman asked, wide-eyed.

"Much bigger," Mary said with a wink, and the crowd roared with laughter. Someone in the back yelled something bawdy, and the policeman scolded him, earning another round of jeers and laughter.

I slipped through the door, into Albin's office.

The outer room was much the same as on my previous visit, though a lamp had been toppled, and there were papers on the floor. Ignoring this, I hurried across the room toward the inner office, where I'd listened to Albin describe the demise of my family. The door was open only a crack, and I silently stepped up and peered inside.

There were three men clustered in the far corner, speaking in low tones. I assumed one was the doctor and the others were police. I couldn't see much of the room itself, though Albin's heavy oak desk had clearly been tipped sideways, its papers and pens spread across the fine rugs, the lamp shattered into tiny fragments. I didn't understand – the floor seemed to be clear. Was I too late? Had the body already been removed?

Then one of the men gestured upward, still speaking, and the others following his gaze toward something on the wall. I eased the door open a little bit farther to improve the angle – and then I saw the body.

The earthly remains of Mr. Albin were draped over the enormous deer antlers above the visitors' chair. He was face-up, but his neck dangled loosely from his torn collar, twisted at a nauseating angle. His clothes were stained red where the antlers had impaled him, and blood dripped soundlessly into puddles on the carpet.

I might have made a sound, or perhaps it was just the motion of the door, but one of the policemen saw me coming and hurried toward me. Mumbling my apologies, I backed away and kept going, pausing only long enough to grab Mary's arm. The young policeman saw me come back through the door and began shouting, but I was running now, pulling Mary after me.

"Was it him?" Mary said breathlessly as we trotted down the street toward the waiting carriage.

"Yes. Victor's barbarian murdered him."

"How do you know?" There had been a few shouts as we left the crowd behind, but no one appeared to be following now. She slowed to a walk.

I told Mary how Albin's neck had been snapped just before he'd been tossed onto a full set of antlers. I tried to be matter-of-fact, but Mary still paled.

"Couldn't someone else have done it?" she asked in a small voice. "Another client, or an angry colleague…"

"Mary, no man could throw his body that high." My voice came out strangely calm and mechanical.

He was nearby.

"You said you visited this Mr. Albin," Mary said, her brow furrowed in thought. "Do you think your attacker was there to ask Albin how to find you?"

"No." My own movements had been distressingly predictable: I'd come home, then gone to see my uncle's solicitor, then holed up at Gray Hollow for months and months. If my attacker wanted to find me, I had not made it difficult. "I am spoiled goods; with too much of my own mind to suit his purposes." The idea almost seemed laughable now, considering my upbringing, but it was true.

"Then why attack the solicitor?"

"Because there is another way to get the instructions for the procedure." Justine had tried to warn me. They all had.

Mary, who was more worldly and clever than Elizabeth could have dreamed, worked it out quickly. "From Victor himself. The creature got his location from the solicitor."

I nodded. My body was not tired, but I suddenly longed to curl up underneath the bridge near Les Clefs and let the leaves cover me until I disappeared.

"He will go to Chillon tonight to question Victor."

Twenty-Four

Heck

I yawned. I couldn't help it.

Caroline paused, raising an eyebrow above her sunglasses. "Are you all right, Heck?"

"Yeah, sorry," I flapped a hand, trying to smother a second yawn. "It's not you, it's the hydrocodone."

"I should let you rest." She started to stand up from her perch on the edge of the bed. "My shift starts soon, anyway."

"But I want to hear about the big showdown!" I complained. "You versus the monster, cage match on top of the Swiss Alps!" I dissolved into giggles at the mental image.

"I'm afraid it didn't work out quite like that," she informed me. "I don't think I would have won a cage match, not after seeing Mr. Albin. Victor's creation was larger and stronger than me in every way."

"Here's what I don't get. You said the creature was in Geneva before you, but then you haunted Gray Hollow for months and months before he attacked the lawyer. So what was he doing all that time you were haunting Gray Hollow?"

"Making his attempts," she said flatly.

I didn't understand, but then, it felt like my thoughts were running at half speed. "Attempts to find you?"

"No, Heck." Her voice was almost gentle. "His attempts to reproduce Victor's process from memory."

Oh.

Caroline went to the balcony curtain, pulling it back. The thick fog had rolled around the ship again, and I stared outside for several seconds before I realized that we were moving.

"When did we leave Ketchikan?" I asked in surprise.

Caroline didn't turn around. "About an hour ago." Her head was pointed at the top of the desk next to the balcony door. I was too low in the bed to see what had caught her attention. "Is this your beau?" she asked, holding up a magazine that had been folded open. It was the Arctic Journal article about Colin, and yes, there was a big photo of him from his university ID.

"Yes, that's him. But no one says 'beau.'"

"Noted." Caroline turned the magazine back toward herself, skimming the article. "He's in trouble with the university?"

"Of course not." I was annoyed. "There's a competing research team challenging some information from Colin's last paper. It's not a big deal."

"Hmm." But she turned and came back to the end of the bed, poised to leave. "Would you like me to turn on the TV? The ship has some movie channels. Or maybe you'd like to sleep."

"Not yet." I wasn't ready to sleep. Or to be alone again. "Hey," I said dreamily, "what's your favorite movie adaptation? The Boris Karloff version? Robert DeNiro's? I think Daniel Radcliffe did one, too."

There was a silence. I opened one eye to see if I'd offended her. It seemed like she was genuinely considering the question.

"*Jurassic Park*," she said finally.

I burst into giggles. Even Caroline smiled. "I like the dinosaurs," she confessed.

"Well, of course. You're made of dead body, not *stone*."

Her eyes went wide, and I was sure I'd overstepped. Then she actually started to laugh. "I can't believe you said that."

"What, your regular friends don't tease you about being undead?"

The smile disappeared as quickly as it had come. "I don't spend much time with friends."

She'd echoed my words, so I repeated hers. "By choice?"

I regretted the question when Caroline's face went still again, the answer hidden away. I waved her on. "Okay, so the creature went to this castle to kill Victor – go on with the story."

Caroline frowned. "That's not quite right, you know," she said. "Killing Victor wasn't the objective. The creature thought that just by being alive and male, he was entitled to a mate who would serve him. Victor was just an obstacle to getting what he was owed." She gave me a sidelong glance. "Two hundred years later, you'd be surprised how many men still believe that particular premise."

I snorted. "Subtle. But Colin's not some basic entitled douchebag. And it's my choice to go see him."

"Fair enough," she allowed. "But have you considered what will happen if things *do* work out with Colin? Where will you live? What will you do for money?"

Now she sounded *exactly* like my mother. "I'm hoping to get work at the university, with Colin," I told Caroline. "We worked together before; that's how we met. I was a big help with his work."

"I see." Her voice had a certain *gotcha* tone I didn't like. "Your memory. Of course he uses you for his research… which has come under attack." Her eyes narrowed. "The article. That's why you're going now, isn't it? You figure you've finally got something he wants."

"He doesn't *use* me," I practically snarled. "I *help* him, and he values me."

"Heck." She leaned forward to make sure I was listening. "You're lying to yourself," she said frankly. "And I've seen what kind of the damage that can do."

I wanted to pull out my hair. "You're just projecting your own mistakes. You don't actually *know* me."

"I know more than you think. Probably more than you'd like." Her voice went whisper-soft, and the look she gave me was pitying in every possible way. "I know that your daughter's dead."

Twenty-Five

Heck

Her words were so soft, but the force of them drove right through my chest, flattening me back against the bed. *I know your daughter's dead.*

"I'm so sorry, Heck," Caroline said. She took her sunglasses off, looking at me with her lovely toxic eyes. Instead of answering, I pulled the sheets, and then the covers, over my layers of clothing. Maybe if I just buried my stupid traitorous skin bag deep enough –

Caroline's infinitely controlled body shifted a little, and for a second I was terrified she would try to retrieve tissues for me again, or worse: hug me. I lowered the blanket to make sure she wasn't coming near me, but no, she put her sunglasses back on and turned toward the window, staring into the fog. It was a relief not to have her eyes on me. "Was it a miscarriage?"

"Not the way you mean." I wiped my cheeks with my sleeve. "My hips separated at twenty-two weeks, instead of during labor. I was using elbow crutches to get around, and my crutch slipped on the ice in a parking lot. I hit my head on the curb. I woke up in labor in the ER."

Caroline swore in French.

I'm sure most women feel ripped in two when they give birth. In my case, though, something more permanent happened. There was a terrifying, uncontrolled sensation of *give* as the ligaments and tendons tore.

163

When I was a little girl there had been a boy on the playground, Ethan, who fell and broke his arm. The bone – ulna? – poked right up out of the skin, and we'd all seen the bloody white chunk of bone, Ethan screaming. I was only six or seven, but I knew that bones weren't supposed to be seen. This was *wrong*, a wrong thing. I didn't have the words for it at the time, but that was the moment I understood there was a natural order, a way things are supposed to be. And, most terrifying of all, the way could be violated.

Giving birth had felt like that. Not like a natural, blessed miracle, the way they said in the parenting class. It had felt like an atrocity. A merciless shredding of my form.

Caroline got up and retrieved a handful of tissues from the bathroom, handing them to me. "Where was Colin during all this?"

I groaned in frustration. "Caroline, I know you claim you were around during the Spiritualist movement, but I would really appreciate if you'd stop channeling my mother."

"I'm sorry. You're right." She sat back down on the edge of the bed. "I'm sure this was very hard for Colin too," she said primly.

"Honestly, it was," I said. "He was so happy when I told him about the pregnancy."

She looked at me with obvious surprise, which made me roll my eyes. "I know. Everyone assumes he didn't want the baby. But Colin *loves* kids, and he thrives on a little chaos." I pictured the day I'd first met him, crowded under the giant globe surrounded by children.

Yes, your dad could get caught up in his work and forgot to have dinner. And we worried about the expense of a baby. But, Maddie, *never* doubt how much we wanted you.

"To answer your question, that weekend he was in Milwaukee for his friend's bachelor party. Everything should have been fine... except I went to the store."

Colin's roommate had moved out of the apartment a few weeks earlier so I could finally move in. As a result, the apartment was missing some things – Colin didn't own a colander, for example, or a bathmat. I'd had the idea that I would get a few things for the place while he was gone.

I just hadn't seen the ice.

Then the ER, the failed C-section. The hemorrhage.

That was on a Friday. For two blurry days, I laid in the hospital bed and fought not to die. Whenever I surfaced, the hospital staff refused to tell me anything about Maddie. They must have been some kind of meeting. It was probably in all their Outlook calendars as "Convince Patient Her Baby's Alive So She Wants to Live."

It worked, too: I thought I was fighting to stay alive for her.

I barely remember my mother arriving. I wasn't conscious during the screaming fight she and Colin had when he arrived at the hospital Sunday night, still drunk. But I remember the ICU doctor who came to tell me my baby was dead. She was only a few years older than me. I still know the pattern of her freckles just as well as I remember every goddamned word out of her mouth.

"An ICU doctor got interested in my case and looked through *all* my health records," I told Caroline now. "She contacted a local pain management specialist who happened to be experienced with EDS."

"What did they say?" Caroline asked me.

I looked at her closely to see if she understood what she was asking me. Caroline just nodded at me.

"He said, 'The pregnancy hormones caused too much laxity in your joints. For a while the baby was able to develop safely, but your body was falling apart around her. I've seen your chart, the history of dislocations, the hypermobility. I wish we'd caught it earlier," I recited. I reached up to brush tears away. "He explained Ehlers-Danlos syndrome to me. And he said, 'Some women with this diagnosis can still handle pregnancy. I'm afraid you're not one of them.'"

"Oh, Heqet," Caroline said. She reached over to rest her hand on my uninjured knee, which was under the covers. "I'm so sorry."

She patted my knee once and withdrew her hand. "But you said Colin broke up with you because he wants more kids, and you can't have them. So why are you going to Juneau?"

"I didn't say I couldn't have more," I snapped. "I said my doctor advised against it. One doctor, at one hospital, in one city."

(Five doctors, in three hospitals, in two different cities…)

"Heck…"

"Just leave," I whispered.

"That's a good idea." She stood, shaking her head again, and stalked toward the door. "Two hundred years, and nothing has changed." It closed silently behind her.

Twenty-Six

Wednesday, day 5 at sea
Pain scale: 7

Dear Maddie,

This morning I thought a lot about what Caroline said about lying to myself. I'm sure she's wrong, and I know exactly who Colin is: an imperfect man in an impossible situation. But I'm not writing these letters –okay, fine, this journal – to reinforce some kind of imaginary tale. So I printed out the following emails in the ship's office center and I'm tucking them into this journal. The first email is from the day Colin broke up with me, and the second is from three weeks ago.

March 25th

Dear Heqet,

I'm so glad to hear you're feeling better. I'm sorry I haven't been responding to your texts or calls, but as you know, the middle of the semester is always hectic, and I wanted to push through these last few weeks. But now I'm writing in hopes that it will give you closure.

I'm writing this email to say goodbye. I'm sorry, Heck, but I know my future includes kids. It has to. I'm sorry that our lives are diverging, but I know you wouldn't ask me to give up on being a father. We were good together in a lot of ways, but ultimately, I'm not sure it would have worked out. I want to be with someone who can keep up with me.

I figure you're going back to live with Leah, so I left a box of your things on her porch. I'll be leaving town myself soon. I truly hope your recovery goes smoothly and you find a great new future for yourself.

Fondest regards, Colin

June 27

Dear Hegel,

I hope you're doing well. I'm writing from my office at the University of Alaska-Juneau, where I'm running their new Arctic Sciences program. I think I got this job partly because of the two papers that you assisted me with, so you should be proud of the work you put in with me.

I know I don't have to tell you how important this work is. The placement of the magnetic pole affects everything from smartphones and satellites to navigation for airplanes and boats. Understanding its movement is crucial to understanding what's going on in the Arctic.

Speaking of which, I'm writing to ask you for a favor. Some researchers in Vancouver are questioning the measurements I took of the rock formations in Greenland. I've spoken to both the university and the journal that published the paper (Arctic Sciences), and I told them about you and your memory. They've agreed that if you can write a report of the data and sign an affidavit that the measurements are correct, they'll support the paper. Can you please provide this? I'd really appreciate it.

Warm regards, Dr. A. Colin Carson

Twenty-Seven

Thursday, day 6 at sea
Pain Scale: 5

Dear Madison,

We're finally here! I woke up from a tangled dream about something dark and ropey like black spiderwebs, and found that the ship had docked in Juneau overnight.

I feel ready. I spent yesterday typing up Colin's notes, resting my knee, and updating this journal. The research is done, and I'll be able to deliver it to Colin in person. Don't worry, I'm not going to walk in and just *throw myself* at your dad. I'm going to be professional, calm, and competent. I'll convince him – no, scratch that, I'll *show* him – that I'm doing much better, and I've really got a handle on my diagnosis now. I'm ready to start a new chapter.

Colin's office hours start at 10. As I write this, it's 9:15, and I've showered, put on makeup, and even done my hair, although my shoulder aches from holding up the hair dryer. For the first time since the hospital, I'm wearing actual jeans over my compression underwear. I had to buy a new pair with a low-rise waist so it doesn't interfere with the majority of my stitches, but I almost look like the old me.

Oh, Maddie, I almost forgot – the sun is out! This morning when I pulled back the curtain for the sliding glass door, I nearly fell over in surprise. I think it's the first time all week there's been anything but gray fog and rain. It's like a sign.

Anyway, I'm heading out now to find your dad. I've got my wallet and pills, a knee brace, the collapsible cane, and this journal, plus a couple of pairs of clean underwear and socks. If it goes *really* well with Colin I'm still hoping to return to the ship for the rest of my stuff, but I have what I'll absolutely need for the next few days just in case.

Off I go to find your dad, Maddie! Wherever you are now, I hope you'll wish me luck.

Love, Mommy

Twenty-Eight

Middle of the night, Thursday-Friday
Pain scale: 6

Here's what happened.

It was easy enough to get a cab at the dock in Juneau, although the driver, an old man with a stereotypical hermit beard, was certainly surprised when I told him my destination. "Not sure why you'd want to see the university," he said doubtfully, one finger poking into the beard to scratch. "Most people wanna see the glacier or the sled dog camps. Or there's a lumberjack show, whale-watching trips, sea kayaking, panning for gold, even a helicopter excursion…"

It had an air of memorization to it – the guy had clearly been getting kickbacks from the cruise lines. "Just take me to the university, please," I said firmly. "I'm visiting a friend."

He lifted his hands from the wheel in a quick gesture of surrender. "Have it your way."

Like Ketchikan, Juneau's downtown area is extremely close to the port, and as we drove by I had to admit that the city looked charming. In the bright sunshine I could easily make out rows of frontier-style buildings, all painted bright Easter-egg colors that were set off nicely by the mountain ranges just behind them. Everything looked clean and pretty, like it had just been hosed off for a photo session. I've lived in Seattle long enough to understand that there's the city you show visitors and the city you don't, but I still think I could see myself living here.

I turned my eyes downward, to my phone. There were a dozen more texts and voicemails from my mother. I skimmed the messages just long enough to satisfy myself that she wasn't going to call any authorities on me.

I started to put the phone down – then had a bolt of anxiety: what if Colin wasn't in today? The school website said he had office hours on Tuesday and Thursday mornings, but it was possible he was home with a cold, or had a special schedule because of exams or something. It would be horrifying to come all the way to Juneau just to miss him.

I looked up his office extension again and dialed, ready to hang up the second he answered.

The phone rang four times, and a girl's wavering voice picked up. "H–Hello?"

I blanched, but only for a moment. Colin had never had an office assistant before. "I'm looking for Colin Carson," I said, trying to sound businesslike. "I'm calling from the University of Wisconsin's Department of Human Resources."

"Oh! Oh my gosh!" The girl sniffed, her voice coming out as a partial sob. "I'm so sorry, you must not have heard."

Something swam loose in my stomach. "Heard what?"

"Colin – Dr. Carson – was in an accident; he's at the hospital. I'm just grabbing a few of his things to drop off for him."

I forgot all about being subtle. "Is he all right? What hospital?"

"They haven't told us much. There's only one here, Bartlett Hospital. He's in the CCU; they won't let students in to see him," the girl added, her voice rising in pitch, as if reporting a grave injustice.

I hung up the phone, yanking my earbuds out so hard that it stung. Then a thought lifted me: When I was pregnant, Colin and I had made each other our emergency contacts in our cell phone health apps. Had Colin remembered to change it? He could be absentminded about that kind of thing; I might be able to get in.

"Change of plans," I said to the cab driver, and then realized I had shouted the words. Meekly, I added, "Please take me to Bartlett Hospital."

When we arrived at the hospital, I practically threw cash at the cab driver and rushed into the Emergency Department. In the back of my mind a little voice reminded me how much my joints would pay for my haste tomorrow, but for now I ignored it.

Inside, I babbled something at the grandmotherly nurse behind the desk, including my name, and she picked up Colin's chart, flipped pages, and ticked off a note. "You're the emergency contact," she said, nodding with satisfaction.

"Yes, thank you!" I said with a rush of relief.

"I can take you to his room."

Wendy, as her nametag said, came around the counter and scanned us through the security doors. I was so focused on keeping up with her that we were through the doors and halfway down the hall before I really registered the familiar smells and sights.

The hospital walls began to tilt and lengthen in my mind. My steps slowed, and I had to rest a hand on one wall just to steady myself from the onslaught of mechanical beeping, disinfectant stink, murmured, worried voices and canned recycled air. The hallway walls had framed prints by Alaskan natives, and the nurse's scrubs featured totem poles, but otherwise I might as well have been right back in Madison.

Up ahead, Wendy turned back to me with an inquiring look. "I… don't like hospitals," I admitted, hunching my shoulders.

She frowned. "Well, I'm sure he'll appreciate your coming," she said pointedly.

Get it together, I told myself. *You're here for Colin, not for you.* I fell into step beside her. "Can you tell me what happened? I didn't get any details on the phone," I added, feeling very clever about my wording.

Wendy had stopped outside one of the patient doors, but now she paused and glanced around. She stepped closer, too far into my personal space, and my stomach lurched.

"They told you he was attacked?" she said quietly.

I shook my head. "I just know that he's hurt."

Wendy straightened up. "He will likely recover, but you should still prepare yourself," she said, her voice not-quite detached. "Both legs are broken: one at the shin, one at the ankle. Two broken ribs. Broken left collarbone. His right hand is shattered; he'll need surgeries for that alone, but not until the swelling goes down."

I put my hand on the railing alongside the wall, feeling dizzy. "Was he hit by a car?"

"His injuries don't support that."

"I thought it was an accident?"

Wendy gave a little snort. "Honey, this was the farthest thing from an accident. Someone beat him like it was their job."

"Is he awake?"

She patted my shoulder, and for once I was too distracted to mind. "He's in and out, with the pain meds. But he's stable." She held up her hands, palms up. "That's about all I can tell you, honey. Let's go in so you can see him. I need to get back to reception."

I nodded, distracted, and Wendy pushed the door open in front of me. Taking a deep breath, I made my feet carry me inside the room.

My first impression was how strange it looked for Colin, *my* Colin, to be lying in a hospital bed with his limbs sticking out in various directions. A blanket covered the lower half of his body, but underneath it, his legs were bulky from casts or braces, with bolster pillows propped underneath to elevate them. His left arm was braced and in traction, but his right hand was trapped in a clear plexiglass box. Inside, the puffy mess of his hand was locked in place with dozens pins. I couldn't look at the box for more than a second before my eyes slid away.

I stepped closer. Colin's torso and chest were wrapped up under his open hospital gown, and above that... well, for a moment I thought he was wearing a purple tie-dyed undershirt, but then my brain supplied the right answer: bruising. He'd been strangled.

I forced my eyes to his face. It was remarkably untouched, except for a single small cut dividing one eyebrow. That was held closed with a couple of stitches and a small piece of white tape. His face was pale and diminished, and they had shaved away part of his beard when they taped his collarbone.

He looked like a stranger. I wanted to run, and was simultaneously shamed by the thought.

"Apollo?" The nurse was gently pushing me forward, like she was positioning a mannequin. "You have a visitor. Hee-quat is here."

"Heck," I said automatically. "And he goes by Colin."

Colin's eyes fluttered once, managed to open. "Heck?" he said hoarsely. "Am I imagining you?"

I shook my head and came closer. "I'm really here."

To my utter astonishment, Colin's eyes filled with tears. "Thank God," he said in a half-sob. He sounded just a little drunk, and I figured that was the painkillers. "I called my parents, but they can't get a flight until Saturday. I thought I was all alone."

Wendy patted my arm, looking absurdly satisfied. To her we must have seemed like two young lovers reunited after tragedy, like a movie. "I'll leave you two to talk," she said crisply. "There's a folding chair for you there, under the TV."

"But..." Now that I'd seen the extent of Colin's injuries I didn't want her to go. But she was already speed-walking through the door.

175

I looked back at the bed, and Colin turned his arm with the forearm cast sideways, palm up, weakly flapping his fingers.

Taking a breath, I set up the chair next to the bed, and carefully took his hand, the one dangling in the air in traction. I worried that it would hurt him, but he squeezed my fingers gratefully.

"How are you here?" he asked in a whisper.

"I'm still listed as your emergency contact," I said dumbly, as if that might explain everything.

Colin wasn't that high, though. He furrowed his brow, winced at the pain. "Is it still Thursday?"

"Yes."

"How did you get here so fast?"

Right. I'd practiced this response, but it was hard to remember my lines now that the stage had changed. "Oh. I'm actually in Juneau on a cruise. And I have this –" I pulled off my backpack and rummaged around inside, producing a file folder. "Since I was here, I brought the notes you asked for. I called your office to see if you were on campus today, and they told me you were here." I set the folder on his tray table.

"Oh, honey," he said in a morphine-slur, squeezing my hand. "Thank you. I can't believe the serend... saran..." His face clouded over. "What's the word?"

"Serendipity."

"Yes, yes!" He sighed happily.

"Col," I said, "what happened?"

"I was attacked," he mumbled. "Out for a run this morning. Been getting back into shape...." He fell silent, letting go of my hand so he could point to a cup of water with a long bendy straw. I picked up the water and held the straw to his lips, then wiped up the drops that spilled down his chin.

"It was just this morning?" I said, confused. Hadn't the girl on the phone said he'd been hurt last night?

Colin sort of blinked his nod. "Yeah. Six or so. Juneau s'posed to be safe. I's running along shore, by th' woods. Thought I heard someone yell for help... in the forest..."

"Oh my god." I smoothed the hair back from his face. "You were robbed?"

"Two guys. Big. They just kept hitting me..." His voice broke at the end, and he squeezed my hand tighter for a moment, his eyes closing.

Guys. A ridiculous suspicion had sprouted in my thoughts, but that one word made me relax. She wouldn't. Of course she wouldn't.

Colin seemed to have drifted off for a moment, but then he opened his eyes with a start, his fingers squeezing my hand too hard. "Heqet," he said suddenly. "You'll stay, right? You'll stay with me? I don't want to be alone when I wake up."

"Of course I'll stay."

He gave me a smile filled with gratitude and love... or maybe just morphine. Seconds later he was asleep.

I just sat there for a long time, listening to the quite beeps and hisses of the machines. It was all so surreal. I'd made this long journey, and spent so much time preparing for a big emotional blow-out conversation about the baby and our feelings and our future. I had been, I realized now, like a lawyer getting arguments lined up for trial. But all I'd done was walk in the door, and Colin seemed ready to pick up right where we'd left off back in April, when it was me in the hospital bed.

I'd gotten exactly what I wanted.

Right?

My thoughts were interrupted by the arrival of another nurse, an Indigenous woman in her forties with a long black braid and a nametag that read Coral. She gave me a conspiratorial smile when she saw that Colin was asleep. "Oh good, rest is just what he needs," she said.

Picking up the clipboard at the end of the bed, she looked at the monitors near Colin's head and made some notes.

"How is he?" I whispered. I wasn't used to being the support person. What should I be asking?

"He's stable." She glanced up. "It'll be a long road to recovery, though."

"Have the police talked to him yet?"

"They've been here, but he sent them away," Coral said matter-of-factly. "Said it's a job for the campus police – but then he didn't want us to call them either."

"What?" I looked at the casts, Colin's immobilized hand. "He said he was mugged. Why wouldn't he want…?"

Coral shrugged. "Talking to police can be overwhelming when someone's in a lot of pain. They can't necessarily think clearly with the pain meds anyway." She put the clipboard back and smiled pleasantly at me. "Don't worry; the police will come back when he's feeling a little better."

A fresh insecurity twisted in my heart. "When will that be? I mean, he's on a lot of drugs… when will he be thinking clearly?"

Coral checked her watch. "I expect him to sleep for the next, oh, three or four hours. He may wake up shortly before then from pain, but he's got a button right there to press." She pointed at a red button on the blankets below Colin's traction arm. "He keeps dropping it, so just hand it up to him."

She turned and started to leave the room. "I'll be back to check in a bit," she called over her shoulder.

And then I waited.

For the first few minutes, I just gazed at Colin's face with a kind of awed gratitude. I hadn't been sure I'd ever be allowed to look at him like this again, to feel his hand in mine.

After thirty-five minutes, though, my own aches began to make themselves known: first in my shoulder, from keeping my arm still so I could hold Colin's hand, and then my knees and ankle joints, from being fused in the same position. I checked my watch, and realized I needed to take some more Advil… but I hadn't eaten all day.

Coral came in again to check Colin's vitals, and I stood up to stretch and get out of her way. My joints were stiff, and there was a moment of awkwardness while I tried to move past her as she tried to take my place. My stomach chose that moment to rumble loudly.

"He'll be out for another couple of hours yet, if you want to run down to the cafeteria," she said.

I wavered. "I'd hate for him to wake up and be alone."

She glanced at the clock on the wall. "You'll be fine. I'll fit him with the call button in case he wakes up in the meantime." She threaded the button through the contraption holding up his arm, so he could easily press it. "Give me your cell phone number, and we'll text you if he wakes up." I thanked her and agreed.

The hospital cafeteria was just like the one at the university hospital in Madison, and like every other hospital I'd been to in my life. For some reason, though, it didn't bother me the way the rest of the building had. Maybe because I never spent much time in the cafeteria when I was a patient.

It was almost noon, so I got myself some coffee and a turkey sandwich, scanning the large room for an empty table. The place was beginning to fill up with medical staff and haggard-looking folks in wrinkled clothes – the family members of the sick and dying.

I didn't want any kind of small talk. I walked stiffly to the farthest corner of the room, where a couple of those awkward cafe-style tables were set up with stools. Then I began to mechanically push food into my mouth, not even tasting it.

I couldn't understand why I didn't feel happier. Of course it was terrible seeing Colin so injured, but his whole face had lit up when he saw me. In a bizarre way, it was like a gift – not only was he willing to accept me back; he needed me. He was grateful I was here.

For now, said the new little voice in the back of my mind. *What happens when he gets better?*

I was so busy staring into space, pondering my trepidation, that I didn't hear her walk up. Or perhaps she was just that quiet.

"Hello, Heck."

I jumped, knocking over the bottle of water on the table in front of me. Quick as a snake, Caroline's arm snapped out and righted it. "Thanks," I muttered, getting a good look at her.

I'd only seen her in her uniform or in careless, baggy clothes that seemed meant to make her look as unattractive as possible. But today she wore expensive athletic leggings and a hoodie made out of that fancy fabric that's supposed to make you run faster and sweat less. Her blonde hair was tied in a tight French braid, and she held a paper cup with a tea bag string dangling down the side. With her massive sunglasses, she looked like a model in the world's nicest ski catalogue.

I managed to swallow the lump of sandwich stuck in my throat, trying to hide how much she'd startled me. I felt my hands clenching under the table and told myself she wasn't going to hurt me in front of all these people. "Are you following me?"

Caroline sat down in the chair across from me. "Yes," she replied, "Well, your cab."

"Why?"

"I wanted to talk to you," she said simply.

During my junior year of high school, my best friend Cherie and I had had a brutal fight and didn't speak for a week–not because we were still upset, but because we were too young and awkward to know how to walk it back. "Um, I'm the same," I said cautiously. "Colin's the one who's hurt."

"Is he going to be okay?" Was it me, or did she seem really intent on the question?

"They think so. But he'll be out for a while. He wants me here," I finished lamely. Why was I explaining myself? Why did I still feel the need to fill silences with this strange woman?

"I see. So you're staying in Juneau, then." It wasn't quite a question, although she did look at me expectantly.

"Yeah. I guess…" The enormity of what I was about to risk, the steps I would need to take to do it, suddenly exhausted me. I felt small. "I mean, I'm not sure how one leaves a cruise. Do you know if I need to talk to someone, or report it or something?"

Caroline shook her head. "I'm sorry, I'm just a bartender."

"Okay. I guess there's probably a number I should call or something."

I was a little surprised when Caroline stood up. "I'll leave you to it then," she said, as casual as could be.

"That's it? You're not going to give me some preachy feminist speech about Colin not deserving me?"

Now I was sure I saw her eyebrow go up. "Would it help if I did?"

"No."

"There you have it then. I'm glad you got what you wanted." She turned to go.

"Wait!" I blurted.

Caroline turned around, eyebrows raised above the rim of the glasses, and I realized I didn't know what to say. For some reason, I wanted Caroline to stay longer. I wasn't sure I even cared why she could heal like she could, or who she really was. There was something unfinished between us.

"If you've got a couple of minutes, would you mind finishing your story?" I asked. "About the creature?"

"Heck…" She studied me for a long moment. "It isn't a happy story."

There were a lot of things I could have said to that, like "no shit," or "I'm not a happy person." But I decided to forgo the glib and tell her the truth. "Maybe that's why I want to hear it."

Caroline nodded and sat back down in her chair. "Where was I?"

"You realized the creature was going after Victor."

Twenty-Nine

Caroline

After we were secured inside the carriage once again, Mary turned her attention to me. "We need to warn the authorities at Chillon."

"And say what?" I asked. I still felt that strange sense of calm. Resignation, I realized. It was resignation. "There is a powerful composite creature coming to attack the lunatic who assembled him out of corpses?"

She fell silent for a moment. "Chillon has plenty of guards," she pointed out. "Their job is to stop intruders. Surely all of them together can overpower him."

I lifted my hands from my lap, flexing the fingers slightly. I thought of Albin's body, then Alice's. Human bodies were so easy for us to break. "How many of them will die in the process?" I wondered. I shook my head. "I must go, Mary."

"No! Don't say that!" she cried. "Why would you save a man who created a monster?"

I suddenly felt exhausted. "Before he was that man," I told her, "he was a boy. A curious, somber little boy who could never understand why anyone's mother should get sick and die."

"Plenty of mothers die. *My* mother died," she argued. "I didn't use it as an excuse to raise the dead."

I looked down at the scar encircling my wrist, remembering the words I had seen in Victor's notes. *New species.* "That wasn't his goal, not really. He wanted to create *new* life."

Her words were almost careless. "He could have done that with you."

I lowered my head to peer through the window at the manor that had been my home. It was no longer early, but a low gray mist hung low over the building, its damp tendrils clinging to the garrets and shutters.

Mary was right, of course: I'd been right there, wanting nothing more than to give Victor a child. Why hadn't that been enough?

"You could leave Geneva," Mary suggested. "If your attacker is no longer looking for you, surely you are free now. You could travel anywhere."

I turned back and smiled sadly at her. The idea should have been delicious and liberating, but it had never occurred to me to crave freedom or independence.

"That was never a possibility," I said. "I'm not like you, Mary. I wasn't raised to think for myself, to invent new ways of living."

I had been conditioned for the hearth and home, the comfort and service of men. In every sense, it's what I had been made for.

I realized that I knew what to do.

Mary started to say something, but just then the carriage jerked to a halt. I looked out the window and discovered we had returned to Gray Hollow.

"It's all right, Mary. "I told her, reaching for the door handle. "I am not afraid anymore."

"But you said he's stronger than you!" she argued, grabbing my hand. It surprised me. "He's more experienced in his body, more used to force, less caring of human life."

"All true," I agreed. I had no delusions about how I'd escaped from the cottage. It had been pure luck. "In a fight, I would have no chance."

"So how will you stop him?"

"I will use what I was given," I said calmly.

The carriage door opened next to me, the driver already extending his hand to help me exit. I turned to climb out, and Mary moved to follow me. I put up a hand to stop her. "No, Mary. This is where we must part."

Her eyes sparked with shock, and she looked past me to the driver. "Would you give us a moment, please?" she asked. He touched his hat and closed the door again.

I sat back down as Mary turned to me. "You shouldn't face Victor and his creature alone," she said stubbornly. "I must come tonight and help."

I smiled, touched by the offer. "You must stay home and take care of your son," I told her. "I would never risk depriving that little boy of a mother."

Mary looked stricken at that. I pressed my advantage. "But you can still help me."

Reaching into my dress pocket, I pulled out the packet of Victor's journals. I had never even untied the string. Even if I had been a reader, there was nothing in there that would help me. "You said you felt as though you were meant to tell this story." I deposited the package on her lap. "Consider it yours."

She gave me a doubtful look, turning the packet of journals over in her hand. "You know this is what I want," she said finally, "but I do not see how it helps you."

"Telling the world about Victor and his folly may prevent others from pursuing the same ends," I said, then added firmly, "Besides, if I fail to stop Victor's creature, your book will ensure that he cannot hide in the fog any longer."

Her eyes filled with tears, but she nodded. "I will write it."

"Thank you," I took a breath. "Now, can you me where to find Victor at Chillon? I have not visited since I was a girl."

Mary nodded her acceptance and began to describe Victor's location. He was not, to my relief, chained to a post with the other prisoners. He had been secured in one of the empty apartments, currently unoccupied while the castle awaited renovation.

When I was certain I understood the simplest way to find my husband, I thanked Mary. There was a moment of silence, neither of us quite sure how to bid farewell to each other. After a pause, she added hesitantly, "What will you do tomorrow?"

The question surprised me. I did not expect to see another tomorrow. It must have shown on my face. "When your business with Victor is finished, you must really leave Geneva," Mary rushed to say. "You'll need a new identity. You cannot go by the name Elizabeth Frankenstein."

"Nor would I want to. She should remain dead."

"We must call you something." Mary looked at me thoughtfully. "I'm named for my mother. What was your mother's name?"

I wasn't sure how to answer. I had never learned the name of the mother who gave birth to me, and I did not remember the mother who took me in after her death.

But, whatever her choices, I had loved Victor's mother with everything I had. "Caroline," I said at last, rapping on the carriage door.

The driver opened it, and I allowed him to take my hand and help me down to the ground. Then I turned around to take one more look at Mary Godwin through the carriage window. "Do take care of yourself, Mary. And of little Willmouse."

She extended her hand, and I took it. "Goodbye... *Caroline*. I hope you find your purpose."

A moment later the driver snapped his reins, and I waved as Mary Godwin rode away, my heart heavy with the knowledge that I already had.

Thirty

Caroline

After Mary left, I strode back into Gray Hollow and began to search each room, as thoroughly as I could. I yanked up floorboards and ran my fingers along crown molding, cut open mattresses and emptied drawers. When I had left no square inch of that house unexamined, I brought my finds to the kitchen and spread them out over the table.

All three male bedrooms had yielded coins, and from my own room and my aunts' things I had necklaces, bracelets, a broken pocket watch with a fine gold chain, and several brooches. Most of the jewelry had been deep in my aunt's chests, held for the day when I wanted to pass it on to my own children with fond stories of my childhood. That would never happen now, but her treasures could still be put to use.

If I had to estimate now, the whole glittering lot of it was probably worth nearly a hundred thousand in modern American dollars, although it was a fraction of what the Frankenstein family once kept around the house. Still I was painfully aware that it was the only financial resources I would be able to glean from my former life. Any future sums would need to be earned or stolen.

I swept the lot of it into the largest of my aunt's handbags, ones she had sewn herself as a girl. Then I went to put on some of young Ernest's black trousers, covering them with Elizabeth's black mourning cloak, the same one I'd worn to William's funeral. I applied a small amount of rouge to bring color into my cheeks, and set my aunt's hat with the veil atop my head. Then, purse in hand, I ventured out into the gray afternoon.

By the time I walked across the drawbridge to Chateau de Chillon, that afternoon in 1816, the island castle had already stood for more than eight hundred years, serving many roles. It was first used to control a major road frequented by pilgrims and merchants, then by the counts of Savoy as they moved around to govern their subjects. When the Swiss conquered the region in 1536, Chillon Castle became an administrative hub, complete with an arsenal and a prison. The castle was conquered again in 1798 by a French-speaking district of Vaud. As the local government evolved and changed, it served as a summer home, then a prison, then a residence again, and a prison again.

In 1816, many of the castle's inhabitants were political prisoners. They were kept in relative comfort in the crumbling old living quarters of the castle – many with their servants in tow. It was very common for these men to pay the guards to allow small comforts and goods to enter the castle. This wasn't considered corruption, because Chillon had changed hands so many times, and the new government of Vaud was so precarious. It probably sounds strange now, but at the time the wardens thought it was only sensible to indulge the political prisoners. It felt like at any moment, their roles could be reversed.

All of this was public knowledge to the residents of Geneva, and that was to my advantage. Fog or not, I knew that my enemy wouldn't risk arriving at the castle before full dark, to reduce the number of people who saw his face and therefore, raised an alarm. I, on the other hand, could approach the castle in broad daylight. As long as I wore my sunglasses or veil, I could still pass for a pretty young woman with money. Someone like that could get nearly anything she wanted at Chillon, short of actually leaving with a prisoner.

I arrived at the chateau an hour before sunset. As I approached the gates, and for the first time since my awakening, I made a conscious effort to duplicate Elizabeth's walk, the poise that spoke of breeding and money. I strode boldly up to the first guard and made my plea: my husband was a captive at the Chateau, I said, and his father had just died. Though his grasp of reality was tenuous, I needed to inform him of this tragic news. I made myself sniffle delicately into a handkerchief. Then, completely unprompted, as though it were the most natural thing in the world, I passed along the coins or jewels.

It was shockingly easy.

I had to repeat this performance several times, of course, for other members of the garrison. Mary had even given me the name Victor had been using, Michael Horton, so it did not take long before a portly young soldier was assigned to lead me to my husband's quarters.

As I followed him through the castle I felt my dormant stomach quiver with a brush of nerves. Or perhaps it was anger? I could no longer tell the difference. Much of my rage at Victor and his lies had subsided after Alice – not so much because I forgave my husband, but because that anger was replaced by my own guilt. Now it was all rushing through me again, and its strength both terrified and provoked me. What if I lost control again? What if I were truly as evil, as vicious, as the other creature?

I wanted a moment to think, to slow myself down, but the soldier had stopped at a door and was already turning the key. "Wait –" I began, but he'd pushed the door open, and I was staring into the dimly lit room beyond.

The apartment was tiny, barren, and decrepit, its only light source a small barred window near the ceiling, and two candles set on the floor on opposite sides of the room. My eyes had no trouble with the dimness, however, and I immediately saw the room's sole occupant: a gaunt man with wild tufts of beard and hollow eyes, who was bent down near the far wall. He was dressed in ragged clothes, his feet crammed into ill-fitting shoes with no socks. When the door creaked opened, he glanced at us briefly, before his eyes returned to the floor. The whole time, his lips moved in a soundless mutter. I didn't recognize him.

I was about to speak to the guard, to tell him this was the wrong apartment, but then my eyes went past the gaunt man and caught the writing that covered the wall beyond him. Chemical formulas, notes, slashes of angry ink – and my own name, scrawled and circled in a number of places. And all of it in Victor's handwriting.

My words caught in my throat.

"He makes the ink himself, out of leaves and other waste. We had to stop giving him paper, though." The soldier shifted his weight from foot to foot. "He went through so much of it, and there was no money, you see. Then he started on the walls." The young man shrugged. "They're planning to renovate this apartment anyway, so the major said it would do no harm."

I took in a breath, the air stinking of mulch and Victor's unwashed body. The anger that had ballooned inside me on the way there had deflated completely at the sight of my husband. The man who had deceived me, who had created the monster that killed me, was not the man in this room.

I forced myself to tear my eyes off my husband and look at the soldier, so impossibly young. "May I have some time with him, please?"

"I'm not supposed to –"

"Do you have a sweetheart?" I interrupted.

He blinked in surprise, but a brief smile flashed across his face before he could smother it. "Yes, Miss."

I pulled out an unadorned gold necklace and tucked it into his hand. He flinched when my cold fingers touched him, but he didn't pull away. "This is for her."

"Yes, Miss." The soldier looked dazed, but he bobbed his head without looking up from the necklace. "I'll return in a few minutes, to see you out."

"Take your time," I said, already making my way toward Victor. I barely heard the door close behind us.

The boy I'd known all my life was crouching now, to add something to his writing with a black charcoal pencil. His fingers were stained dark gray with ink and charcoal. He didn't look up when I lifted the veil off my face. I knelt down and reached for his hands, gently took them in my own. I could not feel subtle changes in temperature anymore, but even I knew they were like icicles.

"Please release me, mademoiselle," Victor said, barely glancing at me. "I must finish my work."

"You already did, *mon mari*," I said, keeping my voice gentle. It was the same tone I'd used a thousand times before, whenever I had to persuade Victor to stop and come to dinner, come play with William, go speak with his father. "Your work is done. You can stop now." I squeezed his hands, just as I always did, and for the first time the gaunt man peered at my face, frowning with confusion.

"Elizabeth?"

"Hello, Victor."

"You're dead. I killed you." He said this in the reasonable tone of one who feels he is being perfectly obvious.

"*He* brought me back."

For a moment Victor's face remained clouded with confusion, and he seemed on the verge of objecting. I opened my mouth to explain further – but what could I possibly say that wasn't obvious already?

Then Victor abruptly dropped his pencil and reached for me. He tore the veil all the way from my head and pulled my face close to his – not to kiss, but to examine my eyes with great scrutiny. Then his gaze moved down to my neck, to the top of my dress. It surprised me when he seized the fabric, but I understood what he wanted, and forced myself to hold still as he held open the dress and peered down at my body with clinical excitement. Even then, you see, I could not deny Victor anything.

He jumped up and ran to fetch one of the candles, but when he returned it was to kneel by my back, tugging at the back of my dress. I let him look at my scars. "He did!" Victor said at last, and the glee in his voice shocked me. "He brought you back, oh, Elizabeth!"

Putting the candle down, he circled to kneel in front of me again, taking my hands. As his fingers enveloped mine, they brushed against the scar around my left wrist, drawing his attention. With a grimace, I allowed him to yank my sleeve back and twist my arm this way and that in the candlelight, looking at the raised scar tissue. "Your left hand was crushed, I remember," he murmured. "He replaced it?"

"Yes. I lost my wedding ring, though."

Victor's head jerked up to look into my face. "So you have retained your memories?" he asked eagerly. "You know me?"

The inside of my rigid body hardened even further. "Better now than I ever have before."

Justified or not, the accusation was a mistake – the clarity and excitement that had entered Victor's eyes vanished, and his expression became vacant again. "Yes, of course," he murmured, cringing away from me to pick up his pencil. "You know what I made, what I began. You've come to kill me, of course you have."

Now it was my turn to flinch, to pull every part of my body away. "Kill you?" I repeated.

Even now, I have to marvel at how the mind can deceive and soothe itself, often at the same time. Since the moment I'd decided to come to Chillon, I had purposefully focused all my thoughts on arriving before my attacker and preventing him from obtaining the instructions for the procedure. I'd never let myself truly consider what to do with Victor Frankenstein.

Some part of me must have understood I had a decision to make. But I hadn't decided.

I hadn't let myself decide.

"I'm so pleased that it is you," Victor said absently, returning to his scribbles. "Give me just a moment to finish this first, if you would not mind."

"I am not here to kill you, Victor."

Now he looked up sharply. "Oh, but you must. It is so fitting that it is you. I'm quite pleased," he repeated. The corners of his mouth twisted in a grotesque, dreamy smile. "How like you, my gracious Elizabeth, to put me out of my misery despite how I've wronged you. A lesser woman – a lesser man, even – might desire to punish me with a long life, but you have always been merciful."

I had no idea what to say to that, but he didn't seem to expect a response. Looking downright cheerful, he lowered himself to nearly a prone position so he could scribble notes onto the wall.

I could only sit there for a moment, blinking. My gaze lifted to the scribbled ramblings of my broken husband. I couldn't make sense of more than a few words… but that didn't mean it was nonsense.

I forced myself to adopt the old, cheerful tone. "What is it you are writing, my dear Victor?"

"It is my formula, I must not forget it," he muttered distractedly. "They have taken everything else, but they cannot have the contents of my brain, not if I make myself remember."

My heart sank as I stared at the scribbling. Victor didn't just know the formula – he was writing it on the walls for anyone to see. Even if I could stop Victor's creation, my own murderer, what would prevent another from using this information?

My eyes traveled further upward, to the small, barred window. Night had fallen, I realized. We had little time.

Then Victor was dropping his pencil, futilely dusting off his filthy hands. "There," he said with satisfaction. "Now you may kill me, Elizabeth." He looked at me with open eagerness, the same little boy who had begged me to play piano for him, to sing, to smile, to lift his spirits. Pity warmed my heart, and I found my decision.

"I won't," I declared, climbing to my feet.

Victor frowned. "You must," he insisted, his expression beginning to grow anxious.

A knock struck the apartment door, and I spun and hurried toward it, thankful for the interruption. "That will be the guard," I said over my shoulder. "We must move you to a new location immediately; you are in grave –"

The door swung before I reached it, and I was once more face to face with my own murderer.

I suppose I had imagined that he would burst through the door, flattening it to the ground, and bound over to seize one or both of us. It never occurred to me that he might knock.

Now he stood there, framed in the doorway, though he had to duck in order to step forward into the room. He wore trousers and a white shirt that was spattered with streaks of dark red. There was more red on his great black boots, of the kind favored by the military men. I said a silent prayer for the friendly young guard who had escorted me to this room.

Due to the angle of the room and our positions near the floor, his eyes went to Victor first. "Hello, Father," he growled.

Victor began to weep. "No, no, no, no..." He shot a pleading look to me, begging me to fix this. "Kill me," he whispered, his voice so low only I could hear.

I stood up slowly, and the creature's eyes flickered over to me, his scarred yellow face going slack in surprise. I had forgotten the blackness of his lips. "You."

For a long moment the three of us were frozen in that tableau: Victor on the floor, and the two of us standing over him: his monsters.

Then my attacker's monstrous face narrowed at me. "I will deal with you momentarily," he spat, stalking forward with his eyes fixed to the wall behind Victor.

He scanned the formulas with great interest, but after only a few seconds he shook his head impatiently. "No, that is not complete!" he raged down at Victor. "I need details, instructions. I cannot duplicate your work without *exact information!*"

Victor was sobbing now, making no effort to stand up. "I won't, I won't, I won't," he chanted, though his shoulders were hunched and his head ducked down. My attacker stepped toward him, reaching down to seize his upper arm. "I shall take you with me then," he thundered.

Victor's terrified eyes found me. "*Please*, Elizabeth," he implored. "You must!"

I found my voice at last. "Taking him won't be necessary," I declared, stepping toward them so I had to tilt my head to stare the creature straight in the face.

His gigantic brow rolled forward in a furrow, skin puckering at the scars. I looked down at Victor, at my feet. "In fact," I mused, and before either of them could react, I reached down, grabbed Victor around the neck, and smashed his head into the wall as hard as I could. I had underestimated my strength again.

Thirty-One

Caroline

Out of respect, I will not describe here what the force of that blow did to Victor's skull. I will only say that it was over in an instant, and I do not think Victor felt even a moment of pain or fear. It was not what I had decided to do, but I cannot regret my choice.

As I had intended, blood and other body matter burst across the wall, covering much of Victor's writing. Only a little of it spattered onto me, but it still took all my composure not to react to the hot spray on my face. I remember a giddy, crazed thought ricocheting through my head: *Now we are a matching pair.*

I almost lost my nerve in that moment, but I made myself think about Justine. William. Alice. The questions I had never asked.

I had not chosen my second life, but I was not innocent in it, either. *Someone needs to atone.*

I lifted my head again to look at Victor's creation, who was frozen in shock. It wouldn't last long – I had been his student for months; I recognized the explosion building on his face. It was time to commence my real plan.

Ignoring the mess on my face, I lifted my skirt and stepped over Victor's body. Then I threw my arms around my attacker, clinging to his middle.

He towered over me by more than two and a half feet; I barely reached his chest. His shirt reeked of dank places and unwashed bodies, but I pretended I was embracing the softest silk.

I had never touched my captor like this. His body was disturbingly solid—not in the sense of musculature, but as though his parts had been harvested during rigor mortis.

"I had given up hope of ever finding you!" I cried into his shirt.

"You...what foolery is this?" he demanded, grasping my upper arms and pushing me away so he could look down at my face. His grip was unyielding, but it was not meant to be painful, either.

"There's no foolery," I told him, forcing myself to stay limp and docile in his arms. "I have been searching for you for months, Gaius."

"You—" he began, then paused and let go of me, looking newly confused. "What did you call me?"

I lifted my eyebrows and bounced on the balls of my feet like a hopeful child. "Gaius? It is the name I thought of for you." I offered a shy smile. "Do you like it?"

As I'd hoped, the discussion of names completely derailed his rage. "Gaius." He looked as though he was tasting the word.

"As in Gaius Coriolanus," I prompted. "From the book you read to me about Roman and Greek philosophers? I cannot recall the title, but I remember Coriolanus was your favorite."

"Plutarch's *Parallel Lives*," he corrected automatically. "Gaius. I *do* like it. You...you may call me that."

I dropped a small, eager curtsy, which brightened his dark expression.

Then his gaze fell on what was left of Victor's body. "Why have you done this?" he demanded, pointing down, as though I were a puppy who urinated in the house.

"Forgive me," I said meekly, allowing my shoulders to hunch forward. "It was jealousy. I did not want you to create another."

"Jealous—" Gaius puffed out his chest, remembering himself. "You deceived me. *Abandoned* me!"

I did not dare meet his eyes. "I was confused," I whispered. "It was so confusing, having you speak to me like an infant when I first woke up."

"So you lied to me?!" He was working himself up now, I saw. "You made me your fool!"

The blue flame in my chest flickered to life, but I forced it out again. I was no longer a captive.

Elizabeth had always been good at making herself cry. With only a little more effort, I managed to force several tears down my cheeks. "Please try to understand, *monsieur*," I said, making my voice quaver, "I didn't know who to trust. Remember that I woke up chained to a wall." I sniffled. "Like an animal."

He stared, the anger he'd been nursing abruptly deflating. "That…must have been a shock," he said grudgingly.

Out in the hall, I could hear shouting. Whatever chaos the creature –Gaius, now– had caused on the way in, it had been discovered.

I tilted my head again and peered up at him through my eyelashes.

"I know there is much we must discuss, *monsieur*, but perhaps we could talk somewhere more private?"

"I do not know Geneva well," he said sullenly.

"The Frankenstein family home is still unoccupied," I offered. "I have been waiting there in hopes you'd return. Perhaps we could move our conversation there?"

There were more shouts, from just outside the door now. Gaius turned toward his massive hands clenching into fists.

I stepped forward, drawing his attention back. "May I take your arm, sir?" I asked. He nodded, looking at me as though I were a sorceress casting a welcome spell.

I held his forearm as we walked out of the room, and made our way toward the castle exit.

Twice, we encountered a small group of soldiers, but Gaius snarled and shoved at them. I wanted to spare as many as possible, but I knew the longer we were in the castle, the more people he would kill, so I wasted no time. I figured out that if I made myself look even the slightest bit distressed at his violence, he gentled slightly. It helped hurry things along.

Once we were across the drawbridge, Gaius grasped my hand and began to run. His long legs were much faster than mine, and for a few minutes I felt like a kite in the air, being pulled along beside him. His strength was sobering, and reminded me that once again, I was walking a tightrope above a monster.

But this time was different, I reminded myself. I had spent twenty years of my human life training to be a human barometer: charming Victor out of his dark moods, entreating him to care for himself, tempting him from his work with laughter and fun. My job was made easier by his awkwardness, his unease in social situations. And he had been raised as a gentleman. Gaius had no such training in flirtation or deception.

I let Gaius into Gray Hollow through the unlocked back door, closing it tightly behind us. When he turned to eye me, still wary, I smiled up at him with adoring submission in my eyes.

I would destroy him.

Thirty-Two

Heck

When my cell phone buzzed in my pocket I nearly jumped out of my skin. I told myself it was just because I'd gone so long without reception on the cruise ship.

Caroline broke off her story. "Hang on," I said, pulling out the cell. There was a text from the nurse's station. "He's waking up," I said, feeling disoriented. I'd been so absorbed in Caroline's story.

I pushed the thought aside and began gathering up my trash. I needed to figure things out with Colin. The cruise ship left in just two hours; I had to know before then.

"Heck, there's something I need to confess," she began, but I was already standing up. I didn't want to hear any more lectures.

"I'm sorry," I told her. "I have to go. Colin needs me."

She didn't say anything, just sipped her tea, like that was exactly what she'd expected from me, but she was disappointed all the same. It was her best impression of my mother yet.

Carefully, so I wouldn't twist anything, I unfolded my legs from the tall chair and stood up. My knee twinged its way through the Advil, reminding me how recently it had dislocated. I could tolerate it.

I started to say, "See you later," then realized I might not. I just mumbled a "goodbye" and left the cafeteria as quickly as I could.

When I got back to the room, Colin's eyelids were flickering, his face scrunching with pain. He'd dropped the call button from his dangling hand, but Coral was standing by his bed, noting something in his chart. She smiled when I came in. "There you are. He's been asking for you."

My heart fluttered. She replaced the clipboard and bent at the waist so her face would be in Colin line of sight. "Colin? You're doing great. I'll be back to check on you in thirty minutes."

His eyes found her, stayed open. "Morphine?" he said weakly.

She checked her watch. "You can push the PCA button in a few minutes." I automatically glanced at the familiar tube that she'd left on the bed: the patient-controlled analgesic pump. I'd learned so much about hospitals this year.

Coral did her brisk-walk thing out of the room, and Colin's eyes shifted slowly over to find me.

"Heqet?" he said, his voice a dazed croak. "I didn't dream you?"

"No, I'm really here." I stepped forward and lifted my fingers to touch his. The hand in the plexiglass box was gruesome, so I focused on his face. "How are you feeling?"

"Awful."

But his eyes were clearer than they'd been earlier. I wasn't going to get a better chance to talk to him, at least not before the cruise ship left. "Is it, um, okay that I'm here?"

The pain didn't leave his face, but his eyes narrowed slightly like he was trying to remember someone's name. "We broke up," he said dully. "I left you in the hospital." His eyes flashed around the room for a moment before landing on my face again. "Oh, gods, I'm so sorry." He sniffled, a couple of tears sliding down the side of this face. "I wouldn't blame you if you told me to fuck off and stormed out of here right now."

I squeezed his fingers very gently, even though my arm was already beginning to ache from holding my own hand up. "It's okay," I said, but the words didn't feel as good as I'd expected.

Colin's eyes filled with tears. "I'm so sorry I left you back then. I love you. Please don't leave," he begged.

I tried to smile at him. I wanted to savor this delicious sense of rightness. He'd rejected me at the hospital, but here I was, forgiving him. This was the fantasy. Our love story could finally resume.

But something made me keep talking. "Colin... do you really want me here...or do you just not want to be alone?"

His expression shifted slightly, and I could tell he was thinking more clearly now than earlier. "Can't it be both?" he said lightly, trying a crooked smile. The one that always made me smile back in return.

When I didn't, his eyes slid away from me. "I love you, Heck – I think I do. But I want a nice, normal wife and my own biological children." He shrugged helplessly. "Maybe it's a guy thing, you know, the desire to pass on the family bloodline? And you..." he trailed off.

"I can still have kids," I argued. I'd practiced this in my head, but out loud it sounded so plaintive. "I can get in shape, you know, and consult the best doctors and specialists. And EDS is being studied right now, who knows where they'll be in two or five years. And there's surrogacy –"

Colin looked uncomfortable. "Yeah, but do you know how much that will cost? And even then, there's no guarantees that what happened with Madison won't happen again. I don't want to go through that again. Or put you through all that," he added.

I'd practiced these arguments, goddammit, but suddenly I found myself not wanting to make them. Not wanting to convince him. I found myself withdrawing my hand.

Maybe it was just too soon after Caroline's story about convincing the creature she cared for him. I was being extra sensitive.

"I'm sorry, I do want you here," Colin added, his fingers tightening to clumsily hang onto mine. I let him. "I love you so much. I'm just really messed up right now, and the drugs don't help." He gave me a beatific smile. "Why don't we worry about the future later? Let's just... see what this is."

I pushed out a breath to keep myself from saying yes. Then I said, "How would that work, though? Are you going to recover here in Juneau, or going back to Madison? Or will you stay with your parents in Green Bay? And where would I live?"

"Heck..." His eyes flicked to the clock on the wall, then dropped to the covers as though scanning for something. "Give me a break, this *just* happened. The doctor said I'm going to need surgeries, and physical therapy, and honestly, I don't have anything worked out yet. But I know I'll need help with my work."

"With your work," I repeated.

Of course. I was Colin's own personal human Dictaphone.

It should have felt good – being needed by Colin had always felt so good before. But suddenly I felt empty. Almost numb.

What was happening?

"Why don't you want to talk to the police?" I blurted.

He blinked at me for a moment, and a voice in my head said, *he's going to lie.* "Because I don't remember anything," he said. "It's all a blur." His uninjured hand moved twitched on the covers. "Do you see that button, for the morphine thingy?" Colin asked. "Not the call button; there's another one."

Without thinking, I moved the sheet aside and picked up the PCA button. I started to put it in his outstretched fingers, but then my hand froze in the air above his. He couldn't move his arm to meet mine. "Heck," he said with a tinge of impatience.

"When I first got here, you told me there were two guys, and they kept hitting you," I reminded him.

"Did I? I don't remember. Anyway, calling the police won't do anything. I have good insurance through the school. It's fine."

I stared at him. "What aren't you telling me?"

"This isn't funny. Heck, give me the morphine thing." He was trying his teacher voice on me, but Colin had never been my teacher. I didn't owe him obedience.

"Why didn't you call the police?" I demanded.

The voice came from the doorway, soft and familiar. "Because I told him not to."

I turned, and saw Caroline leaning against the doorframe, arms crossed casually over her chest.

Thirty-Three

I hadn't even heard the door open.

There was a gasp from the bed, and when I looked back, Colin had gone white-green. He squirmed backward in the bed like he was trying to avoid a particularly large and terrifying spider. It must have hurt his legs, but the hand in the plexiglass box was what pinned him to the spot. "You," he whimpered.

Caroline didn't bother to answer.

"You did this to him?" I asked her. My voice sounded like a stranger's, and I felt lightheaded. A fresh wave of horrified nausea swept over me. "For me? Please don't say you did this for me."

"Not like that. This is what I was trying to tell you in the cafeteria," Caroline said quietly. "I was just planning to talk to him... I lost control."

For a moment I just stared at Caroline, whose sunglasses were pointed at the floor. Was this my fault, because I told her to care about something? Was she really some kind of avenging angel, like Mary had suggested in the story?

The story. The Frankenstein story.

Belief is a funny thing, because although it comes from inside you, it doesn't require your consent. I never agreed to believe that Elizabeth Frankenstein was standing in front of me, two hundred years after telling her story to Mary Godwin. I had, I realized in a rush of clarity, actively fought against that belief. But somehow, it had seeped into me anyway. Because despite all my insistence and rationalizations, I *knew* who I was looking at. And what she was capable of.

I took an instinctive step back, trying to put space between me and her.

"Heck? Do you *know* this girl?" Colin sounded so hurt, so betrayed, that I opened my mouth to lie and say Caroline was some random woman I met on the ship. It would be so easy to call her crazy.

I didn't know what I was going to say until it was already out of my mouth. "Better now than I ever have before."

Caroline flinched, just a little. At least, I thought she did. I suddenly found it intolerable that she got to hide behind those goddamned lenses. Forgetting my fear, I dropped the PCA button and strode over to Caroline. She let me tear off the sunglasses. She was wearing her contacts, so her eyes appeared almost normal, but she hissed at the bright hospital lighting, cringing from the florescent bulbs. "Explain," I demanded.

She didn't answer, just screwed up her eyes in a squint. Impatiently, I reached for the wall switch next to her and flicked off the main overhead light. There was still sunlight coming through the window, and a spotlight over the bed, but Caroline's face relaxed most of the way.

"I just wanted to meet him," she said stiffly, but added, "...at first." Her shoulders were high, and I realized she was defensive. "I wanted to know if he was worthy of your throwing away your life, perhaps literally. I found one of his teaching assistants online, and he emailed me Colin's usual routine. I didn't even have to pay him." She glared past me at Colin. "You're not well-liked here."

I didn't have to look at Colin to know that would sting. He loved being liked.

"Go on," I said to Caroline.

"I left the ship very early and went to the trail where he runs. I expected him to strike up a conversation." That explained her fancy workout clothes. She glared at him again. "He did not disappoint."

Ah. I didn't want to draw this story out any farther. "He hit on you," I said tiredly. "I understand. And I'm not delighted, but we were – are – broken up. That's no reason to –"

"Oh, it was so much worse than hitting on me," she said, her voice taking on a new note now, something low and dangerous. Before she'd been defending her actions, now she was reliving her anger. "I expected him to hit on me; he's the type. We started talking, and he brought you up within the first five minutes –"

"Because I love you," Colin burst out from the bed. "I think about you all the time, Heck, and Maddie too –"

Caroline had been turned toward me, making her case, but that was too much for her. She rounded on Colin, and was at the side of his bed in an instant. I hurried after her, and had to lean forward to hear her say very softly, "Is that why you told me they were *both* dead?"

Colin, for his part, was trying helplessly to scoot back in the bed again, to move as far away from her as he could. He wound up looking like a toddler rocking because they need to pee.

"You said I was dead too?" My feelings couldn't keep up with this conversation; instead of anger I was confused. "Why would you say that?"

"So I would fuck him," Caroline spat. "He's using you and your baby as a goddamned pickup line."

Suddenly the whole scene played in my head: Colin easing up to Caroline, complimenting her form or her jacket, something innocuous. He'd ask if she was a student, and then, as soon as possible, turn the conversation to himself – that he was spending the summer teaching at the university while he mourned the loss of his girlfriend, who'd died in childbirth. Maybe he'd even kick me up to "fiancée," for added dramatic affect.

Later, when they were finished, he'd have the perfect excuse to get rid of her. He wasn't ready for a real relationship – he was still mourning.

"It wasn't like that," Colin muttered, his terrified eyes fixed on Caroline. "You misheard me, I said it was like the relationship had died…"

I was still at Caroline's shoulder, and didn't see the look she gave him. I did see her tiny step forward, and suddenly the monitors all around Colin began to bleep and trill in alarm.

But I didn't move. Because God help me, I believed Caroline. She knew not to believe Colin's story, of course… but how often had it played out just like that with some other woman?

I had to drop into the wooden folding chair before I started swaying. Colin said something, but I just shook my head, not registering it. Lying about me, that was repulsive – but how many times had Colin sold our daughter's memory so he could fuck someone?

Oh, God. I'd been such a fool.

Caroline had leaned over Colin, who looked terrified. "You deserve to know every kind of pain," she told him, her soft voice braided with hate and steel. "You are a small, shallow man who needs to climb over women to feel worthy of what he has been freely given to you. I've met a thousand men like you, and I can tell you this: you are *not* worthy, and you will never be special." Colin shrank back, but she wasn't finished. "What you are," Caroline hissed, "is very lucky I allowed you to live."

"Yes, ma'am." Colin was crying silently, his face gone from white to bright red. He shot me a pleading look, begging me to save him.

I still didn't move. Love can die, I thought in a daze. Not just over months and years, like a cancer. Love can die like a car wreck.

I heard footsteps in the hall then, drawn by the beeping monitors. "In here!" Colin shouted hoarsely, then cringed at

207

whatever he saw on Caroline's face. Carefully, I put a hand on her shoulder, and she turned to me. Her eyes were ablaze, yet somehow tinged with paler blue. In my gut, deep down where my sense of self-preservation was supposed to live, something quivered to life.

Fear, I realized. I knew it was there, in the room, but I didn't feel it. Not from her.

Then the moment snapped like a rubber band. Caroline's eyes lost the bluish tint, and her shoulders relaxed. She turned to face me, and her face slowly crumpled. "I'm sorry," she whispered. "I lost control again. I've never..." She gave a little head shake. "This is why... I'm sorry."

Turning, she practically ran from the room.

Two nurses burst into the room then, and I had to step back while they fussed with Colin's wires and IV, injecting the morphine and speaking to him in soothing voices. I think they might have asked me what happened, and when I didn't answer, they quizzed Colin, who simply shook his head, red-faced. I stopped listening. It felt like I was back in the fog.

Eventually, after his pulse had settled down and the machines stopped screaming, the nurses filed from the room again, looking at me with furtive, confused eyes.

I said nothing.

Then we were alone. Colin looked at me with wide, desperate eyes. "What did you tell her about me?" he said, his voice breaking.

I actually considered the question. "Very little," I said at last. "That we were together, we broke up, I was coming here hoping to get back together."

Admitting the last part felt like...nothing. It didn't matter anymore that I'd been desperate, that I'd come for Colin. It was like mentioning something silly I'd done as a child.

"She must be obsessed with you," he declared, sounding triumphant. "That's gotta be it. I mean, okay, we were chatting on my run, but then she did this to me." He made the arm in traction sway a little, his eyes moving over the other injuries. "There's something wrong with her, Heck. She's too strong. Like, freakishly strong. She's a monster."

I laughed, a dry, broken sound. Colin was staring at me in confusion, like I'd broken away from reality. Maybe I had.

"Heqet!" He looked annoyed, despite his weakness.

I shook myself to attention. "What?"

"You have to call the police. I can't do it; she threatened me, but you can."

"I'm not going to call them," I said, and was surprised at my calm voice. "And neither are you. Not now, not in six months, not in five years."

Now it was Colin's turn to gape at me. "What? I thought… now *you're* turning on me too?"

I sat down in the chair, leaned forward. "Listen to me very carefully," I said. It felt like I was watching myself from somewhere else, but I didn't mind at all. "You will never, ever mention me or my daughter to another woman, ever again. You will never tell a soul about Caroline or what happened. I don't care where you go from here or who you fuck. But you will leave the three of us out of it."

His mouth closed and his eyes narrowed, just a fraction. He didn't say it, but it was written all over his face. Or what?

"If you ever write about us, use us to get laid, or even mention us drunkenly in some bar," I continued, "I'll call the chancellor's office and the student newspaper at every university you've ever worked for, starting with Juneau. I'll tell them how you got one of your employees pregnant, how I had to drop out, and, especially, you leaving me dying at the hospital to have sex with another woman. And after *that*," I paused for a breath, and to smile at him. "That's when I'll start digging through your life for real. I've got a lot of free time now. How long do you think it would take me to find more students that you've fucked?"

His face flickered, and I thought sourly, *bingo*.

209

"Heck, I don't understand where this hostility is coming from," he whined. "All I did —"

"Shut up," I snarled, and he fell silent, his eyes widening with surprise. "I'm not finished. If you ever, ever use Maddie or me again, or try to talk to the police about this attack, I'll also contact Caroline. She has a lot of free time too. And I don't think she liked you much."

Now he went pale. "I — how could you — I never meant —" he sputtered. It reminded me of a robot with dying batteries. It would have been a little funny if I weren't so disgusted — not just with his actions, but because the only thing he seemed to respond to was violence.

So be it.

I reached over and picked up the two buttons he'd dropped on the bed, one for the nurse and one for the pain meds. Gently, so they wouldn't make any noise, I laid them on the tile floor.

"Heck, what are you —"

"One more thing," I interrupted. I picked up the manilla file folder with my typewritten report from where I'd left it on the tray table. I ripped it in half and tucked it under my arm.

"Do your own fucking homework," and I limped out of the room.

Thirty-Four

Heck

I had expected her to be waiting in the hall, but it was empty. I retraced my steps to the emergency entrance, and spotted Caroline standing just outside the sliding door, leaning against the glass.

I limped toward her. My knees and hips hurt, maybe from the hospital chair, or running down the hall. Or maybe for no particular reason at all. EDS is like that. *I've got to get in better shape*, I thought. Maybe it was time to try physical therapy again. If I could strengthen the muscles around my joints, it might put less stress on them.

Caroline's sunglasses turned toward me as she approached, but then she looked down and away, as if in shame. "I'm so sorry," she whispered.

I leaned against the glass next to her. I wished we could sit, but the nearest wooden bench already held a man and woman in their thirties, having their own heated discussion. For a few seconds I just stood there watching them. They were both good-looking, with pale skin and dark hair. As she spoke, he winced and lifted his hand to shield himself from the sun.

"I wonder if that guy's actually Dracula," I mused.

I hadn't meant to say it out loud, but Caroline burst into laughter, a warm, ringing sound that went on and on in great peals of joy.

I smiled. It felt good to make someone laugh like that.

"He's not handsome enough," Caroline said when she'd caught her breath. "She could be one of the brides, though."

I shot her a sideways look, and her smile faded as she shook her head. "I'm the only one like me I've ever met." Her face fell. "Which is probably good, considering. I... lost control in there."

"Everybody loses control sometimes." I shrugged. "And who knows, maybe Colin will come through it a better person."

The tiniest smile bloomed under Caroline's sunglasses. "No, he won't."

"No, he won't," I agreed. "You were right: Colin really is some basic entitled douchebag. He'll use the mugging story to sleep with half the nurses and go right back to who he is." I sighed. "But I don't think he'll use Maddie anymore. And now I'm free of him."

She turned her head, regarding me. "You are, aren't you?"

I nodded. "I don't know why you did that for me, but... thank you."

'You believe I'm who I say I am, don't you?"

"Yes," I said simply.

To my surprise, Caroline reached for my hand then, lacing her fingers through mine. Her hand felt strong and a little cooler than mine, but otherwise it was like holding anyone's hand.

"Even if I still had Victor's notes, I'm almost certain I couldn't reproduce what was done to me," she said without turning her head. "But if I could... would you really want that?"

At that moment, the couple on the bench got up and started down the road, and Caroline gently pulled me off the wall and led me over to sit down. She let go of my hand as we sat. "No," I told her. "I'd be worried that my health problems would come with me, for one thing." I couldn't imagine being trapped for two hundred years in a stretched-out body that never obeyed my wishes.

"Is there another thing?"

We sat there for a few minutes in silence, watching the people scurrying in and out of the hospital. "I don't know if there's anything after this," I admitted. "I don't know if people... go anywhere, you know, when they die. But if we do... I want to go where Maddie is."

"Ah," was all she said.

Beyond the hospital's roof I could see lines of lush green trees rising up the nearby mountains. It was like looking at a vertical wall of green, and so beautiful I wanted to cry. How much of Alaska's beauty had I already missed on this trip? It had been foggy, yes, but I hadn't made any effort to get out of the fog, or enjoy what I could see. I closed my eyes, took in a breath. The air smelled wonderful.

Opening my eyes, I touched my stomach, feeling the scars between the layers of clothing. I grew a tiny human being in there, and she would never get to see this. Never marvel at the wall of green, or breath the crisp scent of Alaskan summer. Tears pricked my eyes. It was just so fucking sad.

"I dream that my baby came to life again," I said out loud, "that it had only been cold and that we rubbed it before the fire and it lived."

"That's from Mary's journal."

I nodded. Mary Shelley had lost four children to miscarriage or illness. "We read selections in college. My stupid memory... anyway. I get why she wrote the book so neither Victor nor the creature is totally vilified. She must have seen the temptation in what Victor could do."

"Oh yes. Mary understood temptation," Caroline said darkly. "She saw a great deal of it, between Percy and Byron." Caroline shook her head.

Percy Shelley had died young, I remembered now, when his boat sank during a storm. I looked at Caroline out of the corner of my eye. No one really knew how it had happened. "Did you ever meet Mary again?" I asked carefully.

"Mary? No." She glanced at me, lifted an eyebrow, then turned to look ahead again. She wasn't going to volunteer anything.

If Caroline had killed Percy Shelley, she wasn't going to say. I didn't ask her directly if she'd killed Percy Shelley. There wasn't enough room in my head for another literary revelation…and besides, I didn't like that I was kind of hoping she'd say yes.

"Do you want to tell me the rest?" I asked her. "About what happened after…um…"

"After I killed Victor, and lured his creation away from the chateau?" she said flatly.

"Yes." I noticed that she didn't use the name she'd given him. That had been part of the con.

Caroline looked straight ahead again. "There's not much to tell," she said at last. "We went to Gray Hollow; I made him a cup of tea, and I charmed him. I told him how sorry I was for leaving him, that I'd panicked back in the cottage. That I would never abandon him again."

"Did he buy it?"

"I sold it," Caroline said flatly. "It wasn't even difficult. He *wanted* to believe that the plaything he'd made out of spite and anger desired him in return. It was just a matter of repetition."

"Jesus," I whispered.

The sleeves of Caroline's workout top had ridden up on her arms, exposing the ugly scar that circled her left wrist. She began to tug carefully at the left sleeve, pulling it down over the old wound.

Without thinking, I reached over and took her left hand, clasping it in both of mine so my palms touched the scar. I left the sleeve where it was.

"I took him to my bed," she said softly, her sunglasses still pointed down at her lap.

"Oh, Caroline."

"It was my choice," she added sharply. "I could have tried something else – bought more laudanum, or tried to catch him by surprise. I've thought of a dozen ideas over the years. But I needed him to trust me completely, and I meant what I said to Mary. I wasn't afraid anymore."

I felt helpless. What could you say to that? I wanted to know if she was okay, but the question was about something that had happened two hundred years ago.

"Was it…very awful?" I asked tentatively.

Her lips lifted in a half-smile that faded quickly. "Honestly? It was mechanics. Anatomy. He didn't hurt me, and it was over quickly."

"I'm sorry," I said softly.

"Don't be. I don't regret it." She let out a little half laugh, as if mocking herself. "It was my first time, you know. With a man. My only time."

"Your *only* time?" I burst out, then dropped her hand to slap both of mine over my mouth.

Elizabeth smiled, but it was tinged with sadness. "Anyway," she said. "It worked – I had convinced him to trust me."

Her voice was steady, but she wiped under the sunglasses with one finger. "It was easy after that. Eventually he fell asleep, and I went to the fireplace in my bedroom, the one that had warmed me every night of my human life. I knew the coal shovel was made of heavy iron."

She gave me a wry smile. "Not fashionable for a young lady' room, but my uncle did not excel at proprieties.

"While he was unconscious, I hit him with the side of the shovel, as hard as I could. Many times. It was very gruesome." Her voice broke on the last word.

Tears stung my eyes again, spilling down my face. I didn't understand it at first – why would the creature's death make me sad?

Then I realized I wasn't crying for him. I was crying for her. For what she'd given up of herself.

When I was sure my voice wouldn't break, I asked, "What happened to Gray Hollow?"

She gave the smallest shudder, as if coming back to the present. "I took the few things I could carry, and I set it on fire."

"That… doesn't sound easy at all," I remarked, earning a tiny smile.

"But seriously," I added, unable to resist. "You *never* had sex again? You never fell in love, or had a one-night stand…?"

She shook her head. "I wasn't designed for love, Hequet. I was made like Eve: for the pleasure of another, and the procreation of a line."

"I'm sorry, but that's bullshit," I objected, turning on the bench to face her now. "He brought you back, and okay, you couldn't be the same person you were, but you're still *a* person. Of *course* you're made for love."

I thought she might snap at me then, but all Caroline said was, "Tell that to Alice Roussel."

I flinched. "You're not him," I said.

"Maybe not. But I could be, at any moment." She touched her chest. "It's always in me."

"You didn't put it there," I reminded her.

For a moment I thought I'd got through to her, but then she shook her head sharply. "Don't make the same mistake Alice did," she warned. "You can't let yourself be fooled by… this." She gestured at her face and clothes.

"I wasn't –"

"We should get going," she said suddenly, rolling to her feet. "The ship leaves in an hour."

The moment was gone. "Yeah. Okay."

I didn't move right away, though. I didn't want to get back on that artificial boat, or go home to my mother and her questions. She'd demand that I take disability and get proper rest until I could jump back onto the career path she wanted. She'd insist it was time to move on, when it already hurt so much just to move.

But when Caroline reached down, I allowed her to pull me up. "There are cabs just there," she said, pointing toward the curb of the connecting street.

We walked over, and the driver rolled down his window to ask our destination. "Take her to the pier," Caroline replied, handing a couple of twenty dollar bills through the open window.

I'd already started opening the door, but now I froze. "You're not coming?" My eyes darted to the hospital entrance – she wouldn't go back in there and...

But Caroline shook her head, smiling. "I have a couple of errands in town," she explained. "I'll catch the next cab. Be right behind you."

"Okay..." That seemed... abrupt. Maybe she just wanted to be alone, after telling me that story.

Before I could react, she had closed my door, given me a smile, and moved away.

Thirty-Five

Heck

When I finally returned to my cabin, I dropped my backpack inside the door, used the bathroom, and then collapsed on the bed, where I immediately fell into a deep sleep.

This time I didn't dream of Maddie, or Colin. My only dream was a brief sensation of standing in a field of ripe lavender, a breeze blowing at my summer dress.

I woke disoriented, registering only that it was dark outside the patio window, and cool in the room. Reminding myself to go slowly, I stretched my arm up and felt for the little switch on the wall, the one for the reading light. I flipped it up, squinting in the sudden brightness, and fumbled for my phone to check the time. Nine pm. The ship had set sail hours ago.

I sat up. My body was stiff, with various joints reporting their complaints, but I ignored them. In the center of the desk, there was an unmarked white envelope, centered perfectly. It was weighted in place by a sprig of bright purple lavender.

That hadn't been there when I walked in. As tired as I'd been, it was impossible to miss, in the dead center of the desk.

Someone had been in my room while I slept.

Caroline?

Flipping back the covers, I approached the envelope cautiously. When I reached the desk I could turn my head sideways to see the door to my cabin. Yes, I had bolted it. The noise of the bolt flipping would have woken me, so how the hell...?

I snatched up the envelope as though it were a snake that could bite. Tearing it open, I pulled out a few sheets of folded paper – and immediately fumbled it. The pages wafted down to the floor.

"Calm down, Heqet," I told myself, lowering my body to the carpet to retrieve the damn letter. The envelope had contained two handwritten sheets of paper, plus what looked like a printout of an email. The email page had been on the bottom, but it caught my eye first, simply because the name in the "From" window was so familiar: Margaret Alice Saville, PhD.

My mother. I looked at the date. She'd sent the email the day after I'd asked for her cruise ship points and she turned me down.

The day I went into her account and stole them.

Dear Elizabeth,

I must apologize right from the start: I don't know what you're calling yourself these days, so I'm using your former name instead. Please forgive the omission.

I know we haven't spoken in some time, but I'm writing about my daughter, Heqet. She's had a lot of medical difficulties this last year, and now I'm afraid she's throwing away her life to pursue a boy – the same one who caused a lot of those difficulties.

It's partly my fault, I'm sure. Her father pushed her so hard, and in the end I picked up all his worst habits. She won't listen to me, and I'm afraid any attempts to convince her to change course, so to speak, will only drive her farther away.

Heqet is boarding a cruise ship in a few weeks, and I'm hoping with your connections you can do something for her –

as you once did for me. Happy to discuss further at your earliest convenience, on the phone or in person.

As always, you have my deepest gratitude, Maggie

I stared at the email in shock. I didn't even know what to react to first. My mother knew Elizabeth/Caroline? Caroline called her *Maggie*? I hadn't heard a single person call her anything but "Margaret" or "Dr. Saville" since my dad died.

Then the rest of the words caught up to me. My mother had known what I was doing. So she'd… sent Caroline after me?

I should have listened to all those voicemails.

My fingers shook slightly as I dropped that sheet on the desk and turned to the handwritten letter, which I was probably supposed to read first.

Dear Heck,

I won't be joining you on the way back to Seattle. This morning's activities got out of hand, and I don't think it's safe for me to be near people right now, especially not you and your mother. I'll take some time away.

I realize, of course, that you probably have a hundred questions for me, but I'm afraid I'm only going to answer two of them.

The first question is simple, and yet vastly complicated.

Why you?

When I said I'd found my purpose, I wasn't talking about charming the men who made me. I was thinking of what I'd been brought up to do. I was raised to care for others, and it is the one part of me that remained hard-wired into my changed body. I never did find poor Ernest, so after Victor's death there was no one left from Elizabeth's life to care for.

I did, however, have a debt to repay. You could call it an atonement.

When I was sure my husband's creation was dead, I traveled to Chambéry, France. It was still a very small city back then, and it took only a few days of inquiring after tailors before I was able to locate Luc Durand, and then his wife, Jeannette. The first time I saw Jeannette I nearly cried. She looked exactly like an older version of Alice.

Luc was an apprentice tailor at a notable men's store, so I took work as a seamstress at a lady's tailor nearby. I had never held a job in my life before then, but I was surprised to find it very tolerable. My new body had nearly endless stamina, and I did not get sore from the long hours of craning my neck, or bleed when I stuck my thumb... which was very often at first. My fine motor skills did eventually improve, with practice.

I found lodging not far from the Durand's apartment, and quietly monitored the family. Whenever I could, I did small favors for them, leaving firewood or fresh milk. I struck up a neighborly friendship with Jeannette and found more ways to help. I kept away from the children – I was too frightened to repeat what had happened with their aunt – but I baked bread, knitted socks, and fetched firewood. Jeannette often praised my tirelessness and generosity, but I always brushed it away, insisting that I was a lonely old maid and I appreciated her company.

Inside, I was often sick with guilt at what I had taken from them. Alice should have gone to live with Jeanette. It was Alice who should have been there helping her sister, planning her own life parallel to her family's. Eventually I learned to live alongside my guilt. Not with it, and not past it, but alongside.

I could have gone on like that forever, I think, but after nearly fifteen years in Chambéry, people were talking in earnest about my youthful features. I knew I had to leave.

I moved to Lausanne, but I continued writing to Jeannette. I worked nonstop, sending as much of my earnings as I could as anonymous gifts to the Durands. I required so little, and could work such long hours, that I was able to make a striking difference in their lives.

Jeanette died at sixty-two, shortly after Luc. After her passing, I returned to Chambéry, introduced myself to Antonin and his little sister, Alice, as a distant cousin, and began the pattern anew.

This, you see, has been the work I chose for my long life: taking care of Alice's family.

After just a few decades, there were enough descendants of the Roussel line that I could spend five or ten years keeping an eye on one relative, and when my lack of aging became suspicious, I would move on to another heir, another branch of the family. This suited me. It kept me from getting too close to anyone I might hurt.

I followed various family members as they spread across the globe, preferring to stay close to those who lived in northern climates. I always worked, and often found good jobs because I wasn't bothered by cold, illness, or exhaustion, nor do I get sick. I have been a miner, a truck driver, a window washer, and dozens more. I've worked in factories and firms, skyscrapers and ships. Eventually I learned to invest, and my money grew exponentially.

Two things have remained constant over all that time: I keep a watchful eye out for anyone trying to replicate Victor's work, and I look after the Roussel descendants. Today there are eighteen living descendants of the Roussel family, including Alice's great-great-great-great niece, Margaret, and her only daughter – Heqet Saville.

I've watched you all your life, Heck, though always from a distance. My brief interactions with the Roussel descendants always occur after they reach adulthood, for obvious reasons, and for the most part I keep my role in their lives anonymous. I must say, it was a great pleasure to spend real time with you this week. You were the first descendant to see my physical abnormalities, and therefore get the whole story. It made me miss... well. Things I've never really had.

You, or rather your ex, also made me remember why I have this transient way of life. The last thing I ever want to do is hurt you.

Now for the second answer: Go ahead, if you want to. No one would believe it was true, and it might help you. And that is, after all, my job.

Please take care of yourself, Heqet. It may take some time to figure out how to do that, but after meeting you, I have faith that you can build yourself the life you need.

But if you find that you cannot, look into the shadows, the fog. I'll be there, keeping watch.

Caroline

PS: If you'll accept one gentle piece of advice: perhaps consider a name change. It made a great difference for me.

I let the paper slip through my fingers, watching it waft down onto the carpet. I felt like I'd been tasered. I was descended from Alice's family? Caroline had watched me grow up?

And what did that mean, "Go ahead if you want to?"

My nose suddenly stung with lavender, and I looked at the blossoms on the desk, which were nearly at my eye level. Lavender is made of tiny purple petals. When my eyes lowered, I saw tiny grains of purple standing out against the navy carpet. I crawled awkwardly across the carpet, following the makeshift trail, until I nearly ran my head into the glass sliding door. Then I sat back on my heels.

I hadn't bothered to lock the sliding door. My cabin was on the twelfth deck.

"Holy shit," I whispered.

Struggling to my feet, I grabbed my cane and made my unsteady way toward the door. I knew she wasn't going to be tending bar – but I needed to be sure. It still seemed possible that I'd just... lost my mind.

The observation deck was packed with families, laughing and enjoying the long-awaited sunshine. I ignored all of them, forcing my tired, stiffening body to lurch toward the adult bar where I'd seen Caroline working. I hadn't gone inside before, but as I went through the door I barely registered the surroundings. They seemed more or less the same as the bar outside, only without children present.

As I dropped onto a stool, a young African bartender approached the other side of the bar. He was smiling pleasantly, in the same empty, wooden way of all the employees. "What can I get you, miss?"

"I, um," I had to stop and swallow, wishing I'd prepared a story in advance. "I can't remember what it's called, but the bartender who helped me the other night made something special for me. I think her name is Caroline. Is she working tonight?"

The young man was already shaking his head. "I'm sorry, miss. No one by that name works at this bar." The polite smile, all teeth. "Perhaps you were in one of the restaurants?"

I placed my hands flat on the bar, slightly dizzy. "No, I'm sure it was here," I insisted. "Dark-haired woman, very pretty, about my height? Always wears sunglasses?"

I saw the recognition in his eyes, and pounced on it before he could lie. "You do know her! Is she working tonight?"

"Ah, no miss." He leaned forward, the smile shaky but holding. "She is not technically an employee. She is one of the shareholders on the cruise line."

I gaped at him. "Excuse me? Why on earth would a shareholder be tending bar?"

His smile broadened now, and he gave a carefree shrug. "She likes to keep her hand in, eh? She says she came up on the ships, and likes to remind herself. But she comes and goes as she pleases."

"I see," I said, feeling dazed. Caroline really was gone.

I was alone.

Epilogue

Seven Years Later

The 1:30 mat class is surprisingly packed, for a weekday, until I remember that today is some kind of bank holiday. Martin Luther King Jr? President's Day? I can't remember. I don't have to pay attention to office holidays.

My instructor, Christen, is particularly peppy this afternoon, probably hyped about having new customers. Christen and I went on two dates shortly after I moved to town, but decided we are better as friends. She remembered to save my favorite spot for me, though: near the back of the studio, far from the music speakers and close to the mirror so I can check my form. I thank her as I roll out my mat, and Christen grins and does a graceful little curtesy before bouncing to the front of the room to start class.

I envy the curtsy and the bounce, but not as much as I used to. I am stronger now. On my stomach, beneath my scars, I have a visible two-pack. This summer Mom and I are planning to spend a week in the Grand Caymans, and I told her I'll wear a bikini to the beach. I haven't decided yet if I'm lying.

Some days Christen has us use props, but today she clearly wants to keep it simple for the newcomers, mats only. We run through all the usual paces: the Hundred, the Fabulous Five, roll-up, saw, spine stretch, side series. I can do all of them – or at least, a version of them – except any of the planking, because it hurts my shoulders. Sometimes my other joints ache, but I have learned to distinguish between pain that's just pain and pain that's doing damage. I am fine.

Christen flits around the mats suggesting adjustments, calling out the next position like the dance teacher she used to be. When I first started coming here, she often hovered near my mat, close enough to help me figure out the modifications that didn't hurt my joints, but I know them all by heart now. When she calls side plank I lay down along my side instead, lifting my head and my feet to form a sort of smile with my body. This pose is called banana, and the goal is to keep your sideways body straight, as though you're between two panes of glass. Pilates is big on imagery and metaphor, which is probably part of the appeal for me.

Christen happens to be wandering past during my banana, and she makes a little pleased noise. "Good job, but don't forget to squeeze that bottom glute," she reminds me.

I smile, just managing not to topple sideways. This is our whole teacher-student relationship – actually, it's a microcosm for all of Pilates: you work and work on your form, and just when you think you're in perfect alignment, there's something else to fix. I like that, because it means no one is really an expert. No one is without the ability to improve.

After class, I go out to the street to put the mat in my car trunk, exchanging it for my work backpack.

This part of Ann Arbor is full of funky coffee shops and cafes, plus places like this that teach barre, Pilates, and yoga. I chose this studio because of its proximity to Common Grounds, my favorite coffee shop and unofficial office. I've got a client meeting there in 30 minutes, which will give me plenty of time to settle in and order tea.

Common Grounds was a hundred-year-old house before it was renovated to include a kitchen, bar, and coffee counter. I love it because the food and drinks are good, and because of the many, many seating options: along one wall there are traditional cafe booths, while a huge open area in the center holds retired kitchen tables from every era. I would say there are chairs to match, but the not-matching is the whole point. I can pick a chair with arms, which helps my shoulders, and drag it to a table with feet, which makes my knees happy. If there's a day when I don't feel up to any of the chairs, well, there's always a booth or even the couch in the back.

I call a quick hello to the barista, Isabel, and pull the chair I want to my favorite table by the window. Before I can go to the counter to place my order, though, my cell phone buzzes, and I dig it out of my sweater pocket.

It's a video chat from Cherie. The tables closest to me are empty at the moment, so I hit the button to answer the call, dropping down into my chair. "Hey, Cherie."

My old friend's face fills the screen, though her dark red hair appears to be alive, chunks of it swirling and straightening on their own accord. "Hi – hang on," she says, and the picture tilts wildly for a few seconds while she props it on the counter. Cherie takes a step back, allowing me to see the two-year-old in her arms, yanking on Cherie's hair.

"Hey," I say, smiling. "Hi, Lucy. How are you today?"

"Pretty hair," Lucy says, her attention fixed on the task at hand.

"She's 'doing' my hair," Cherie explains with an eye roll. She winces in pain as Lucy tugs again.

"I see that. Momma's hair is very pretty, Luce. I think you've got it just right. You should leave it just like that."

Lucy pauses, examining her work, and decides that I am right. "'Kay!" She wriggles, and Cherie sets her down on the floor. Lucy scampers out of frame, off to play with her toys or maybe try to do the dog's hair next.

"Thanks," Cherie says, leaning her upper body over the counter and rolling her eyes. "I have no idea why she only listens to you, but at least she listens to someone."

"Well, she knows I'm her godmother," I remind her. "She's probably hoping if she's nice to me I'll randomly show up at your house some night with a fabulous ballgown."

Cherie is running her hands through her hair, trying to tame it enough for a ponytail. "This kid would probably be more excited about staying up until midnight playing with mice. What are you up to? Coffee shop again?"

"Yep. Client meeting in a few minutes."

"Ah." Cherie's done with her hair, but as a mother she must by law always be doing at least two different tasks, so she starts wiping the kitchen counter with a tired-looking sponge. "New client? Old client?"

"Brand new. First meeting."

She actually pauses, raising an eyebrow mischievously. "Anyone I'd know?"

"Absolutely." I give her an exaggerated wink, and she pretends to pout. We've had this conversation a dozen times, since I started ghostwriting full-time. Cherie knows that I have to sign an NDA, but she can't resist asking. My part of the game is pretending I only work for huge celebrities.

"Okay, well, I'll let you go make a good impression. When are you home again?"

"Um..." I squint at the ceiling for a second, trying to remember. "Easter."

"Another month," she groans. "Do you realize that every month you're gone is a month in which I have to *pay* for babysitting?"

I blow her a raspberry, and we hang up.

At the counter, I get my tea latte and bring it back to sip as I review my notes. A few minutes later I see my client come in. I've seen pictures of her online, of course, but it wouldn't have been difficult to identify her anyway: a young woman in her late twenties, raven-dark hair and haunted eyes. Insanely thin, poor posture, shoulders hunched in defeat – Christen would be appalled. She's wearing four-inch heels and a tailored dress that seems out of place in this homey, mismatched environment. I think it might be Diane von Furstenberg, but I don't have much of an eye for high fashion, even now that I can afford it.

I wave at her, half-standing, and she gestures toward the register to indicate she'll get a cup of coffee first. This gives me time to put my notes back in their folder and pull a clean pad of paper out of my work bag, along with a nice pen. I've discovered that the clients feel more comfortable when I look ready to take notes, even though they've been told in advance I won't need them.

When she has her coffee she strides over, already extending her hand. "Hi," she says, forcing a weary smile. "I'm Megan. Elizabeth, right? You look just like your publicity photo."

I stand and shake her hand. "It's great to meet you. Please call me Beth."

I sit back down and pick up my tea, giving her a few seconds to get settled in. Then she picks up her coffee and clutches it with both hands like someone might try to snatch it away. "Thank you so much for meeting with me," she begins. A blush creeps over her cheeks. "I'm a huge fan of yours. *Lady Lazarus*, I mean, although I really liked the biographies you did on that Olympic ice skater, and the director."

I raise my eyebrows. "I know, you can't confirm you ghostwrote those," Megan says with a smile. "It's kind of funny; the publisher puts all these restrictions on you, but then they go and tell their other clients so we'll agree to work with you."

I smile and give a little shrug to get past it. "When is your book due?" I ask.

She makes a face. "Two months. And I'm... nowhere. I sit down to write Dave's story, and the words are in my head, but on the page they look stupid. And I can't figure out the order of anything, you know, and I keep hearing Dave's voice saying what he would want or wouldn't want..."

Suddenly her eyes redden, and without thinking I reach out across the table and cover her hand with mine.

Megan is a pediatrician, a mother of two, and the widow of David Rowland, a quarterback for the Detroit Lions who died on the field last year after a traumatic brain injury. According to my research, before that they were the rare NFL couple with a true fairytale romance: college sweethearts who married after graduation and had two kids while Megan finished med school and David signed with the Lions. Since his death, Megan had been a vocal advocate for banning violence in America's most popular sport.

She takes a napkin from the dispenser on the table and swipes at her eyes. "I'm sorry. Anyway, the book. I mean, I knew it would be hard to write about Dave, but it's more than that. I'm just... stuck."

"Maybe," I say carefully, "the problem is that you're trying to write David's story, when you should be writing yours."

She blinks and looks up at me, her head cocking slightly like a curious retriever. "My story? Who cares about my story?"

I pull out my notes. "Our mutual boss, for one. I've already talked to Calleigh about it."

Calleigh LaFontaine is the senior editor in charge of biographies, and my employer. She wasn't initially crazy about my pitch for Megan's book – the straightforward biography of an NFL star sells a lot better than anything that reeks of "activism" or "romance." But I convinced Calleigh that there was a market for a more complex narrative.

"Megan, I've looked into you, and you are impressive as hell in your own right," I went on. "You're a doctor, for crying out loud –"

She lowers her eyes. "Only thirty hours a week."

"Yeah, and why is that?" I say, because I know the answer.

She gives me a tiny smile. "So I can take care of the kids, and run Dave's charity."

I lean back. "Exactly. I think your book needs to be about you –yes, your love story with David, but also your lives together, the sacrifices you both made, and your relationship.

Plus everything you've done since his death to change NFL regulations."

She blinks at me. "My agent says they don't want an 'activist' book." She puts air quotes around the word.

"I'm not suggesting you write a manifesto. I'm suggesting you tell people a story. Your story. And I can help with that."

It is beautiful, the slow, escalating way her whole face lights up. "I love that," she says softly. "This is exactly why I picked you."

I smile back. I don't have the heart to tell this grieving woman that I was the one who picked her. Whenever I'm ready for a new book, Calleigh sends me a dozen pitches to choose from. Even those have already been winnowed down, since after fifteen books together she's starting to understand my priorities. My base is in Ann Arbor, but I will travel anywhere that's not hot. I don't work with criminals, and with *very* few exceptions, I only write for women.

The meeting with Megan Rowland lasts another twenty minutes, most of which are spent coordinating our schedules. This is the only part of the meeting when I actually do take notes, because although I will remember everything I've heard out of Megan's mouth, schedules are easier to cross-reference on a piece of paper. We'll video chat nearly every day, and meet once a week in person, mostly at her place in Detroit. My time is flexible – Pilates classes run every day and most nights – so we can work around her schedule and her kids' schedule.

When the conversation winds down, Megan reaches into her big Prada tote and shyly pulls out a hardcover copy of my first book, *Lady Lazarus*. "I know it's kind of tacky to ask, but... would you mind signing this?"

"Of course! It's not tacky at all." I move my mug aside and pull the book toward me, picking up my good pen. It's been a long time since I held the hardcover copy, and I take a moment to touch the cover, running my fingers over the art deco-inspired graphic of a woman rising from a pool of blackness. I always thought it was a little garish, but then, in the first draft the woman was rising out of an actual grave. I had to fight against that, and a whole bunch of other marketing choices, particularly their chosen title: Bride of Frankenstein. Caroline would have hated that.

I turn to the title page. When I was on the book tour I was surprised to find that the book was a favorite read in many grief support groups. Maybe they use it as a jumping off point to start a conversation about the ethics of medicine or something.

I write:

To Megan, may your book find you the peace that this book brought me. Elizabeth H. Saville.

I close the cover slowly, to buy an extra few seconds for the ink to dry, then hand the book back to Megan. She puts it in her bag and begins to stand up, but hesitates. I see the question coming, but I'm used to it by now. "If you don't mind me asking... how come you never wrote another novel?"

I give her the same answer I've given everyone else for the last six years. "I guess I never found the right muse. Maybe someday I will."

We say goodbye, and Megan glides out of the coffee shop on her high heels, looking taller and lighter than when she walked in.

There are a few emails I need to write, and some billing to log, so I stay on for a bit at the coffee shop. I work better here than at home. By the time I close my laptop and walk back out to my car, the sun is going down. The street isn't deserted, exactly, but it's the in-between time, before the college kids and hipsters come out for dinner. My car is one of only a handful left on the street.

I fumble in my jacket pocket for keys, but stop, pausing right in the middle of the sidewalk. There is a stillness in the air, along with the scent of spring flowers and car exhaust. Unlocking the car, I drop my backpack in the trunk and then turn in a full circle, examining the shadows.

I see nothing, but it never hurts to try. I've tried so many times before.

"Please come out," I call, to no one in particular. I've tried so many lines over the years: jokes, pleas, even outrageous false statements, when I felt like amusing myself. But the last year or so, I've settled on one simple, truthful sentence. "I miss you."

Resting my butt in the trunk of the car, I wait. I let the tiny ember of hope in my chest stay alive, and I close my eyes, breathing in the moment. *It's okay*, I tell myself, in preparation for the inevitable disappointment. *You are okay.*

I don't realize I've said it out loud until a familiar voice responds, a foot away from me. "That's not much of a mantra."

My eyes fly open and this time, *this one time*, she is there.

Caroline is wearing jeans and a black canvas jacket, her dark hair pulled back in a simple ponytail. Her glasses are yellow now, not dark, so I can see her eyes. They are amused and sad at the same time, because humans are infinitely complicated and our goddamn feelings are so big.

"I shouldn't be —" she begins, but then I throw my arms around her with such intensity that she has to take a step back, letting out a surprised laugh.

"Shut up," I tell her happily.

Her body softens, and her low voice is in my hair. "I'm so proud of you, Heck," she says, and though no one has called me that in years, I don't correct her. "You built the life you needed."

I pull back to see her face, though I cling to one of her hands as insurance. I am determined that she won't run away again. "There was a piece missing," I tell her.

It is so wonderful to see her eyes as I say this, and see the idea catch and perch tentatively, like a butterfly. It is the longing face of a child who knows she shouldn't have the sweet, but wants it terribly anyway. "Heck, I..."

"Probably haven't had a vacation in ages," I finish for her, grinning. I have been thinking about this moment for years, and now that it's here I am flying. "And I've got plenty of money, thanks to you. What do you say? Paris? Montreal?"

She studies me for a long moment, and then allows herself to smile. It's like the sun coming out. "I've always wanted to see Iceland," she admits.

I stand up from the trunk – carefully, still very carefully – and pull her toward the passenger door. "As long as it's not on a cruise ship."

About the Author

Melissa F. Olson is the author of seventeen books in the Old World urban fantasy series, the comic book *Archaic*, and numerous short stories and novellas, including the Nightshades trilogy for Tor.com. Her journalism and academic work has been published in The International Journal of Comic Art, the compilation Images of the Modern Vampire, Litreactor.com, and Tor.com, among other places.

Melissa has been a writing teacher, English professor, and TEDx presenter, but she now divides her time between writing and conventions, where she speaks about issues related to genre, feminism, writing, and parenting. Read more about her work and life at MelissaFOlson.com.

ALSO FROM NEWCON PRESS

ANIMALS – Geoff Ryman
From the multiple award-winning author of *HIM*, *Was* and *The Child Garden* comes a powerful new novel. *ANIMALS* tells the chilling tale of a family caught at the heart of a terrifying and transformative epidemic. Geoff Ryman delivers an astonishing fusion of beautiful writing and pure horror as the world we know falls apart.

The Hamlet – Joanna Corrance
A fabulous tale that dances between horror and science fiction with an added dash of weird. Screens go blank, radios go silent, and a government announcement advises everyone to stay indoors. The residents of a rural Scottish community abandon their picnics and return home. Everyone can sense that something is wrong...

Rowany de Vere and a Fair Degree of Frost – Chaz Brenchley
A graduate of the Crater School and of Oxford, Rowany has taken up service on Mars. As a spy. Her mission is to escort a prominent defector, to see him safely across the hostile surface of Mars, pursued by Russian agents. Success will require every ounce of her wits and her training, but, as it says on her card, she is Rowany de Vere. Of the Colonial Office.

The Creator – Aliya Whiteley
When Phillip receives a distraught call from his sister-in-law, Patricia, to say that his brother is dead, he doesn't hesitate in dashing to her side. Little does he imagine the tragedy and horror that awaits, as he uncovers what really happened to Reynold – the genius behind ThinkBulb, the invention that changed the world – and where his latest obsession has led.

Into the Dark – Patrice Sarath
Patrice Sarath is an award-winning filmmaker and author living in Austin, Texas. This, her debut collection, gathers her finest short fiction from the past two decades and more, adding a brand new story for good measure (which is currently being adapted into a film). Contemporary fantasies, deep space skulduggery and so much more...

www.ingramcontent.com/pod-product-compliance
Lightning Source LLC
Chambersburg PA
CBHW020639260626

47157CB00008B/2828